Praise for *Because They Wanted To*

"Subtle and elegant . . . she sees what's worth saving in these outsiders lives, and as much as they mourn, these stories are also a jeremiad against the modern world's assault on the soul."
—Ann Powers, *The Village Voice*

"It is the essence of Mary Gaitskill's fiction to acknowledge all the impulses at war in the human heart, and to deliver them to her readers in the form of compelling, evocative art."
—Jessica Treadway, *The Boston Globe*

"Soulful, erotically charged . . ."
—Virginia Heffernen, *The Boston Phoenix*

"[A] stunning new short-story collection . . . Gaitskill's vignettes—and her complex, memorable characters—perfectly capture the delicious impossibility of our postmodern, post-feminist, postqueer existence."
—Jeannine DeLombard, *Out*

"Better than any other writer working today, Mary Gaitskill comprehends the spiritual and emotional malaise of American life at the end of the millennium. . . . Surely, there have been few stories this brilliant published anywhere in the past five years."
—Chauncey Mabe, *Ft. Lauderdale Sun-Sentinel*

"Her dark humor, her ambitious, novelistic delineation of character, her resonant language, and startling insights make her stories linger as examinations of old-fashioned universals: pain, suffering, compassion, redemption."
—Katherine Price, *The Memphis Commercial Appeal*

Also by Mary Gaitskill

Veronica
Bad Behavior
Two Girls, Fat and Thin

Because they wanted to

Stories

Mary Gaitskill

Simon & Schuster Paperbacks
New York   London   Toronto   Sydney

SIMON & SCHUSTER PAPERBACKS
Rockefeller Center
1230 Avenue of the Americas
New York, NY 10020

SIMON & SCHUSTER PAPERBACKS and colophon are registered trademarks
of Simon & Schuster, Inc.

For information about special discounts for bulk purchases,
please contact Simon & Schuster Special Sales:
1-800-456-6798 or business@simonandschuster.com.

Designed by Sam Potts
Manufactured in the United States of America

7   9   10   8

The Library of Congress has cataloged the
hardcover edition as follows:
Gaitskill, Mary.
Because they wanted to: stories / Mary Gaitskill.
p. cm.
I. Title.
PS3557.A36B43   1997
813'.54—dc21   96-46337
CIP
ISBN-13: 978-0-684-80856-7
ISBN-10:   0-684-80856-4
ISBN-13: 978-0-684-84144-1 (Pbk)
ISBN-10:   0-684-84144-4 (Pbk)

Some of these stories first appeared in slightly different form in the following publications: *The Threepenny Review* ("Tiny, Smiling Daddy"), *Elle* ("The Blanket"), *Fourteen Hills* ("Comfort"), *Mirabella* ("The Girl on the Plane"), *Esquire* ("Kiss and Tell"), and *The New Yorker* ("Turgor").

Excerpt from "East Coker" in *Four Quartets*, copyright 1943 by T. S. Eliot and renewed 1971 by Esme Valerie Eliot, reprinted by permission of Harcourt Brace & Company.

"Day-O" (The Banana Boat Song). Words and music by Irving Burgie and William Attaway. Copyright © 1955; Renewed 1983 by Lord Burgess Music Publishing Company (ASCAP) / Cherry Lane Music Publishing, Inc. (ASCAP). Worldwide rights for Lord Burgess Music Publishing Company administered by Cherry Lane Music Publishing Company, Inc. All Rights Reserved. Used by Permission.

Contents

Acknowledgments

I would like to thank and acknowledge the following people: Laura Miller, Pat Towers, Deborah Garrison, Becky Saletan, Henry Dunow, Will Blythe, Frank Kogan, Ephrem Korngold, Karen Everett, Knight Landesman, Mieke Van Hoek, Barbara Cooper, and The Better Off Dead Poets Society.

The most outlandish people can be the stimulus for love. . . . A most mediocre person can be the object of a love which is wild, extravagant, and beautiful as the poison lilies of the swamp. A good man may be the stimulus for a love both violent and debased, or a jabbering madman may bring about in the soul of someone a tender and simple idyll. Therefore, the value and quality of any love is determined solely by the lover himself.

It is for this reason that most of us would rather love than be loved. Almost everyone wants to be the lover. And the curt truth is that, in a deep secret way, the state of being beloved is intolerable to many.

—Carson McCullers,
The Ballad of the Sad Café

Because they wanted to

Tiny, Smiling Daddy

He lay in his reclining chair, barely awake enough to feel the dream moving just under his thoughts. It felt like one of those pure, beautiful dreams in which he was young again, and filled with the realization that the friends who had died, or gone away, or decided that they didn't like him anymore, had really been there all along, loving him. A piece of the dream flickered, and he made out the lips and cheekbones of a tender woman, smiling as she leaned toward him. The phone rang, and the sound rippled through his pliant wakefulness, into the pending dream. But his wife had turned the answering machine up too loud again, and it attacked him with a garbled, furred roar that turned into the voice of his friend Norm.

Resentful at being waked and grateful that for once somebody had called him, he got up to answer. He picked up the phone, and the answering machine screeched at him through the receiver. He cursed as he fooled with it, hating his stiff fingers. Irritably, he exchanged greetings with his friend, and then Norm, his voice oddly weighted, said, "I saw the issue of *Self* with Kitty in it."

He waited for an explanation. None came, so he said, "What? Issue of *Self*? What's *Self*?"

"Good grief, Stew, I thought for sure you'd of seen it. Now I feel funny."

The dream pulsed forward and receded again. "Funny about what?"

"My daughter's got a subscription to this magazine, *Self.* And they printed an article that Kitty wrote about fathers and daughters talking to each other, and she, well, she wrote about you. Laurel showed it to me."

"My God."

"It's ridiculous that I'm the one to tell you. I just thought—"

"It was bad?"

"No, she didn't say anything bad. I just didn't understand the whole idea of it. And I wondered what you thought."

He got off the phone and walked back into the living room, now fully awake. His daughter, Kitty, was living in South Carolina, working in a used-record store and making animal statuettes, which she sold on commission. She had never written anything that he knew of, yet she'd apparently published an article in a national magazine about him. He lifted his arms and put them on the windowsill; the air from the open window cooled his underarms. Outside, the Starlings' tiny dog marched officiously up and down the pavement, looking for someone to bark at. Maybe she had written an article about how wonderful he was, and she was too shy to show him right away. This was doubtful. Kitty was quiet, but she wasn't shy. She was untactful and she could be aggressive. Uncertainty only made her doubly aggressive.

He turned the edge of one nostril over with his thumb and nervously stroked his nose hairs with one finger. He knew it was a nasty habit, but it soothed him. When Kitty was a little girl he would do it to make her laugh. "Well," he'd say, "do you think it's time we played with the hairs in our nose?" And she would giggle, holding her hands against her face, eyes sparkling over her knuckles.

Then she was fourteen, and as scornful and rejecting as any girl he had ever thrown a spitball at when he was that age. They didn't get along so well anymore. Once, they were sitting in the rec room watching TV, he on the couch, she on the footstool. There was a Charlie Chan movie on, but he was mostly watching her back and her long, thick brown hair, which she had just washed and was brushing. She dropped her head forward from the neck to let the hair fall between her spread legs and began slowly stroking it with a pink nylon brush.

"Say, don't you think it's time we played with the hairs in our nose?"

No reaction from bent back and hair.

"Who wants to play with the hairs in their nose?"

Nothing.

"Hairs in the nose, hairs in the nose," he sang.

She bolted violently up from the stool. "You are so gross you disgust me!" She stormed from the room, shoulders in a tailored jacket of indignation.

Sometimes he said it just to see her exasperation, to feel the adorable, futile outrage of her violated girl delicacy.

He wished that his wife would come home with the car, so that he could drive to the store and buy a copy of _Self._ His car was being repaired, and he could not walk to the little cluster of stores and parking lots that constituted "town" in this heat. It would take a good twenty minutes, and he would be completely worn out when he got there. He would find the magazine and stand there in the drugstore and read it, and if it was something bad, he might not have the strength to walk back.

He went into the kitchen, opened a beer, and brought it into the living room. His wife had been gone for over an hour, and God knew how much longer she would be. She could spend literally all day driving around the county, doing nothing but buying a jar of honey or a bag of apples. Of course, he could call Kitty, but he'd probably just get her answering machine, and besides, he didn't want to talk to her before he understood the situation. He felt helplessness move through his body the way a swimmer feels a large sea creature pass beneath him. How could she have done this to him? She knew how he dreaded exposure of any kind, she knew the way he guarded himself against strangers, the way he carefully drew all the curtains when twilight approached so that no one could see them walking through the house. She knew how ashamed he had been when, at sixteen, she announced that she was lesbian.

The Starling dog was now across the street, yapping at the heels of a bow-legged old lady in a blue dress who was trying to walk down the sidewalk. "Dammit," he said. He left the window and got the afternoon opera station on the radio. They were in the final act of *La Bohème*.

He did not remember precisely when it had happened, but Kitty, his beautiful, happy little girl, turned into a glum, weird teenager that other kids picked on. She got skinny and ugly. Her blue eyes, which had been so sensitive and bright, turned filmy, as if the real Kitty had retreated so far from the surface that her eyes existed to shield rather than reflect her. It was as if she deliberately held her beauty away from them, only showing glimpses of it during unavoidable lapses, like the time she sat before the TV, daydreaming and lazily brushing her hair. At moments like this, her dormant charm broke his heart. It also annoyed him. What did she have to retreat from? They had both loved her. When she was little and she couldn't sleep at night, Marsha would sit with her in bed for hours. She praised her stories and her drawings as if she were a genius. When Kitty was seven, she and her mother had special times, during which they went off together and talked about whatever Kitty wanted to talk about.

He tried to compare the sullen, morbid Kitty of sixteen with the slender, self-possessed twenty-eight-year-old lesbian who wrote articles for *Self*. He pictured himself in court, waving a copy of *Self* before a shocked jury. The case would be taken up by the press. He saw the headlines: Dad Sues Mag—Dyke Daughter Reveals . . . reveals what? What had Kitty found to say about him that was of interest to the entire country, that she didn't want him to know about?

Anger overrode his helplessness. Kitty could be vicious. He hadn't seen her vicious side in years, but he knew it was there. He remembered the time he'd stood behind the half-open front door when fifteen-year-old Kitty sat hunched on the front steps with one of her few friends, a homely blonde who wore white lipstick and a white leather jacket. He had come to the door to view the weather and say something to the girls, but they were muttering so intently that curiosity got the better of him, and he hung back a moment to listen. "Well, at least your mom's smart," said Kitty. "My mom's not only a bitch, she's stupid."

14

This after the lullabies and special times! It wasn't just an isolated incident, either; every time he'd come home from work, his wife had something bad to say about Kitty. She hadn't set the table until she had been asked four times. She'd gone to Lois's house instead of coming straight home like she'd been told to do. She'd worn a dress to school that was short enough to show the tops of her panty hose.

By the time Kitty came to dinner, looking as if she'd been doing slave labor all day, he would be mad at her. He couldn't help it. Here was his wife doing her damnedest to raise a family and cook dinner, and here was this awful kid looking ugly, acting mean, and not setting the table. It seemed unreasonable that she should turn out so badly after taking up so much of their time. Her afflicted expression made him angry too. What had anybody ever done to her?

He sat forward and gently gnawed the insides of his mouth as he listened to the dying girl in _La Bohème_. He saw his wife's car pull into the driveway. He walked to the back door, almost wringing his hands, and waited for her to come through the door. When she did, he snatched the grocery bag from her arms and said, "Give me the keys." She stood openmouthed in the stairwell, looking at him with idiotic consternation. "Give me the keys!"

"What is it, Stew? What's happened?"

"I'll tell you when I get back."

He got in the car and became part of it, this panting mobile case propelling him through the incredibly complex and fast-moving world of other people, their houses, their children, their dogs, their lives. He wasn't usually so aware of this unpleasant sense of disconnection between him and everyone else, but he had the feeling that it had been there all along, underneath what he thought about most of the time. It was ironic that it should rear up so visibly at a time when there was in fact a mundane yet invasive and horribly real connection between him and everyone else in Wayne County: the hundreds of copies of _Self_ magazine sitting in countless drugstores, bookstores, groceries, and libraries. It was as if there were a tentacle plugged into the side of the car, linking him with the random humans who picked up the magazine, possibly his very neighbors. He stopped at a crowded intersection, feeling like an ant in an enemy swarm.

15

Kitty had projected herself out of the house and into this swarm very early, ostensibly because life with him and Marsha had been so awful. Well, it had been awful, but because of Kitty, not them. As if it weren't enough to be sullen and dull, she turned into a lesbian. Kids followed her down the street, jeering at her. Somebody dropped her books in a toilet. She got into a fistfight. Their neighbors gave them looks. This reaction seemed only to steel Kitty's grip on her new identity; it made her romanticize herself, like the kid she was. She wrote poems about heroic women warriors, she brought home strange books and magazines, which, among other things, seemed to glorify prostitutes. Marsha looked for them and threw them away. Kitty screamed at her, the tendons leaping out on her slender neck. He punched Kitty and knocked her down. Marsha tried to stop him, and he yelled at her. Kitty jumped up and leapt between them, as if to defend her mother. He grabbed her and shook her, but he could not shake the conviction off her face.

Most of the time, though, they continued as always, eating dinner together, watching TV, making jokes. That was the worst thing; he would look at Kitty and see his daughter, now familiar in her withdrawn sullenness, and feel comfort and affection. Then he would remember that she was a lesbian, and a morass of complication and wrongness would come down between them, making it impossible for him to see her. Then she would just be Kitty again. He hated it.

She ran away at sixteen, and the police found her in the apartment of an eighteen-year-old bodybuilder named Dolores, who had a naked woman tattooed on her sinister bicep. Marsha made them put her in a mental hospital so psychiatrists could observe her, but he hated the psychiatrists—mean, supercilious sons of bitches who delighted in the trick question—so he took her out. She finished school, and they told her if she wanted to leave it was all right with them. She didn't waste any time getting out of the house.

She moved into an apartment near Detroit with a girl named George and took a job at a home for retarded kids. She would appear for visits with a huge bag of laundry every few weeks. She was thin and neurotically muscular, her body having the look of a fighting dog on a leash. She cut her hair like a boy's and wore black sunglasses, black leather half-gloves, and leather belts. The only remnant of her beauty was her erect, martial carriage and her efficient movements; she walked through a room like the commander of a guerrilla force. She would sit at the dining room table with Marsha, drinking tea and having a laconic verbal conversation, her body speaking its precise martial language while the washing machine droned from the utility room, and he wandered in and out, trying to make sense of what she said. Sometimes she would stay into the evening, to eat dinner and watch *All in the Family*. Then Marsha would send her home with a jar of homemade tapioca pudding or a bag of apples and oranges.

One day, instead of a visit they got a letter postmarked San Francisco. She had left George, she said. She listed strange details about her current environment and was vague about how she was supporting herself. He had nightmares about Kitty, with her brave, proudly muscular little body, lost among big fleshy women who danced naked in go-go bars and took drugs with needles, terrible women whom his confused, romantic daughter invested with oppressed heroism and intensely female glamour. He got up at night and stumbled into the bathroom for stomach medicine, the familiar darkness of the house heavy with menacing images that pressed about him, images he saw reflected in his own expression when he turned on the bathroom light over the mirror.

Then one year she came home for Christmas. She came into the house with her luggage and a shopping bag of gifts for them, and he saw that she was beautiful again. It was a beauty that both offended and titillated his senses. Her short, spiky hair was streaked with purple, her dainty mouth was lipsticked, her nose and ears were pierced with amethyst and dangling silver. Her face had opened in thousands of petals. Her eyes shone with quick perception as she put down her bag, and he knew that she had seen him see her beauty. She moved toward him with fluid hips; she embraced him for the first time in years. He felt her live, lithe body against his, and his heart pulsed a message of blood and love. "Merry Christmas, Daddy," she said.

Her voice was husky and coarse; it reeked of knowledge and confidence. Her T-shirt said "Chicks With Balls." She was twenty-two years old.

She stayed for a week, discharging her strange jangling beauty into the house and changing the molecules of its air. She talked

17

about the girls she shared an apartment with, her job at a coffee shop, how Californians were different from Michiganders. She talked about her friends: Lorraine, who was so pretty men fell off their bicycles as they twisted their bodies for a better look at her; Judy, a martial arts expert; and Meredith, who was raising a child with her husband, Angela. She talked of poetry readings, ceramics classes, workshops on piercing.

He realized, as he watched her, that she was now doing things that were as bad as or worse than the things that had made him angry at her five years before, yet they didn't quarrel. It seemed that a large white space existed between him and her, and that it was impossible to enter this space or to argue across it. Besides, she might never come back if he yelled at her.

Instead, he watched her, puzzling at the metamorphosis she had undergone. First she had been a beautiful, happy child turned homely, snotty, miserable adolescent. From there she had become a martinet girl with the eyes of a stifled pervert. Now she was a vibrant imp, living, it seemed, in a world constructed of topsy-turvy junk pasted with rhinestones. Where had these three different people come from? Not even Marsha, who had spent so much time with her as a child, could trace the genesis of the new Kitty from the old one. Sometimes he bitterly reflected that he and Marsha weren't even real parents anymore but bereft old people rattling around in a house, connected not to a real child who was going to college, or who at least had some kind of understandable life, but to a changeling who was the product of only their most obscure quirks, a being who came from recesses that neither of them suspected they'd had.

There were only a few cars in the parking lot. He wheeled through it with pointless deliberation before parking near the drugstore. He spent irritating seconds searching for *Self*, until he realized that its air-brushed cover girl was grinning right at him. He stormed the table of contents, then headed for the back of the magazine. "Speak Easy" was written sideways across the top of the page in round turquoise letters. At the bottom was his daughter's name in a little box. "Kitty Thorne is a ceramic artist living in South Carolina." His hands were trembling.

It was hard for him to rationally ingest the beginning paragraphs, which seemed, incredibly, to be about a phone conversation they'd had some time ago about the emptiness and selfishness of people who have sex but don't get married and have children. A few phrases stood out clearly: "... my father may love me but he doesn't love the way I live." "... even more complicated because I'm gay." "... because it still hurts me."

For reasons he didn't understand, he felt a nervous smile tremble under his skin. He suppressed it.

"This hurt has its roots deep in our relationship, starting, I think, when I was a teenager."

He was horribly aware of being in public, so he paid for the thing and took it out to the car. He drove slowly to another spot in the lot, as far away from the drugstore as possible, picked up the magazine, and began again. She described the "terrible difficulties" between him and her. She recounted, briefly and with hieroglyphic politeness, the fighting, the running away, the return, the tacit reconciliation.

"There is an emotional distance that we have both accepted and chosen to work around, hoping the occasional contact—love, anger, something—will get through."

He put the magazine down and looked out the window. It was near dusk; most of the stores in the little mall were closed. There were only two other cars in the parking lot, and a big, slow, frowning woman with two grocery bags was getting ready to drive one away. He was parked before a weedy piece of land at the edge of the lot. In it were rough, picky weeds spread out like big green tarantulas, young yellow dandelions, frail old dandelions, and bunches of tough blue chickweed. Even in his distress he vaguely appreciated the beauty of the blue weeds against the cool white-and-gray sky. For a moment the sound of insects comforted him. Images of Kitty passed through his memory with terrible speed: her nine-year-old forehead bent over her dish of ice cream, her tiny nightgowned form ran up the stairs, her ringed hand brushed her face, the keys on her belt jiggled as she walked her slow blue-jeaned walk away from the house. Gone, all gone.

The article went on to describe how Kitty hung up the phone feeling frustrated and then listed all the things she could've said to him to let him know how hurt she was, paving the way for "real communication"; it was all in ghastly talk-show language. He was unable to put these words together with the Kitty he had last seen lounging around the house. She was twenty-eight now, and she no longer dyed her hair or wore jewels in her nose. Her demeanor was serious, bookish, almost old-maidish. Once, he'd overheard her saying to Marsha, "So then this Italian girl gives me the once-over and says to Joanne, 'You 'ang around with too many Wasp.' And I said, 'I'm not a Wasp, I'm white trash.' "

"Speak for yourself," he'd said.

"If the worst occurred and my father was unable to respond to me in kind, I still would have done a good thing. I would have acknowledged my own needs and created the possibility to connect with what therapists call 'the good parent' in myself."

Well, if that was the kind of thing she was going to say to him, he was relieved she hadn't said it. But if she hadn't said it to him, why was she saying it to the rest of the country?

He turned on the radio. It sang: "Try to remember, and if you remember, then follow, follow." He turned it off. The interrupted dream echoed faintly. He closed his eyes. When he was nine or ten, an uncle of his had told him, "Everybody makes his own world. You see what you want to see and hear what you want to hear. You can do it right now. If you blink ten times and then close your eyes real tight, you can see anything you want to see in front of you." He'd tried it, rather halfheartedly, and hadn't seen anything but the vague suggestion of a yellowish-white ball moving creepily through the dark. At the time, he'd thought it was perhaps because he hadn't tried hard enough.

He had told Kitty to do the same thing, or something like it, when she was eight or nine. They were sitting on the back porch in striped lawn chairs, holding hands and watching the fireflies turn on and off.

She closed her eyes for a long time. Then very seriously, she said, "I see big balls of color, like shaggy flowers. They're pink and red and turquoise. I see an island with palm trees and pink rocks. There's dolphins and mermaids swimming in the water around it." He'd been almost awed by her belief in this impossible vision. Then he was sad, because she would never see what she wanted to see. Then he thought she was sort of stupid, even for a kid.

His memory flashed back to his boyhood. He was walking down the middle of the street at dusk, sweating lightly after a basketball game. There were crickets and the muted barks of dogs and the low, affirming mumble of people on their front porches. Securely held by the warm night and its sounds, he felt an exquisite blend of happiness and sorrow that life could contain this perfect moment, and a sadness that he would soon arrive home, walk into bright light, and be on his way into the next day, with its loud noise and alarming possibility. He resolved to hold this evening walk in his mind forever, to imprint in a permanent place all the sensations that occurred to him as he walked by the Oatlanders' house, so that he could always take them out and look at them. He dimly recalled feeling that if he could successfully do that, he could stop time and hold it.

He knew he had to go home soon. He didn't want to talk about the article with Marsha, but the idea of sitting in the house with her and not talking about it was hard to bear. He imagined the conversation grinding into being, a future conversation with Kitty gestating within it. The conversation was a vast, complex machine like those that occasionally appeared in his dreams; if he could only pull the switch, everything would be all right, but he felt too stupefied by the weight and complexity of the thing to do so. Besides, in this case, everything might not be all right. He put the magazine under his seat and started the car.

Marsha was in her armchair, reading. She looked up, and the expression on her face seemed like the result of internal conflict as complicated and strong as his own, but cross-pulled in different directions, uncomprehending of him and what he knew. In his mind, he withdrew from her so quickly that for a moment the familiar room was fraught with the inexplicable horror of a banal nightmare. Then the ordinariness of the scene threw the extraordinary event of the day into relief, and he felt so angry and bewildered he could've howled.

"Everything all right, Stew?" asked Marsha.

"No, nothing is all right. I'm a tired old man in a shitty world I don't want to be in. I go out there, it's like walking on knives. Everything is an attack—the ugliness, the cheapness, the rudeness, everything." He sensed her withdrawing from him into her own world of disgruntlement, her lips drawn together in that look of exasperated perseverance she'd gotten from her mother. Like Kitty, like everyone else, she was leaving him. "I don't have a real daughter, and I don't have a real wife who's here with me, because she's too busy running around on some—"

"We've been through this before. We agreed I could—"

"That was different! That was when we had two cars!" His voice tore through his throat in a jagged whiplash and came out a cracked half scream. "I don't have a car, remember? That means I'm stranded, all alone for hours, and Norm Pisarro can call me up and casually tell me that my lesbian daughter has just betrayed me in a national magazine and what do I think about that?" He wanted to punch the wall until his hand was bloody. He wanted Kitty to see the blood. Marsha's expression broke into soft, openmouthed consternation. The helplessness of it made his anger seem huge and terrible, then impotent and helpless itself. He sat down on the couch and, instead of anger, felt pain.

"What did Kitty do? What happened? What does Norm have—"

"She wrote an article in *Self* magazine about being a lesbian and her problems and something to do with me. I don't know; I could barely read the crap."

Marsha looked down at her nails.

He looked at her and saw the aged beauty of her ivory skin, sagging under the weight of her years and her cockeyed bifocals, the emotional receptivity of her face, the dark down on her upper lip, the childish pearl buttons of her sweater, only the top button done.

"I'm surprised at Norm, that he would call you like that."

"Oh, who the hell knows what he thought." His heart was soothed and slowed by her words, even if they didn't address its real unhappiness.

"Here," she said. "Let me rub your shoulders."

He allowed her to approach him, and they sat sideways on the couch, his weight balanced on the edge by his awkwardly planted legs, she sitting primly on one hip with her legs tightly crossed. The discomfort of the position negated the practical value of the massage, but he welcomed her touch. Marsha had strong, intelligent hands that spoke to his muscles of deep safety and love and the delight of physical life. In her effort, she leaned close, and her sweatered breast touched him, releasing his tension almost against his will. Through half-closed eyes he observed her sneakers on the floor—he could not quite get over this phenomenon of adult women wearing what had been boys' shoes—in the dim light, one toe atop the other as though cuddling, their laces in pretty disorganization.

Poor Kitty. It hadn't really been so bad that she hadn't set the table on time. He couldn't remember why he and Marsha had been so angry over the table. Unless it was Kitty's coldness, her always turning away, her sarcastic voice. But she was a teenager, and that's what teenagers did. Well, it was too bad, but it couldn't be helped now.

He thought of his father. That was too bad too, and nobody was writing articles about that. There had been a distance between them, so great and so absolute that the word "distance" seemed inadequate to describe it. But that was probably because he had known his father only when he was a very young child; if his father had lived longer, perhaps they would've become closer. He could recall his father's face clearly only at the breakfast table, where it appeared silent and still except for lip and jaw motions, comforting in its constancy. His father ate his oatmeal with one hand working the spoon, one elbow on the table, eyes down, sometimes his other hand holding a cold rag to his head, which always hurt with what seemed to be a noble pain, willingly taken on with his duties as a husband and father. He had loved to stare at the big face with its deep lines and long earlobes, its thin lips and loose, loopily chewing jaws. Its almost godlike stillness and expressionlessness filled him with admiration and reassurance, until one day his father slowly looked up from his cereal, met his eyes, and said, "Stop staring at me, you little shit."

In the other memories, his father was a large, heavy body with a vague oblong face. He saw him sleeping in the armchair in the living room, his large, hairy-knuckled hands grazing the floor. He saw him walking up the front walk with the quick, clipped steps that he always used coming home from work, the straight-backed choppy gait that gave the big body an awesome mechanicalness. His shirt was wet under the arms, his head was down, the eyes were abstracted but alert, as though keeping careful watch on the outside world in case something nasty came at him while he attended to the more important business inside.

"The good parent in yourself."

What did the well-meaning idiots who thought of these phrases mean by them? When a father dies, he is gone; there is no tiny, smiling daddy who appears, waving happily, in a secret pocket in your chest. Some kinds of loss are absolute. And no amount of self-realization or self-expression will change that.

As if she had heard him, Marsha urgently pressed her weight into her hands and applied all her strength to relaxing his muscles. Her sweat and scented deodorant filtered through her sweater, which added its muted wooliness to her smell. "All righty!" She rubbed his shoulders and briskly patted him. He reached back and touched her hand in thanks.

Across from where they sat had once been a red chair, and in it had once sat Kitty, looking away from him, her fist hiding her face.

"You're a lesbian? Fine," he said. "You mean nothing to me. You walk out that door, it doesn't matter. And if you come back in, I'm going to spit in your face. I don't care if I'm on my deathbed, I'll still have the energy to spit in your face."

She did not move when he said that. Tears ran over her fist and down her arm, but she didn't look at him.

Marsha's hands lingered on him for a moment. Then she moved and sat away from him on the couch.

Because
They
Wanted
To

Elise sat in the free medical clinic, studying the support group flyers on the bulletin board. There were support groups for gay youths, lesbian youths, bisexual youths, prostitutes and junkies and people who had AIDS. She did not belong in any of those categories, and even if she did, she did not think she would want to go to a support group. But she liked the idea that they were there, just in case. She sat rhythmically bumping her bare, filthy heels against the rungs of her chair. Although she was moving, she gave an impression of unusual stillness. She seemed hidden, even though she was sitting right there. Her nose and lips were small and finely drawn. Her large eyes were receptive and guarded at once. Her features were pretty, but there was something crumpled, almost collapsed, in her. At the same time, she had something that was very erect and watchful, something that didn't yet show on her face. She sneezed into her hand and reached into the back pocket of her torn jeans for a wadded tissue, which she vigorously dug into both nostrils, then returned to her pocket. She sniffed daintily. She hadn't bathed for a while and she smelled bad, but she didn't know it.

Elise was sixteen, and she had run away from home. She had come from Marin County to Vancouver. She had been getting money by begging on the street, and while she always got enough to

25

buy the fried food and packaged snacks that she liked, she wanted to find a job. It was hard because she didn't have any papers that said she was a Canadian of legal age. People said those papers were easy to fake, but so far she hadn't figured out how.

She had gotten across the border by hitching a ride with two men who were taking horses to Vancouver for a big horse show. They had hidden her in the back of the van with their horses. The older of the two was fat and English, and the younger was slim and wiry, with bitterness and happiness wound together in his own special shape. They seemed pleased that she was hitchhiking. They seemed to think it was very funny.

"Doesn't she remind you of one of those silent-movie stars?" said the younger one. "Sort of passive and ephemeral?"

The older guy glanced at her with a luxuriant turn of his thick neck. "Yeah," he said, "she's like that."

They asked her how old she was, and she said eighteen. They said that just before they crossed the border, they'd stop and let her get in back with the horses. If the guards looked in back, they'd say she was there to groom the horses for them. But, they said, she absolutely had to be eighteen, or they could really get in trouble. She promised that she was. But the border guards didn't even look in the back of the truck.

When the men let her out in Canada, they invited her to come eat with them at a diner that had a rotating sign shaped like a half-moon on top of it. The men ate sandwiches filled with meat and mayonnaise and little sliced tomatoes abundantly dripping out. Elise had a strawberry milk shake and a piece of blueberry pie. The men ate with a gusto that almost disgusted her; it made her want to draw back fastidiously, but it also made her want to join in and have gusto too. "You know," she said, "I'm not really eighteen. I'm sixteen." There was silence. The big English guy stopped eating. Elise loudly sucked up the last of her milk shake.

"Fucking hell," said the Englishman. "Fucking little liar."

"You selfish bitch," said the young one. "Do you know how much trouble we could've been in? They'd of held us back and we'd miss the show!" All his happiness was gone, and his bitterness was coming ~~out in a straight line~~. "You can just get your stuff out of our truck and get your ass back on the highway," he said.

They went out to the parking lot, the young man strutting with anger. "And another thing," he said. "When someone stands you a meal, you're supposed to say thank you." He threw her backpack on the ground.

She walked away so upset she trembled. She didn't understand why they had gotten so mad when they'd thought everything else was so funny. She was a liar and a selfish bitch and rude. But then a woman in a fancy car had stopped to pick her up and Elise had sped away like she didn't have to be those things anymore. She'd been glad she'd lied to those jerks.

A nurse with big white legs and blond hair on her arms came out with a file folder and said, "Elise?"

Elise followed the nurse back into the examining room. She took off her pants and put on a paper gown, and a woman doctor with a sad, handsome face came in and shook her hand. The doctor talked to her about AIDS and asked her questions about sex. She took blood from her arm and asked her to lie down for a pelvic exam. During the pelvic exam, the doctor asked her if she'd ever seen the inside of her vagina. When she said no, the doctor asked if she wanted to look. The doctor seemed to think it was a good idea, so Elise said okay. She lifted her head and looked in the mirror that the doctor was holding between her legs. The doctor smiled encouragingly. Elise thought that the doctor was doing this because she was trying to encourage Elise to relate to her body in a caring way, so she looked with what she hoped was a caring expression. It was a rather startling sight, probably because of the metal thing. "Thank you," she said. Fleetingly, she thought of the men with the horses and how they'd feel if they could see how polite she really was.

When she went back out into the waiting room, a group of people were clustered about the receptionist's desk, so she had to wait a moment to make another appointment. As she stood there, she looked again at the support group flyers on the bulletin board. A small piece of torn-out notepaper with pink writing and drawings of flowers and a cat caught her attention. "Baby-sitter needed," it said.

[handwritten margin note, right side: WHY MEDICINE ANSWERED]

[handwritten margin note, bottom: PLOT FORWARD]

"Good pay, friendly environment. No phone. Apply in person." Elise recognized the street address; it was near Pigeon Park, only a few blocks from where she was staying. She asked the receptionist how long the ad had been there.

"Baby-sitting?" The woman looked up, alarmed. She had a tiny green tear tattooed under one dark eye. She got up and went to the bulletin board. "Who put *that* there?" she demanded. She tore the ad off the board, crumpling the flowers and the little cat into a ball. "That shouldn't even be here," she said.

But Elise remembered the address, and she went there straight from the clinic. The address was a tenement building in a slum with a dull, vaguely benevolent character. A family of foreigners sat on the front steps, drinking and spreading their lives out for anyone to see. The father sat holding a beer can between his big knees. He was sweating through his undershirt. There were patches of black hair on his fatty upper arms. He seemed intensely aware of Elise, even though he looked away. Inside, the foyer was close and full of innocuous smells made big and nasty by the heat. The glass in the door had been shot at and taped up. Elise pushed a dirty little button and a woman's voice came furrily through the intercom. She had to come down to let Elise in.

She was very small and thin, and she seemed to flicker in the dark hall. Even from a distance, her personality shot off her body. When she opened the splintered door, her smile was tremulous and tight. She was about twenty-five. She made Elise think of a small, bright fish darting through deep water.

"I'm Robin," she said as they walked up the stairs. "I'm so glad to see you. I couldn't afford to run an ad in the papers, and I wasn't sure who would see the ones I put up." Her voice was light and excited; it pulled on Elise with the tactile intelligence of a small child who wants something. "You're exactly the kind of person I was hoping for, thank God." She rounded a corner and looked back at Elise, her eyes wide and one hand on her heart.

The apartment was a large room. There was a sink and a hot plate and a furiously humming refrigerator. The bathroom door was open; it looked like it was the size of a closet. Two little boys, about six and four, looked at Elise, the younger one peeping from behind his brother. There was an infant lying on the king-size bed in a diaper, softly jerking its limbs with the private movement of its thoughts. Robin offered Elise a chair with a vinyl seat and sat on the bed.

"You see the situation," she said. She looked Elise in the eyes, as if acknowledging something she'd prefer not to mention directly. "We're from Sacramento," she said. "And I'm going to tell you the truth. We're here illegally. I just drove us across the border. I said we were shopping and kept going. I had to leave because my husband was abusing me and he was starting to hurt the boys. I couldn't stand it anymore." She sat very straight, with her legs tautly crossed. "I was afraid all the time," she said. "I didn't want the boys to . . . to . . ." She made a strange crumpled gesture.

There was a silence. The children were in the corner playing with their toys, but Elise felt their attention on their mother.

"I'm an American too," she said. "I ran away from home too."

To her surprise, Robin smiled. "So we have something in common," she said. "Were your parents abusive?"

Elise hesitated. She pictured her father sitting in his armchair, looking miserable.

Robin held up her hand. "It's okay," she said. "You must've had your reasons. You can tell me later if you want, and if not, that's okay."

Elise said she had done a lot of baby-sitting but hadn't taken care of an infant before. Robin said that it was okay, that she would make up some bottles of formula before she left in the morning. She would show Elise how to change diapers.

"There's one thing, though," she went on. "I know it's bad, but I can't pay you for at least a week. I don't even have a job. That's why I need a baby-sitter. I need to find a job. Until then I need every penny for food. I know it's asking a lot. But if you can just stick with me for a few weeks, I promise I'll take care of you."

"Okay," said Elise. She felt irritated with herself for saying it; she wasn't sure why she had.

"Thank you," said Robin. "I know it sounds flaky, but I'm a good judge of people. I feel I can trust you. Only two other people have come by, and they were just . . ." She gestured with distaste. "Druggy, crazy. I was getting frantic, you understand."

Elise nodded. She felt as if Robin had reached out and grabbed her.

Robin asked if she could start the next day at nine o'clock. She said she had a job interview at ten. "I think I'll be back around three," she said. "But if he offers me a job right away, I'll take it. Then I probably won't be back until six or so."

It did not occur to Elise to ask what kind of job it was, or why the interview was being conducted on Sunday morning. Robin introduced the children. The oldest boy's name was Andy and the little one was Eric. The baby was Penny. The boys looked at Elise gingerly, as if she might do anything.

Elise left feeling strange about the arrangement. She was glad she had a job, but she didn't like having to wait for money. The family on the porch registered her departure. The little girl crouched and stared up at her as if from the bottom of a pit.

She went back to the flat she was sharing with a guy named Mark. She had not known him until four weeks ago. He was the friend of a girl in Seattle named Wren, and when she told him that Wren had given her his address, he let her in. He was a pale, exhausted twenty-five-year-old with an air of affable ruin. He offered her a cup of tea. They sat together in the living room and talked while he sewed leather patches onto his jeans with dental floss. He told her he had come to Vancouver to stop using heroin and to recover from romantic disappointment. He sewed very deliberately, as if each fine, repetitive movement replenished his faith in the bodily truth of his existence. He told Elise that his roommate had gone to London for the summer; she could stay in his room. She had been sleeping there since then. The sour, musty little mattress was covered by a faded flannel sheet with blue sheep on it. Instead of a blanket, there was a heavy pink curtain that she slept under. Once she got used to it, she'd come to like its exaggerated scratchiness.

She found Mark in the kitchen, drinking tea out of a flowered china cup and reading an article about an actress who had been a porn star at the age of twelve. She told him about the baby-sitting job, the abusive husband and the no money at first.

"It sounds fucked up," said Mark cautiously. His face had the abstract look of someone who has just categorized something and then quickly stepped away from it.

"I think she's just freaked out," said Elise.

30

"I guess she would be." Mark scratched his stomach and blinked at the sunlight trembling on the table.

For some reason, this conversation made her more determined to make the job work. She lay in bed that night, imagining herself going to the apartment every day, playing with the children and caring for them. She imagined greeting Robin as she came home from work with that tremulous smile on her face, her shoulders drooping as she stooped to take off her shoes. They would form a team. Elise would save money. Years later, Robin would still write to her to tell her how the kids were doing. Elise lay awake under the curtain all night, thinking these thoughts and listening to people walk up and down outside the window. Every now and then, one of them would yell terrible abuse, and she would strain to hear it.

In the morning she had some of Mark's bread and cheese for breakfast, along with olives snuck from an old jar, and left to baby-sit. There were only a few people on the street; they seemed random yet deeply set in their private purposes. Two men with big blunt faces walked along drinking beers and talking about how some ridiculous awful thing that was always happening had happened again. "Pop goes the weasel!" said one. "Yeah, pop goes the weasel," said the other. A pretty, peevish young man in a dress and a wig swiftly padded along in his stockinged feet, his tiger-striped pumps and matching purse in one hand. A middle-aged woman carrying three heavy bags pressed forward as if she had decided that no other direction was allowed.

The front porch of Robin's apartment building was bare except for a child's red plastic bucket with some dirty water and a dead goldfish in it. Robin let her in, greeting her as if they were both already far away in some happy future. The two boys, however, were sitting at a rickety table eating bowls of cereal, and the baby was sitting up on the bed, flailing its tiny fists at the present. The older boy, Andy, stopped his spoon in midair and watched her. His eyes made her feel guilty, even though it wasn't her fault.

"Penny's just dropped a load," said Robin, "so I can show you how to change her."

They sat on the bed, and Robin laid the infant on her back, supporting her head with one slim, splayed hand. She unfolded the diaper as if it were a little paper puzzle. The smell of perfect shit rose into the air. The baby's private body was blank as the flesh of a plant. She kicked her legs, working the fierce new engine of her body. Robin's hands were deft and quick, and Elise thought their movements pleased the baby. Elise expected that Robin would want her to redo the diaper, to show that she had learned, but instead Robin just smiled and said, "See?" The baby gurgled at her mother's big smile. Robin showed her the bottles of formula she had prepared and told her how to heat them. Then she opened a badly dented tin cupboard and showed her a jar of peanut butter, some bread, and a yellowing orange that they could eat for lunch.

"I know you'll do great," said Robin. She turned to the boys; her smiling profile tingled wildly. "Be good for Lisa," she said.

When she left, the air felt roiled, like water in the wake of a furious propeller. Elise sat on the bed. The boys sat at the table with their eyes down. Eric, the little one, fiddled with his spoon as if he were rubbing a secret comfort spot. Elise looked at the baby; it dispassionately stared back. She looked at the boys. She had lied about her baby-sitting credentials; she had had very little experience with children. She went and sat at the table with them.

"Hi," she said.

She felt something move between the brothers, invisible and cellular. Andy looked up and back down. Eric watched him.

"Do you like animals?" she asked.

"Um hm," said Andy. His brown eyes showed intelligence and strength, veiled by a thin, protective opacity.

"We have a cat," she said. "His name is Blue."

"We have a dog at home," said Andy.

Eric looked up suddenly and said, "His name is Roscoe."

"He's a genius," said Andy. "For a dog."

They both looked at her. Eric had a delicate elfin chin. His intelligence seemed more fragile than his brother's.

"Blue was an orphan when we found him," she said. "He was living with his brothers and sisters under a deserted house."

"What's an orphan?" asked Andy.

"Children with no parents. The mother cat had left them, and my brother Rick found them when his friend's dog ran up to the house and started barking because he smelled cats. Blue was just four weeks old, but he came out and stood up to the dog. He arched his back and spat, and the dog was so surprised he just stopped. Rick saved the litter and we adopted Blue."

She expected them to cheer Blue, or to ask about him, but instead they abruptly slid off their chairs and ran to play with their toys. She was puzzled and even a little hurt; she thought they would like the story. She walked over to where they played and crouched beside them. They had a strange assortment of toys, some of which weren't even toys. They had rubber dinosaurs, colored rocks, a metal truck, a turtle with hair, a cymbal with a pink elastic wrist strap, a stuffed dog, a battery-operated gorilla, a knotted leather cord with two marble balls on either end, a wind-up chickie, and a ceramic mermaid. Alex had the metal wind-up chickie and Eric had the mermaid. They talked urgently in cartoon voices and marched their toys around so that they acted out a story. They talked loudly, as if they were putting on a show for her and, at the same time, using their loudness to shut her out. On impulse, she picked up the gorilla and made it walk up to Eric's mermaid. "Hey, good-lookin'," she said. Eric tensed. "Hey," she said. She wiggled the gorilla. Eric ignored her; she blushed. She felt as if she were trying to squeeze into a spot too small for her. She decided to do the dishes, even though there were only two of them.

She washed the cereal bowls with a little bit of green steel wool. Then she wiped the counter with it. She looked at the baby, who wasn't doing anything. She sat at the table by the window. On the table was an old digital clock and an empty bud vase made of clouded plastic. The clock said 9:41. Elise looked out the window. There were people out walking around now, and she watched them. Normally at this time of day she would be walking up and down Granville, asking people for change. Most of the panhandlers her age sat on the sidewalk and begged in groups. They sat huddled as if they were glad to have arrived at the absolute bottom, where it was nice and solid and they could sit. They sat huddled as if protecting something very special, and their begging seemed like an afterthought. Elise much preferred the walking method. People were more apt to give you money if you went up to them and asked them for it, and besides, she liked the big dumb rhythm of everybody going in the same two directions and, inside that, all the tiny, concentrated rhythms of different walking styles. She liked moving quickly in and out of other people's rhythms.

Sometimes she'd have a conversation with someone who gave her money or insulted her, and for a moment that person would loom out of the generality with a loud blare of specificity and then fade back as Elise walked on. Once, she had approached a young guy who had come out of a fast food store and was opening the box of fried chicken he'd bought there. He gave her a dollar. He said he was giving it to her because she reminded him of a girl he knew in San Francisco. "She's a sex worker," he said, "a pros-tee-tute." He dragged the word out singsong style and smiled at her with an aggressive, bristling air as rank and particular as a deep body smell. "I've thought of doing that," she said. His aggression turned into surprise and then into a funny, sour acceptance. He asked her if she wanted some chicken. She said yes and tore all the fried juicy skin off the breast. "Hey," he said, "it's no good without the skin," but he still let her sit with him and eat, even though she'd ruined his chicken.

Andy ran over to her with his metal chickie. "This is Jago," he said. "He's a fighter orphan bird. When the hunters come into the forest to get birds and they see Jago, they scream and run away!"

"Oh!" said Elise.

"You pretend to be the hunter," said Andy. "You're coming in the woods and you see this bird and you don't know it's Jago so you start to shoot, okay?"

Elise pretended that her finger was a gun and pointed it at the metal chick.

Andy flipped up one of the chick's metal wings to reveal *Jago* written on the underside in felt pen.

Elise waited.

"It's Jago!" prompted Andy.

"Oh, no!" said Elise. "Jago!"

Andy ran back to his game in triumph.

Little kids always wanted to set things up so they got to yell a certain satisfying thing or to make you yell it. When she was little, she or her brother Rick would yell something like, "Why did Miss Grinch and Miss Butt take all their clothes off?" and the other would yell back, "Because they wanted to!" Then they would roll around, tickling each other and giggling, yelling more questions and yelling the same answer again and again.

The sunlight shifted, and the surface of the table became warm and bright. Elise extended her arms into the warmth; her pale arm hairs stood up in the air, and the sight made her feel tender toward herself. All those thousands of tiny hair follicles, each earnestly keeping its special hair going. She lifted her arm and rubbed the soft hairs against her lip. Outside, a child flashed down the street, waving something bright in his hand.

When she was seven and Rick was eight, they would dress in skirts and hats and dance around the mulberry bush in the backyard of their old house, picking the berries and singing, "Oh, we haven't got a chance for our vegetables! For our vegetables!" Their mother had taken pictures of them in their outfits, each holding a plastic bucket of mulberries. Elise stood with her stumpy little legs apart and made her stomach stick out on purpose. Rick posed with one hand on his slim hip, his smile innocent and arrogant and glad. His bare legs were long and finely shaped and made him look more delicate than he was.

With a soft blending motion, that memory turned into another one. She and Rick cuddled on the couch while the family watched TV. Their mother sat on the end of the couch with her legs tucked up under her; Rick leaned against her hip and Elise sat against him. They were eating sticky refrigerator cookies and watching *It's a Wonderful Life*. Through her thin nightgown she could feel his warm haunch and his bare foot, cool and faintly sweaty against her thigh. He was radiant, thoughtless, quick, and very male. His heart was tender, but the rest of him was darting around too fast for him to feel it. Elise could feel it, though. Their mother's old knit afghan covered their laps and legs, and while their heads were busy watching TV and eating the special cookies, under the afghan she was knowing him and letting him know her, in an invisible way too complicated for words. Meanwhile, their father presided in his leatherette recliner.

Their little brother, Robbie, sat close to the TV, but instead of watching the movie, he was concentrating on his red crayons and his drawing. They were safe in their lair.

It was very hot in the apartment, hotter than outside. She was already sweating around the waistband. She glanced at the boys; she wished she could take off her shirt but she wasn't sure it was right, even though it was natural.

In Seattle, she had stayed for a few weeks in an apartment with ten other kids. It was okay to take off your shirt or change your clothes there, whether or not you were having sex with anyone. She'd had sex with a boy named David who stayed there sometimes. Even before that they saw each other naked sometimes because they liked each other so much, like brother and sister. He had green eyes with black eyelashes, and a wine-colored birthmark on his prominent right hipbone. He had written a whole page in his journal about her and then read it to her. But the day after they slept together, he took acid and went off with some other guys to steal animal statuary, and she never saw him again. It was all right; she understood that they were both traveling. But she wished she had an address where she could write to him.

"No! No! No!" Eric's whine was smothered and aggrieved. Elise sat up and listened alertly to see if Andy was picking on him. "Okay," said Andy. "Now they're going to attack the mall." "Okay," said Eric. Elise relaxed.

Rick had picked on Robbie a lot when they were little. Before their parents got divorced, he picked on him just by laughing at him. Then the divorce happened. The children went to live with their mother, even though she couldn't afford them. Everybody was upset and unhappy. Their mother cried all the time. Elise had bad dreams. Robbie wet the bed. Rick began hurting Robbie. He slammed the car door on his leg. He punched him in the stomach while he was asleep. He peed on his drawings.

Their mother would yell and then she'd cry, and for a while Rick would try to be nice to Robbie. He would put his arm around his little brother and share his ice cream cone and smile like they were in a secret league together. There would be two feelings in his eyes when he did this. One of the feelings was mocking, as if his kindness was just another, more complicated version of his meanness. But the other feeling was pure sweetness for Robbie. It was so sweet Rick couldn't resist feeling it, and so sweet that he couldn't quite stand feeling it. So he would just taste it, like a piece of candy, and then throw it away. But Robbie couldn't help reaching out for the sweetness. He would look up at Rick and then look down and reach for the ice cream cone and politely eat at it with the shy tip of his tongue. Rick would look at him, and tenderness would shimmer under his eyes, trying to get out. But then he would go back to being mean again.

Their mother would yell when Rick was mean, but she loved him too much to really punish him. She loved his boyish arrogance and his radiance. When he bragged about winning in sports or outsmarting somebody or even being mean, she would look at him as if he had something she needed more than anything in the world. And he would bathe in her look. She would come up behind him and stroke his hair, and he would act like he wasn't paying attention, but really he would lean into his mother, welcoming her. She would ask him to do things: Open a can, carry a bag of groceries, kill a big bug, rub her feet with oil. And he would do it with an air of chivalry, even though she was the bigger and stronger one. Maybe their mother had been afraid that if she lost the meanness, she'd lose the chivalry, and she couldn't bear to lose that. But she loved Robbie too, and she was frightened by the way Rick treated him.

So she got cheap state psychiatrists to look at Rick and Robbie. Once a week they would go to a clinic to be examined, while Elise sat in the waiting room with her mother. Elise didn't mind going to the clinic. She kind of liked sitting on the orange furniture in the lounge, eating candy out of the machine at the end of the hall and observing the mentally ill people who went in and out. She liked her mother's certainty that, finally, she was accomplishing something.

But the psychiatrists didn't find anything wrong, and things went back to normal. Then Rick hung Robbie upside down in a neighbor's barn and made him swing back and forth until Robbie's head hit the wall and his forehead cracked open. When their mother saw, she screamed and put her hand over her mouth; then she turned and hit Rick in the face. She bundled Robbie up and carried him to the house, his forehead bleeding onto her pink blouse, one leg hanging limp off to the side. She didn't cry; she made choking, struggling noises that were terrible and female. Elise ran after her; Rick just stood there.

That night Elise had a dream about Robbie. She was in the fifth grade, and had just learned about how Mount Vesuvius had erupted. In her dream, a volcano had erupted in San Anselmo, and their father came in the car to save them. While they were driving to safety, Elise looked back and saw that they had forgotten Robbie. He was running after the car, screaming for their father to stop. Elise held her hand out the window for him to grab, but their father wouldn't slow down.

Her dream came true, sort of. Their father married a woman who owned and operated a salon where she tattooed color onto women's faces so that they would look like they had makeup on all the time. It was decided that Rick and Elise should go live with their father and his new wife and her daughter, Becky, while Robbie stayed behind with their mother. It wasn't until years later that it had occurred to Elise that the barn incident had something to do with this arrangement.

"I'm cutting his head off! I'm cutting his head off!" yelled Andy.

"No!" Eric's voice had a shrill, stubborn push.

Swiftly, Elise crossed the room. "Don't cut off his head!" she said.

There was a burst of silence. Elise felt the boys shrink deeper into their privacy. Stiffly, they moved their toys. She felt embarrassed. She thought of saying, "Be nice to Eric," but she was too embarrassed. She stood over them, feeling she couldn't move until something else happened.

"What are you playing?" she asked.

Andy looked up. "The turtle is trying to cut off the mermaid's friend's head and Jago is coming to help," he explained patiently.

"Oh." She relaxed. They relaxed. She stood there a minute in the new atmosphere. Then she went to check on Penny. The baby was still just lying there. Elise sat on the bed, feeling that everything was okay. She had shown authority and made contact. She thought about picking the baby up and walking back and forth with her, but she'd never picked a baby up before. Instead, she put her hand on Penny's stomach and rubbed her. The baby smiled and made sounds that were like light, tumbling bubbles. Nervously, Elise stroked the exquisite little forehead. The baby looked at Elise solemnly and then drew her gaze back inward as she returned to the business of creating a person who could survive in the world. Elise looked out the window. Two shabby old women wearing brimmed hats stood on the pavement, talking. They touched each other and smiled and nodded vigorously.

It was funny, thought Elise, that she had told the children "we have a cat" when she wasn't with her family anymore. He wasn't her cat now. They hadn't discovered Blue under a porch with an orphaned litter, either. And he had never faced down a dog. He was an expensive Persian cat from a breeder. Their father had bought him as a special gift for their stepmother, Sandy.

When she and Rick moved in with their father and Sandy, their father had said to her, "Now you'll have a sister," as if she had always wanted one. But she had not wanted, at the age of eleven, to have a nine-year-old stranger dropped into the middle of her life. It was like suddenly having to live with somebody who sat across the room from her at school.

But Becky was nice. She was diffident and she always shared. She was also weird, or, as her own mother said, "neurotic." She picked the fur off her stuffed animals. All her animals were bald. Her mother said it was because she needed to "act out her anger" at her parents' divorce. It didn't look like anger to Elise. Becky would sit with an animal and suck her thumb and pick the fur off it with two fingers, collecting it in her palm until she had a handful. Then she'd put it in a blue plastic bucket called "the picky bucket." If you wanted to torture Becky, and Rick and Elise sometimes did, you could threaten to dump the pickies in the toilet or throw handfuls about the room while Becky screamed and ran around trying to catch them. Even when she got older and stopped picking the animals, Becky kept the overflowing picky bucket under her bed. Then her mother found them and threw them away, because she said it was "over the top" for Becky to have them. For a while after that, Becky defiantly picked the stuffing out of the mattress and dropped it on the floor, but she was really too old by then, so she didn't do it long.

Elise came to like Becky and to feel protective of her shy peculiarity. But she was more impressed by her stepmother. Rick had hated

Sandy from the beginning, but Elise found her too strange and fascinating to hate. Sandy was a little younger than their mother, but she had a bright, bristling competence that made her seem older. She was thin and her stomach was hard and she'd had her face tattooed so that she appeared to be wearing full makeup all the time. Even when she got up in the morning, her lips were bright red, her cheeks were pink, and her eyes were outlined in black. "I fixed it so I wouldn't have to wash my face off at night," she said. She said it with brisk self-deprecation, as if her face, everybody's face, was a vaguely ridiculous thing that could come off at any moment. She also said it with pride that she'd acknowledged the problem and then gone right in there to fix it. Her whole being seemed to be bursting with self-deprecation and pride and the need to fix things.

Their father may have gotten Blue as a present for Sandy, but he had grown to like the cat more than anybody did. He thought it was soulful and beautiful. He brought Blue special treats and talked to him, even sang to him. Blue would be resting on the floor, and their father would bend over to look the cat in the face and he would sing: "Six foot, seven foot, eight foot—bunch! Daylight come and Blue wants to go home!"

Rick despised it when their father did that, and would imitate him viciously. Elise defended their father and reminded Rick that he had been in Vietnam, where he'd risked his life and fought.

"Yeah," said Rick. "The retards are strong."

This was the thing he said when somebody who was ugly or unpopular did something smart. He could say that and take anything away from anybody. When she was younger, it hurt her to hear Rick talk about their father this way. But when she got older, she saw what he'd meant; their father *was* kind of a retard. She remembered him at the dinner table, yelling.

"You think you're such a bunch of smart, tough feminists!" he yelled. "But you don't know anything! About men, about sex!" He grabbed the edge of the table and lunged over his dish. "There's guys out there who would cut your bowels out to have it!"

Elise looked at Rick and rolled her eyes. Becky, who was fourteen, began to cry. "See!" said their father. "The big feminist! Crying!" But his voice wobbled on the second exclamation, as if it was embarrassed, and his last word was almost sorry about the whole thing. He withdrew into his chair, wiped his mouth, and ate with the slightly offended air of someone who just wants to mind his own business.

If Sandy had been there, he would never have said those things. But she was at a codependency meeting, which was why he was in a bad mood to begin with.

Elise looked at Becky so she would see that Elise didn't look down on her for crying, but Becky was busy composing herself and didn't notice. Elise was angry and disgusted that their father had made Becky cry when he had actually been yelling at Elise for talking about a woman on TV who'd been saying that if girls wanted to dress like prostitutes, they should learn to act like prostitutes. Becky sniffed, tucked her fine red hair behind her ears, and took up her silverware with the delicate resolve of a young cat. Elise furtively tried to meet her brother's eye so he would see how contemptuous she felt, but Rick was too deep in his own special contempt to respond. He stroked his dyed black hair and fidgeted disdainfully as if trying to locate some small spot worth being in, even though he knew such a spot didn't exist, at least not among *these people*. One cuff of his angora sweater slid down over one long, severely articulated hand, adding to the exquisite quality of his disdain. Elise felt a pang of admiration for him. She felt dejected that he wouldn't look at her, but she didn't blame him. He was seventeen, and not necessarily interested in looks across the dining table, and anyway, if she were as beautiful as Rick, she thought, she'd be stuck-up too.

The next day Elise was watching TV with Becky and Rick when their father walked through the room in a state of mild, enchanted absence. He looked as if he were in a private landscape, a place of secret relief only he knew about. He passed Becky, and as he did, he reached out and, with one finger, playfully stroked the bridge of her nose and said, "Ski nose! Ski nose!" She giggled and forgave him. He patted her shoulder and moved on. Elise had boiled with anger.

Andy and Eric ran around the room, happily screaming. Andy waved the knotted leather cord and banged the marble balls together. Eric beat the cymbal with a colored rock. Their energy unspooled crazily and spilled all over the room. Andy ran up to Elise like a kitten dancing around a cat. He held up the banging balls and gave a shrill little scream and hopped around. Eric looked on. Elise smiled uncertainly. She wanted to answer their excitement, but she felt too big and stiff. She couldn't remember that kind of excitement and was tentative and vulnerable before it. The boys ran to the bed and chased each other around it, yelling and banging. Elise remembered jumping up and down on the mattress with Rick, yelling, "Because they wanted to!" The boys pounced on the bed and rolled around, tickling. A little strip of feeling wiggled free inside her. She burst off the chair and jumped on the bed, grabbing Andy and tickling him. He squealed and turned in to her embrace with a shy, writhing twist. Penny began to scream. Everything closed up.

"Stop it," said Elise. She sat up and pried Andy off her. "Be quiet now."

The boys looked down nervously. Elise put her hand on Penny and made her rock on the squishy mattress. The baby kept screaming. Elise felt a hard little hiccup of fear. The boys slid off the bed and went away. Her fear got bigger. Frightened, she slid her hands under the baby and took it in her arms. Penny bellowed and wet through her diaper. Elise didn't know what to do. She didn't remember how to change the diaper. She walked the length of the floor with the baby, turned and walked the other way. Her heart pounded. Maybe Penny would stop screaming before the pee got sticky and itchy. Then Elise could think about the diaper. She tried to walk slow and soothingly.

Sometimes her father would run around and scream because the dog down the street wouldn't stop barking. For a while, she would come home from school every day and would find her father yelling about the dog and her stepmother pretending not to hear him. Elise would go upstairs and knock on Rick's door, and he would let her in, putting on a show of reluctance but smiling. "Hi, Leesy," he would say. He would sit on the bed and play his guitar, hunching in on himself as he sang her a song. Or they would sit on his orange pile rug, eating candy corn left over from Halloween and making fun of their father for going crazy over the dog.

"I'm going to kill him!" screamed their father. "I'll beat his skull in!" There was yelling and scuffling, and then the back door slammed.

42

"Yeah, right," said Rick.

But when the dog stopped barking, they were fascinated and nonplussed. If their father had beaten the neighbor's dog to death, what would happen next? "They'd put him in jail," said Elise. "Nah," said Rick. "Just a fine, but it would embarrass him."

They filed down the stairs in excited apprehension. Elise looked back at Rick; he put his hands over his mouth and bugged out his eyes. He meant to be funny, but with his smirking mouth covered, his distended eyes had the flat hysteria of a mask.

"If he kills that fucking dog I'll divorce him, and I mean it. I mean it! It's not normal! What kind of person would go after a dog with a golf club?"

"An asshole," said Rick.

Sandy banged her hand on the counter and yelled, "Shut up!" Her voice broke; she had hit her hand hard enough to hurt it.

Their father came in the back door. His face wore an expression of gentle puzzlement, his golf club was dozing in his hand. He looked as if he been holding a baby against his breast. "That poor sonofabitch is lonely," he said mildly. "When he saw me coming, he started jumping up and down, wanting me to play with him. No wonder he barks! They've got the sad bastard on a short leash, walking around in his own shit." The frilly green curtain on the back window flared out behind his armpit, the little brass bell attached to the curtain rod dangled above his head. Elise thought of the frilled collar and silly hat of a clown. "I just petted him for a few minutes," he said. "And listen, he's still quiet." He came into the kitchen and put his golf club in a corner. It immediately fell down; he gently muttered "Shit" and bent to stand it up again, and Elise was stricken with unbearable pity. It hit her so fast, she didn't have time to be furious or contemptuous. She looked at Rick and saw that under his look of bored distaste was a rigid muscular contraction, like a grimace of pain or rage. For a second, it was as if she was seeing through him to his skeleton. Then it was over, and he was Rick again. He was putting Pop-Tarts in the microwave, his long, agile hands moving like they knew nothing about pain or rage.

Her chest sweated from holding Penny against it. The baby's crying had become a steady contemplative grumble, as if she had found an engrossing pocket of misery and was digging around, exploring.

The rhythmic little sobs penetrated Elise and attached her to the baby. She sat on the bed and rocked. The attachment was mutual and interlocked. It made Elise feel relaxed; no matter what happened, it would be all right. She thought: formula. Robin had left a bottle of formula on the counter so Elise wouldn't have to heat it again. Still holding Penny, she walked to the counter and got the bottle. Penny took the nipple in her mouth with a neat little grab. She sputtered, panted, then sighed and quieted as she earnestly sucked.

As soon as Penny stopped drinking, she wet herself again. She didn't seem to care, but still Elise thought she'd better try to change her. Carefully she laid the baby on the coverlet. She undid the soaked diaper and took it off. Penny kicked and waved. Elise wet a threadbare washcloth at the kitchen faucet and wiped the baby. Carefully she put a new diaper on. She wasn't sure it was on exactly right, but it would do until Robin got back. She rinsed the washcloth and hung it on a tiny metal rack.

Andy came over. "We're hungry," he said. There was a reproachful little push in his voice, and no wonder: it was two o'clock. She got bread and peanut butter and dishes out of the cabinet. The dishes were cheap and bright-colored. There were three cups, two with flowers on them and one with a picture of a hippopotamus carrying a balloon. Elise imagined Robin in the Salvation Army, picking out cheerful dishes; she felt protective allegiance. She stood at the counter, making them all sandwiches. The linoleum on the counter was cracked and faintly buckled. There was moist black mold where the counter met the wall, and a sour smell in the drain. The odorous dirt was lush and dense. It made her feel rooted to the floor and to the making of the food. She thought of her mother, standing at the counter, making food. Mostly she thought of her mother's hips, big and strong and set right against the counter.

She cut each sandwich into four squares and the orange into eight wedges. She poured everybody a cup of milk, and they all sat down to eat. The boys ate with concentrated faces, as if they were exaggerating their satisfaction on purpose, reassuring themselves that it really was good, that there would always be sandwiches and milk for them. Elise remembered the time she and Becky got up before everybody else and made themselves tea and peanut butter sandwiches; it wasn't that good, but they relished the meal because they wanted to. She remembered herself and Rick and Robbie sitting at the breakfast table while their mother hurried around the room in her open coat, fixing pop-up waffles in the toaster. Their mother was always late for work. She poured their little glasses of juice with a quick, jerking motion. She put their plates before them with such force that the food almost slid off. All her movements were like the tail end of a great, bursting effort, like a grab for a lifeline in a midair leap. The children ate breakfast in the center of this surging effort. Unknowingly they aligned with it. They supported their mother with the fierce secret movements of their breath and blood.

If Elise could have written her mother a letter, she would have told her that she remembered how hard she'd worked to get breakfast on the table in the morning and how good her breakfasts were. She would tell her mother she missed her. She would tell her she had a job as a baby-sitter.

Eric looked at her. "When is our mommy coming?" he asked.

Elise looked at the clock. With a strained click, one white digit became another. It was two-forty. "She could walk in any minute," she said, "but if she doesn't, she'll be back in a few hours."

Eric looked confused, then disturbed. He licked his finger and picked at the bread crumbs on his plate with it. Andy began a loud singsong chant.

"She'll be home soon," said Elise. "Don't worry."

Andy sang louder and more insistently. He stood up in his chair and thrust his lips in the air like a singing snout. Well, Elise could sing too.

"Six foot, seven foot, eight foot—bunch! Daylight come and Blue wants to go home!"

Andy stopped with his mouth open, his eyes bright and askance. He grinned, jumped off the chair, and sang his crazy noises right at her. He paused.

Elise stood up; she waved her arms and wagged her butt. "Come Mister Tally Man, tally me banana—daylight come and I want to go home."

The boys grinned delightedly. Eric gave a high squeak; he darted forward and grabbed her thighs, butting her with his head. She wobbled and sat down, unbalanced and abashed by the sudden burst of feeling. He climbed up on her lap and groped her body like a busy animal. Andy jogged up and down, yodeling triumphantly. Eric planted his knee on her thigh and squeezed her breasts with both hands. That startled her. Boys weren't supposed to do that, but he was only four. She wasn't sure what to do; it seemed mean to make him stop, but if she let him do it, he might think he could do it to anybody and he'd grow up to be the kind of guy who grabs women's boobs on the street. Then Andy came over and grabbed at her too. She sat for a moment, perplexed. If Robin walked in, would she think that Elise was molesting the children? She put her hands on their shoulders and gently pushed. "Hey," she said, "stop it." They clung stubbornly. She pushed them again, harder. Eric put his face against her and let out an angry, pleading little grunt. The sound shocked her, and she hesitated. Then Andy lost interest anyway. He let go and went off toward his toys. Eric sighed and relaxed against her. Tentatively, she stroked his head. Then she stroked his back.

When she looked at the clock, it was past three. Robin must've gotten her job. Maybe it was a waitress job and they'd hired her on the spot. Elise imagined Robin changing into a soiled, ill-fitting waitress uniform in a dressing closet filled with odd furniture, forgotten sweaters, and a bucket with a dry mop in it. Her small limbs would be bristling with tension and determination. She would smooth the uniform in the depressing mirror and remind herself to smile. She would work frenetically, trying to do too much at once. The manager would yell. She would work through the break, sneaking olives and maraschino cherries from the condiment tray.

Or maybe she hadn't gotten the job. Maybe she had just decided to go for a long walk in the park, eating cheap candy out of a bag. Elise liked to do that. Sometimes when she was finished panhandling, she would take the long walk around Stanley Park, even though she'd been walking all day. It would probably be a treat for Robin to do something like that, after being cooped up in the apartment for days.

But six o'clock came and then six-thirty, and Robin didn't come back. Elise wondered how, if she'd gotten a job, she could know exactly when she'd get home anyway. What if the job had started at three? What if it was a long shift? What if she'd applied for a waitress job and didn't get it, and then looked at the paper and saw one of those "escort" ads? She pictured Robin in her little summer dress, talking to an escort service man. She pictured Robin sitting and holding her purse with both hands, her knees together and her calves splayed out, one foot tucked behind the leg of her chair.

One night when Elise was begging in San Francisco, a man asked her if she would blow him for twenty dollars. He must've heard her asking other people for money, because she hadn't asked him. She hesitated. She had never blown anybody before. "Okay," he said. "Thirty." "Okay," she said. They had to walk a few blocks to get to his car. She saw that he wore nice pants and shoes. She asked him what he did. "Never mind," he said. He had a sour, contracted little face that reminded her of a cat spraying pee on something to mark it. Elise didn't mind the mean expression; there was even something intriguing about it. It looked like it came out of a small, deep spot that was always the same.

When they got in the car he started to drive. "Are we going back to your place?" asked Elise.

"No," he said. "The park."

For the first time it occurred to her that something bad might happen. She had read in a magazine that according to experts, rapists and killers are less likely to attack people they can identify with on a human level. So she began talking to him about her boyfriend, even though she didn't have a boyfriend. She thought it might remind him of being in love.

"He doesn't like me to do this," she said. "But we need the money so much. He's trying to get a band together."

The man didn't say anything. Light played on his face. He looked like he was alone in the car, thinking about something he didn't like. He drove deep into the park, where there wasn't any light. He stopped the car and took a ten-dollar bill out of his wallet and put it on the dashboard.

"If it's good, you'll get the rest of it," he said. Then he unzipped his pants and said, "Go for it."

Elise hesitated. She felt insulted, and she wasn't sure what to do.

She considered telling him that she'd never blown anybody before; it didn't seem like a good idea. She curled her legs up under her, bent, and tucked her hair back. It couldn't be that difficult.

But it was. Her jaw hurt, hairs kept getting down her throat, and it went on and on. Finally he said, "Oh, Jesus Christ, just hold still and open your mouth." He grabbed her hair in his fist and furiously worked his hand. There was a horrible taste, and she reflexively spat. He yanked her head up and jerked her over to the other side of the car. Pain tingled across her scalp. She reached for the bill on the dashboard. He swung wildly; he meant to slap her face, but she moved too fast and he just clipped her chin with her fingers. He snatched the bill on the backstroke and crushed it in his hand.

"No," he said. "That was shit." Outraged, he groped between the seats and extracted a packet of Kleenex. He yanked one out with such force that the packet flew into the back seat. He wiped himself furiously. "You were shit," he said.

"That's not fair," she said. Her voice was light and shaky, and her heart patted fast and high in her chest. "I mean, you got off." Her voice was still light, but now it was stubborn too.

He paused in his wiping and half turned. The air between them went into a slow, palpable twist. "You little cunt," he said. His voice was very quiet. "I should beat the shit out of you."

If he grabbed her, she would poke out his eye. She would kick and bite and scratch. Her mind sped up and ran too quickly for her to hear it. She waited.

He threw the bill at her. "Get out," he said.

As she walked, her mind stopped racing and she began to think. She didn't know where she was going, but she felt heady and feverish with clarity. She would not be frightened. She would be all right. It was so cold her teeth chattered, but that was all right. She walked a long time. Sometimes she heard voices, and she knew she was passing near groups of people who couldn't hear her. She felt safe and private in the dark.

She emerged on Haight Street. A caravan of street people were arrayed across the edge of the park. She could see them huddled in ragged groups, their belongings on the ground in bundles. Some people walked between groups with a feisty, rakish air. Dogs trotted about, wagging their tails and sniffing people. The scene had a muddy, pushed-down feeling, but inside that was something raw, volatile, and potent as electricity; it could go in any direction, and it was hard to tell which it would be. She walked by a bright-yellow shirt that had been used to wipe somebody's butt. She realized she was trembling.

"Hi." A woman wearing a purple jacket walked up to her. "Do you need anything?"

"What?"

"Like condoms or . . . anything?" The woman had a nervous little face and funny looking glasses. Her jacket had "Youth Outreach" written on it. "Um, alcohol pads, bleach, a toothbrush? A cookie?"

"No, thank you," Elise had said.

It was getting dark. Through the screen, Elise could feel that the air had cooled, but the apartment was still very hot. It was seven-thirty. Andy and Eric were yelling at each other. In a minute, they would start hitting. Elise felt anger come up in her and then go back down.

"Come on," she said. "It's time for dinner."

Andy threw his toy truck on the floor so hard it dented the wood. "When is Mommy coming?"

"Soon," she snapped. Except that she didn't realize she had snapped.

Andy and Eric kept fighting at the table, until Andy kicked his brother and Elise yelled "Stop it!" as loud as she could. Then they sulked. This time, they didn't eat as if they wanted to like the food. They seemed disappointed in it. Elise was sorry she didn't have anything better to feed them, and she was also irritated at having to eat peanut butter again herself. She would rather have had pie or candy bars, and if she had gone out panhandling, she would've been able to. She hoped Robin was working for an escort service, because then she'd bring home enough cash to give Elise some.

After dinner, she heated the formula and fed Penny. The baby was sleepy and docile. She was very wet again, but she wasn't complaining, so Elise didn't change her. She had agreed to stay only until six anyway; Robin could change her when she got home. Penny released the nipple of her bottle with a guttural chirp; a sparkling thread of spit spanned nipple and lip, then broke and fell down

Penny's chin. Elise patted it dry with a Kleenex. She put her hand on the baby's stomach and rocked her.

She thought Robin must sleep in this bed with Penny, curled round her protectively as you would sleep with a kitten. Eric and Andy must sleep with them too. The bed was big, but still they would have to sleep close. She wondered if they wore pajamas. That would be uncomfortable in the heat, but it might be even more uncomfortable to touch sticky naked limbs. She pictured them all lying together, the children asleep and Robin awake and blinking in an oscillating band of street light. She wondered if Robin had a light, lacy gown to wear, or a nylon shortie.

Fleetingly, she thought of her mother in the short cotton gowns she called "nighties." She wore them with a white rayon peignoir that she had bought when she was eighteen. Elise remembered her mother's short, thick calves, the little hood of fat covering each round knee. Her mother's legs were middle-aged and ugly, but there was something childish and sweet about them.

Every summer Elise went to stay with her mother. She lived with a man who had custody of two sons from a previous marriage because their mother spent so much time in mental hospitals. Elise liked the man and the sons okay. Robbie had turned into a strange, fat kid who read philosophy books that were beyond his age range, but she liked him too. She spent her summer days sleeping late, making blender drinks, and staying out late with her friends. She would come in after midnight and find her mother sitting in the warm dark, watching a late-night talk show in her peignoir and a nightie. Her mother would turn her head to greet Elise. It was too dark to see her expression, but Elise saw in her profile a mix of love and sadness, of gratitude to see her daughter arrive home safely and forlorn bewilderment at the way everything had turned out. The expression repelled Elise and then drew her in. She would go into the kitchen and make them both hot chocolate. They would sit at opposite ends of the couch, drinking cocoa and commenting about the people on the talk show. They showed off for each other, trying to be smart. Elise's repulsion would slowly dissolve into deep comfort, becoming part of and affecting the texture of the comfort.

When the talk show was over, her mother got up and turned on the light and came to kiss Elise good night. Her peignoir would open slightly as she bent into the kiss, showing her neck and sun-reddened upper chest. The diaphanous yoke of her gown was embroidered with small, plain flowers bearing four round petals apiece. Elise imagined how much her mother must've liked the peignoir when she bought it. She imagined her putting it on for the first time, her shy vanity at the way it looked with her skin and chestnut hair. Her mother had been beautiful, and her beauty still whispered in her eyes and skin. When she wore the peignoir, her whispered beauty aligned itself with the coarse redness of her middle age and made it better than beautiful.

A breeze came into the room and dispersed the heat. There was a burst of fractious traffic noise, people honking and playing their radios loud. Someone screamed at someone else that he was a moron, a jerk-off, a spastic freak. Under the light across the street, a girl Elise's age was walking in a short, filmy dress that played about her slim legs. There was a funny strut in her hips and haunches, as if she was very proud and very ashamed at once. She turned around to smile at someone behind her, and the light caught her teasing eyes and dark, shoulder-length hair in motion about her face.

Elise wondered how her mother would react if she knew about the man in the park. She couldn't picture any reaction. She could only envision her mother sitting on the couch, waiting for her daughter with that stoic look of love and sadness. It was a look that was already hurt too much to be surprised by the man in the park, a look that even anticipated him. It was the shadow of the way she used to look at Rick.

Elise thought of her father. She imagined him walking around the house with his fists balled, yelling that the world was a shit pot and his daughter was a whore. But that image quickly dissolved to an image of him sitting alone on the edge of his bed with his head in his hands. She imagined him feeling the way she felt when she had walked through the park alone. He would feel shocked and scared and angry. But he would hold on. Inside, he would have a hard little rock of love for her, and he would hold on to it.

Like an echo of that image, she thought of Robbie, crouching by the TV and doing his drawings while the world threatened to crush him. She thought of Becky, moving through the room with her light-footed, absent grace. She thought of Rick turning away from her, except she only pictured one shoulder and the side of his face, as if he were someone she'd dreamed of and forgotten.

It was eight-thirty and dark outside. "That bitch," whispered Elise. "Where is that fucking bitch?"

Andy ran up with a tiny red thing in his hand. "This is Little Friend!" he said. "He's in big, big trouble! He's always, always lost!"

"Oh!"

"Hide him!" said Andy. "You hide him and we'll try to find him!"

She put Little Friend beside one of the kitchen table legs; it took them a surprisingly long time to find it, and when they did, they wanted her to hide it again.

"Put him someplace bad!" they said. "Someplace scary!"

She put him in the sugar bowl. They looked all over, screaming, "Little Friend! Little Friend!" until Penny woke and began to mumble irritably.

"Be quiet," said Elise sharply.

Eric quieted, but Andy kept screaming.

She knelt and grabbed him by the shoulders. "If you want to play you have to be quiet. Okay?"

He looked at her to see if she meant it. She tried to seem stern, but it was halfhearted and he could tell. As soon as she let go, he began to yell again.

"All right," she said. "I don't want to play." She went and sat by the window. In the window across the street, a woman was standing at a table and folding clothes. Even from a distance Elise could see that she was frowning resentfully. The boys yelled and ran. She ignored them. It was nine-thirty.

At her father's house, Elise had liked to climb on the roof at night. Her father's upstairs den had a sunporch affixed to it, a small, roof-tiled square with a wooden railing that they lovingly called "the balcony." One evening she discovered that if she stood on the railing she could get up on the roof, using her sneakers for traction. She climbed right to the top of the house and straddled it, gazing about the neighborhood. She felt very pleased with herself; with a slight maneuver, she had made a special pocket hidden in ordinary life.

The roof had a number of peaks and flat surfaces, and she explored them all. She found she could sit comfortably outside Rick's room and look in. She could see part of Becky's room, and she could look right into the bathroom. Eventually, she grew bold enough to spy on her family. This gave her a strange pleasure she could not have explained. She could see Becky walking around the room listening to music, not dancing or singing but just pacing with an intent, furiously inturned face. She watched Rick while he wrote a song, crouching on the floor and rocking himself, gazing up with big, rapt eyes as he worked his lips, his pencil poised above the page. She watched her stepmother use the toilet. She watched her father sit on the tub and pare his nails. Seeing these things made her feel closer to her family than she did when she was in the same room with them. It made her like them more.

But they got suspicious when they kept hearing muffled noises overhead, and one night her stepmother went out and saw her on the roof. Then they were all mad at her.

"God," said Rick. "What a freak!"

"This is not normal behavior," said their stepmother. "This is sick."

Their father stood and wiped his mouth.

It was ten o'clock. Andy grabbed her arm and yanked it. "Come on!" he said. "Hide him again!"

"No," she said, and she pushed him.

He thrust his little face into the air and sang his nonsense song as loud as he could. Penny began to scream.

Elise stood. "Stop it," she said.

"Daylight come, banana wanna go home!"

"Shut up!"

"Daylight come daylight come!"

She slapped him in the face. She slapped him so hard his head snapped around. He shut up. He looked up at her and smiled, tremulously.

"I said stop it," she said.

He put his thumb in his mouth and went and sat in an armchair in the corner. Eric went and sat with the toys. Elise sat back down. She hoped Penny would stop crying without her having to do anything. It was after ten o'clock. She didn't know what to do. She got up and put an unfinished bottle of formula back on the stove to heat. There wasn't much of it left, she noticed.

Her stepmother loved it when things were sick. Her favorite books were true-life stories about drug-addicted fashion models who died horribly or prep school boys who turned out to be murderers. She loved TV movies about people who seemed okay until they became obsessed with a coworker and wound up killing everyone in the office. She was always saying, "That's not normal!" in a thrilled, disapproving voice. She could say it about a magazine story that described a jealous wife who stalked her husband's lover so she could make her get on her knees and stick a gun in her mouth. She could say it about Becky sitting in her room and playing the same song over and over again.

She disapproved, but part of her seemed secretly to sympathize with the sickness. It was like she thought everybody had it, and the best you could do was to cover it up, and sometimes it would just come boiling out anyway. Then you had to point at it and condemn it, even though you knew you had it too.

Once, Elise heard her talking to a client about the woman's stepdaughter, who was crazy even though she was on Prozac. Elise had stopped by the salon to borrow some money, and she had to wait because Sandy was tattooing the client's lips. The client's lips were swollen and bleeding from the needle, but she wanted to talk anyway.

"I just feel so bad and so helpless. It turns out she's been cutting herself like that for at least a year. All over her arms and her stomach, with a razor."

"You know," Sandy had said, "there's a whole article on it in *Focus* this month. It's just fascinating. It says they do it to distract themselves from the terrible pain they feel inside."

Penny didn't want to take the bottle. Elise pushed the nipple against her lips again and again, but she kept turning her head and crying.

"Come on," Elise whispered, low and angry. "Shut up, come on." It wasn't fair, she thought. It was ten-thirty. She didn't know what to do.

She thought of her father yelling at Rick. "You vain, conceited little prick!" he screamed. "I'd like to see you out in the trenches with the artillery coming in! What would you do, little prick? Dye your hair?" He crouched over Rick so that he could yell at him better. "Nobody out there would give a fuck about your hair!"

She slammed the bottle on the little bedside table. She yanked the diaper off the baby. Penny screamed angrily. Elise stopped. She put her hand on Penny's stomach. "I'm sorry," she said.

When she had finished the bottle, Penny was quiet. It was eleven o'clock. Elise walked up and down the room. If Robin came home now, Elise was going to yell at her. She went to the dresser and began opening the drawers, starting with the top ones. She saw Robin's nylon underwear, a grubby address book, a rubber band, a button with thread still attached. Eric was looking at her from the floor; when he saw she saw him, he looked away. She found a piece of paper; it was the torn-off half of a form letter asking for money for breast cancer research, with phone numbers and a grocery list written on it in chartreuse ink. There was a ballpoint on the bedside table. She sat on the bed, turned the letter over, and wrote on the back: "It is 11:00 and I am leaving. You said you would be back at six and you are five hours late. Almost anybody else would've left after two hours late. I took this job for no money and I did everything I said I would do. What you've done is wrong. You have acted like an asshole. I'm sorry to do this, and I hope nothing bad has happened to you. But I have to leave. I am not coming back tomorrow."

She put it on the table. First she put it down flat, then she stood it up between the clock and the bud vase. She decided to wait just five more minutes. The noise from the street was a cool, soothing mumble. The breeze from the window was almost chilling on her lap. Andy had fallen asleep in the armchair. Eric was moving a toy around and humming softly to himself. She thought about herself in the future. She could only imagine loud music and quickly changing pictures, like an advertisement for something on TV. That was okay;

it seemed like fun. She imagined herself having fun, then making money, then going back home and buying everybody presents. She imagined how grateful they'd be.

It was eleven-thirty when she left. Penny was deep in her thoughts. Andy was asleep. Eric was still playing and humming to himself. She crouched beside him to say goodbye. He looked at her with somber eyes. He looked like he'd just recognized her. "Bye," he said. She touched his arm; he looked down.

The hall was hot and stuffy. It felt like she was already miles away from the apartment. She padded quickly down the stairs. When she reached the next floor, she saw that the people in the apartment directly under Robin's had left their door wide open. She looked in and saw a group of men sitting in shirtsleeves around the kitchen table, playing cards. They had big arms and broad, jovial faces. A woman with her back to the door was moving vaguely at the sink. The men laughed and drank as they played. "Excuse me," she said.

A man got up and came to the door. His face was pockmarked, with little whiskers in the pocks. "Yes?" He was foreign, she couldn't tell which kind. He wore a red kerchief around his neck, and his nose was big.

"There's kids in the apartment right above you. I've been taking care of them all day, but now I have to go. I don't know where their mother is. She said she'd be back, but she's not, and now I have to go. Could you be sure they're okay?"

He put his hand on his chin and looked past her as if considering.

The woman glanced past the man at Elise; from her expression, it seemed that Elise made no sense to her.

"One of them's only a baby."

"Okay," said the man. He pointed upstairs and nodded. "I check."

When she got home, she found Mark sitting in the living room, sewing patches on his jeans. She told him what had happened. "What do you think I should've done?" she asked. "Do you think it was okay to leave?"

He shrugged. "What else could you do? She didn't come back." He concentrated on his pants, very meticulously working the needle. "She shouldn't have left you there like that."

Elise sat on the couch. "Well, but one of them was a baby."

"You told the neighbors. They'll be okay."

"I guess." She stared at the frayed old carpet. There were tulips on it. She felt grateful to be back in her living room, even though it wasn't really hers. "The thing is, I don't know what I'm going to do. I can't keep panhandling forever. I have to find work somehow."

"You'll find something," said Mark. "It'll be all right."

She sat a moment. "I once blew a guy for money," she said. "In San Francisco. It was a nightmare. He said he'd give me fifty bucks, but he only gave me ten, and then he hit me."

"Yeah?"

"And he tasted funny too. Like there was something wrong with him."

"Elise, God, you shouldn't let 'em come in your _mouth_."

"Well, I didn't _want_ to; it just happened."

Mark put down the pants and thought. "Well," he said, "this girl who sells roses in Gas Town has been paying me twenty dollars to clean them for her. Like, take off the thorns and the old petals? If you wanted to help me, I could pay you five dollars. Do you want to do that?"

"Yeah," she said. "Okay." She sniffed. "Thank you, Mark."

"It's okay."

She went into the kitchen and raided the refrigerator. She got olives, cheese, tiny green peppers, and cold white rice from an old Chinese take-out box and put it all on a plate and carried it to her room.

The next day she walked by the apartment building, on the opposite side of the street. There was no one sitting on the porch. She looked up at Robin's window; it was open, as it had been when she left. She pictured Robin coming home and screaming, "Oh, my babies!" She pictured Andy and Eric at the foreign man's table, eating dishes of ice cream. Then she turned the corner and headed for Granville Street, her rubber dime-store sandals hitting her dirty heels with each fleet step.

Orchid

Margot had not seen Patrick for sixteen years, so it was a mild shock to run into him in Seattle, on the sidewalk outside an esoteric video rental store. She had stopped to halfheartedly examine the items of clothing a street vendor had arranged on a large blanket on the sidewalk in front of the store, as well as on some auxiliary coat hangers hung on a parking lot fence. She was considering buying a used print blouse, and thinking how ridiculous it was for someone her age to make such a purchase, when a big man in an expensive suit spoke her name. He was thin-skinned and pale like an old onion, his forehead large and strangely fraught. The muscles of his brows and eyes were tightly bunched together, and their combined expression extended all the way out to the tip of his long nose. She wondered how this oddball knew who she was, but then he extended his hand to her with the debonair fatuity of a very handsome man, and she recognized him. Patrick had been quite a beautiful boy.

"What're you doing here?" Her voice came out high and flirtatious, and she blushed. "I mean, in Seattle?"

"I moved here three years ago. I moved from San Diego."

They stood there smiling, their hands still clasped. The wind blew trash about their feet; Patrick shook his ankle to release a piece of pink cellophane, turned his head to watch it run up the street, then turned back to her and grinned. "You'll never guess what I'm doing now."

"I'm a social worker," she blurted. "How about that?"

His smile surged again and she felt a pulse of warmth come through his hand into hers, then fade quickly, as if a cat had leapt onto her lap, changed its mind, and leapt off. "That doesn't surprise me. I mean, it's great, but—you know what?—it's also funny, because I'm a psychopharmacologist."

"No!"

"Isn't that a kick?"

Margot and Patrick had met when they were undergraduates at the University of Michigan. He was studying to be an actor and she was studying English lit. Margot was generally more interested in girls than in boys, but she, like everyone, had been arrested by Patrick's attenuated, almost feminine appearance. He had pale-brown hair, full, blurrily defined lips, and wide hazel eyes with blunt, abundant lashes. His skin was live and sensitive as the surface of a breathing young plant. He had a curious, light-footed poise, which in certain acute moments he would discard with a subtle inward movement, as if startled or disgusted or fascinated by something only he could see.

He said that almost immediately after graduating he'd landed a supporting role in a popular movie Margot had never seen, and that "people" had gotten "excited" about him. But when he moved to Los Angeles, he found Hollywood too horrible to bear. "The vanity," he said, "the falsity. It's so base, I can't even tell you. You lose everything, you turn into this creature. I lost the ability to act. I'd go meet these people and do these readings and I'd just choke." Like a fastidious girl, he tucked a piece of pale hair behind his ear. "Maybe if I'd hung in, I would've adjusted and I'd be a star by now. But at a crucial moment my mother died, and I sort of flipped out. She'd always wanted me to go to medical school. So I became a psychopharm." He shrugged, almost apologetically. "It's boring, but it's good because I'm really helping people. It's really good to be helping people. You know?" There was an unctuous inflection in his voice that to Margot seemed a poor cousin to his former grace.

60

They stood and talked for several moments, each moment a triangular wedge that started small, widened, and reached a set limit. He asked if she was "with someone." She was not; in fact, a woman named Roberta, whom she had been planning to move in with, had recently dumped her for someone else. Patrick, on the other hand, had just left a relationship with a phlebotomist—a "total masochist" whose life was a vector of disaster and misery—for a chiropractor named Rhoda. Now Rhoda wanted to marry him, and even though he loved her, he knew it would never work out.

"She's a wonderful kook," he said, "but she's a kook. She goes on goddess retreats and Tibetan bell festivals. But _I'm_ actually more open-minded than she is. Her friends are shocked that she's involved with a psychopharm." He laughed, Margot thought nervously. "They solemnly come up to me and say, 'You've got a long path ahead of you.' I mean, please." He sighed. "She's at a harmonic convergence retreat now, trying to get 'centered' enough to leave me. But I'm afraid I'm just going to pull her back." He sighed deeply and then blinked as if suddenly aware that they were in public. "Am I telling you more than you need to know?"

"No," she said. "It's good to see you, Patrick."

They exchanged numbers and agreed that maybe they should eat dinner together. Margot walked away in a mild disorientation that lasted some blocks. She looked into the coffee shops she passed every day as if she hadn't realized what they were before. Listlessly dressed young people sat in them, their expressions hovering between public and private. Their coarsely groomed young faces appeared deliberately inchoate, as if in passive resistance to their own identities. A cosmetic redhead stared back at Margot, her gaze a slim, tingling thread of sensory thought. She self-consciously stroked her dyed hair. The sleeve of her loose pink sweater fell to the elbow of her slim forearm. Margot suddenly remembered the street vendor's little print blouse and reversed her steps back into the wind.

In Ann Arbor, Margot had answered an ad for a roommate and, as a result, had moved into a house with Patrick, his sister Dolores, and a perpetually consternated math major named Donald. The house was small, but an inept system of hallways gave it a neurotic, spindly sprawl. Margot's room was a humble cube with three brown cork-board squares affixed to one wall in a slanting shape of dumb symmetrical ascension. One of the house phones sat on a crippled little table outside her door, and since the math major, Donald, shared the first floor with her, it was he that she most often heard, usually having the same dark, fiercely muttered conversation, apparently with the same loathed person whom he invariably hung up on. Whenever Margot remembered the house, she thought of it as dark and a little too cold; she remembered squatting over the heat vent in her room in the morning with big wool house slippers on her feet, working up to getting dressed.

But the kitchen was large and bright, and it was there that the household gathered for its disorganized breakfasts and late-night snacks. At first it was Dolores whom Margot most noticed. Dolores was twenty-eight, which Margot thought was fascinatingly old and ruined. She was tall, with narrow hips and shoulders but a lot of fat on her rear. She had a pained, sardonic countenance, and her skin was prematurely lined. She had just been released from a mental hospital, where she had been sent after she had pulled most of the hair from her head. She took lithium and wore a head scarf to hide her scalp. She had an air of ridiculous tragedy that reeked of affectation, but Margot admired it anyway. At breakfast she ate an orange, coffee, and toast soaked with expensive European butter, which she would sprinkle with salt. As she leisurely ate, she would glue false fingernails to her fingers and then paint them with red polish. Her gestures were very elaborate and fine.

Donald, the math major, watched her with bemusement and, Margot thought, perverse, furtive attraction enlivened by a little hot streak of disgust. Patrick did not watch her, but Margot felt his attention sometimes touch his sister, quickly, like a traveling drop of light, as if he were checking to be sure she was still there. He sat at the table in a torpid slouch, but his hazel eyes were live and expectant. He held his limbs, especially his hands, in peculiar twists that made Margot imagine his inner muscles in secret shapes of furious discord, but his posture was light, lax, and happy. She knew that his mother sometimes sent him bottles of Valium or Xanax, because she had once been present when one of his would-be girlfriends intercepted a care package and dumped the contents in the toilet. But she didn't think his languor was drug induced. It seemed more the product of an unusual distribution of self, as if, by some crafty manipulation of internal circuitry, he'd concentrated himself in certain key psychic posts and abandoned the vast regions he didn't want to be in. These empty spaces had an almost electrical allure, more highly charged than his distinct presence in the areas he occupied. Men didn't like him very much, but whenever the phone rang, it was almost always a girl for Patrick.

Margot's apartment was cold when she arrived. She turned on the heat and then went through all the rooms, turning on the lights. She put her pink flannel robe over her clothes and made herself a dinner of sliced carrots, a ham sandwich, and a Styrofoam cup of take-out vegetable soup. She put the sandwich and the carrots on a turquoise plate and the soup in a burgundy bowl. She put out a folded napkin and a spoon and vitamin capsules. She poured herself half a glass of red wine. She sat down, and suppressed pain oscillated through her in a slow, hard wave. When she had told Patrick that Roberta had left her, she had seen a faint look of satisfaction move in his eyes—satisfaction not at her loss but at seeing the Margot who was familiar to him, stalwart in a state of loss. His look almost made her bitter. But at the same time, she felt that something in her voice had invited it.

She poured lots of salt on her ham sandwich and allowed her little dinner to comfort her. It was one of the things she and Roberta were good at: small, comforting dinners. Roberta had been gone for six months, and it was still difficult for Margot to sit down to eat by herself. Still, she was determined to do it, and her determination felt good to her. It made her feel like a tenacious animal, burrowing a home in hard, dry soil. And that, of course, had been what Patrick had heard in her voice.

She remembered very well the moment when she and Patrick had become friends. She had been sitting in her room on a rainy afternoon, and he had knocked on the door to ask if she wanted to go to the Brown Jug to have coffee with him. She remembered thinking that coffee with Patrick might be an event and then being irritated at herself for the thought.

They had to walk some blocks to get to the Brown Jug. The rain had just stopped, and the air was cold, silken, and insinuating. Patrick hadn't worn a scarf, and to protect his throat he held his coat close around his neck with one hand in a gesture of artificial privation that seemed a calculated counterpoint to the abundance of his lips and eyes. He drew her into conversation with a gentle solicitousness that was both seductive and condescending. The condescension made her unsettled and gruff, but then a little tendril of seduction would creep out and wrap itself about her wrist, and to her embarrassment, she would find herself talking brightly, her words done up in fancy shapes to impress him. He listened to her with a tense receptivity that made her embarrassment strangely thrilling. The conversation was static and vibrant at once, like a suspension bridge humming with hidden electrical energy.

The rain had surfeited the grass, and each bright blade was alert and full of tender resolve. She commented on the beauty of it. Patrick said that when he was in the third grade, he would walk to school in the winter and imagine that the grass was crying out to him for help from under the snow. Sometimes he would reach down and dig out a blade or two and put them in his warm pocket with an odd, almost erotic burst of feeling at the random, humanitarian rescue. He would imagine what the rescued grass must feel like, huddling in his pocket, gratified, yet bewildered and fearful in the stifling lint-ridden warmth. Once he actually brought one home and laid it to convalesce in a tiny matchbox stuffed with cotton.

"You must've been very disappointed when it died," said Margot.

"Oh," he said, "I didn't really think it was alive."

His tone was light and delighted; it seemed as if it could turn in an infinite number of directions at once, all of them easy. Margot was quite taken with him; he was not what she had expected.

When they got to the diner, they ordered coffee and sweet, gelatinous pies. The tone of their conversation changed. Seated and eating, Margot no longer felt the solicitousness or the light changeability she had sensed during the walk. Patrick just looked at her and talked about nothing. Her mind wandered, taking in the shabby, genial diner with pleasure. On the walls there were cheap paintings of landscapes and animals that nevertheless looked as if the artists had cared about them. There were plastic flowers on each table. The sugar containers had big lumps of stale sugar in them. Their waitress was a small woman in her thirties with beautiful, fierce eyes. One of her legs was withered, but her carriage was determined and erect. Patrick said, "It's just that I feel so invisible. I just feel so invisible."

Margot blinked and stared at him. His bright-orange shirt was open to his exquisite collarbones. His long, subtle hands looked hypersensitive against his cheap coffee cup. He was outrageously fine and fair. "What do you mean?" she said. "What on earth do you mean?"

She didn't remember his answer, or even if he had one.

She got up at six in the morning so that she would have time to eat a nourishing breakfast and prepare a sack of wholesome lunch food. She made herself a porridge of four kinds of whole grain mixed together in the blender. She thought of a former client, a fragile widower named Thomas, whom she had persuaded to make at least one daily meal for himself. On his second breakfast he had dropped his bowl of oatmeal, and she had been unable to make him try to cook again. As Margot remembered him, she felt an intense rush of loyalty and protectiveness bordering on love.

She turned on the radio. People were talking about whether or not the nation's children were being doped up with Ritalin on account of an attention deficit disorder vogue. "It's a brave new world!" yelled a caller. "And you people . . . you . . . "

Margot put a lot of butter, honey, and milk in her cereal. She was the only person she knew who still used whole milk, and she was inexplicably proud of that tiny fact. She sat down and dug in. At least she hadn't spilled _her_ cereal.

She arrived at the bus stop just in time. The bus was crowded, and she had to stand with people pressed so closely about her that she barely needed to grasp the handrail. She was held and rocked in the warm, undulant mass as the bus chugged up hill and down, stopping and jerking exhaustingly. Through the damp cloth and wool of their sweaters and coats, Margot felt people striving hard inside the bone and muscle of their bodies. They seemed horribly tense and mostly unhappy, but there was courage in their tension, and even hope.

"Stupid cunts. Stupid cunts are running the world." The passenger seated before Margot glared up at her like an insulted snake. "It's cunts in the command seat," he said.

"Yes," she said. "It really is. And most of them are guys."

He wrinkled his brow and retracted. The Asian woman to Margot's right tried to withdraw from her in distaste but got squashed against her instead as the bus wheezed uphill. Margot's stop came, and she burst from the bus feeling energized by the little exchange.

The morning was a chaos of bad news and mix-ups. A client who'd been socked on the nose by another client in a support group was threatening to sue the clinic. There were six messages on her voice mail from a client who said his son's foster parent was trying to kill the kid. Two of Margot's clients had been denied further visits by their HMOs because they had "improved," meaning that they hadn't attempted to kill themselves recently. Margot waded in, negotiating the snarl of emotional currents that vied and buzzed against each other like agitated snakes. She sorted them, one at a time, handling each furious, vibrating strand with care, allowing some to careen past her.

She ran out of steam in the middle of a session with a thirty-seven-year-old woman who, although she knew she was pretty for her age, was having suicidal thoughts because she didn't look like a supermodel. "I know it's stupid," she said. "I'm embarrassed even to mention it. But it's all I can think about." In spite of her embarrassment, it was all she could talk about too. "I don't just want to look like that, I want the whole world to *be* like that."

"Like what?" asked Margot.

"Static. With no feelings except, like, if it's your birthday you're happy, if your mom dies you're sad." She paused, as if she'd just remembered something. "I mean, I know the models themselves aren't like that. They probably have the same stupid, ugly problems I do. It's more the world as they represent it. Without any fucking awful complexity. Without any of this filthy shit." She indicated her thigh with a backhanded slap.

After this session, Margot stopped for a snack of orange sections and cheese cubes in the lounge, where she listened to a social worker named Georgia say awful stuff about a colleague she referred to as "the big fat cow pig." Then she went to the rest room, where two other social workers were talking about a woman who'd been in earlier, trying to have her daughter committed. "I don't know about the kid," said one, "but I'd sure like to put Mrs. Bitch away." Margot washed her hands and pressed a wet paper towel against her forehead and temples. She looked at herself in the mirror, resolutely hooked her hair behind her ears, and for some reason thought again of Patrick.

Emerging from her room for late-night toast, she would pass his girl-friends in the hall on their way to the bathroom, or meet them smoking cigarettes in the kitchen. She remembered a beautiful girl named Helen, who had long brown hair and a funny habit of picking up random objects and immediately putting them down as if suddenly stricken with disappointment in this speckled ashtray or that empty fluted cup. Most of the girls seemed unhappy, but their unhappiness seemed integral to them, and in some curious way strengthened Margot's impression of their integrity. They would look at Patrick as if calmly measuring the distance between him and them, as if they knew that his little area of private space was closed to them, but that was all right because they had their own little area they were planning to go back to once they got what they came for—although of course it often didn't work out that way. Margot remembered one girl in particular, a girl she had glimpsed on her way past Patrick's barely opened door. She had been sitting on Patrick's worn mattress, waiting while he did something at the other end of the room. Her arms were wrapped across her torso, each hand grabbing the opposite small shoulder, and one small, gray-socked foot covered the other in a pathetic gesture of protection, but her downturned angular little face was proud and beautiful and full of tense, ready feeling. One month later the girl called Patrick and cried so loud and hard that Margot heard the sobbing as she squeezed past Patrick sitting on his haunches in the dark, narrow upstairs hallway with the telephone receiver between his cheek and his graceful shoulder, listening with a look of rapt, sensual sorrow.

For Margot, it had been quite a display. Although she could be attracted to males or females, she had little luck with either; her shy flirtations tended to be muffled failures, which started, then ended, with puzzled indifference, embarrassment, and trailing irresolution. It was almost a relief for her to witness romantic shenanigans, just to know that they actually happened. At least that was how she had felt at first.

The rest of the day she had an intake phone shift. It was an uneventful few hours, except for a slightly unusual call from a young man who said he was phoning not because he had a problem but to ask for advice about a disturbed woman who was harassing him. She had been calling him and writing rambling, nonsensical letters, and finally he'd had it out with her on the phone. He was worried, he said, about what she might do next.

"Let me be sure I understand," said Margot. "Does this woman want to make an appointment, or . . . ?"

"She was the girlfriend of a friend of mine, and then they broke up and I started fucking her a little bit." He appeared not to have heard her question. "And then I realized she was really sick—she was on all this medication and shit. I thought maybe it was the medication that was making her weird, so I told her maybe she should stop. She did stop, and she got so fucked up she couldn't get out of bed. Then I got interested in somebody else, and so I told her, and she just wouldn't leave me alone. First she sent me this crazy letter, and I just went and put the envelope she sent it in on her mailbox."

"You . . . wait. If you could tell me what you want me to help you with, I could—"

"I'm trying to! So then she called me, really mad because I left her an empty envelope, and I just—"

"Well," said Margot, "it—"

"I didn't have a pen! I didn't want to be rude to her—I mean, she's so sick already. So I left the envelope so she'd know I'd gotten her letter."

Margot was eating dinner when Patrick called, but she picked up the phone anyway. His voice was shy and warm. "I've been thinking about you all day," he said. They talked while she ate with one hand, intermittently tucking the receiver between her shoulder and her head so that she could carve and salt her fancy take-out chicken thigh.

"I was remembering how we used to talk," he said. "It always made me feel better talking to you, especially about relationships. And I wondered if you knew that."

Margot mumbled how she'd been thinking about him too. Her mumble was also shy and warm. It was unusual, her thing with Patrick, she thought. But it was good.

"You always helped me figure out what I was really doing. Guys sometimes aren't very clear about that."

She hadn't remembered doing that, but she liked the idea that she had. As if to reinforce the idea, Patrick began describing in further detail the relationships he had mentioned while they were standing on the street. It wasn't entirely true that he'd broken it off with the masochistic phlebotomist, he said. Tricia still called him in the middle of the night when she was "in crisis" and came by his office in sexy dresses for free Prozac. Last week she'd sent him a birthday card that had a picture of an emaciated kneeling woman with her head thrown back and a tortured look on her face. "God knows where she found the thing. It was repulsive, actually. But still, it hit me right in the gut. I even brought it to the couples therapy that Rhoda and I are doing."

"Why?"

"To illustrate what I'm not getting from Rhoda." He paused self-consciously. "It may've been an unkind thing to do. I mean, I don't want that from Rhoda, but I want her to understand that need in me because it's part of who I am. And she just can't. I mean, her card was generic flowers and a love message." He sighed. "Underneath all the New Age goofiness, she's just totally suburban, you know?"

"So are we, remember?"

Patrick was silent for a moment. Margot salted her oily tomato salad.

"You're right," he said. "That sounded ridiculous. What I meant to say is, she's really conventional."

"Patrick," she said, "how's Dolores?"

"Oh." She almost heard him wince. "I don't know. Isn't that awful? We haven't had much contact over the last five years. I know she's living in some slum in Miami, probably working as a waitress. She's a total alcoholic. Last time I talked to her she was having an affair, if you could call it that, with this fourteen-year-old Latin kid who couldn't speak English. She rear-ended somebody because she was driving around drunk with her pants down and the kid's face between her legs, and I mean so drunk that when she got out of the car, she forgot to pull her pants up and she fell and broke a tooth. That was the last time I talked to her. Since she stopped speaking to my dad, I'm not even sure where she lives. It was just too much, you know? It was painful."

Margot remembered Dolores sitting at the table, affixing her false fingernails, holding her hand at a distance and appraising it with an arched, theatrical brow. She remembered Patrick's attention on her, a drop of traveling light. "Could you get her number for me?" she asked. "Could you try? I don't know what I'd say to her at this point, but . . ."

"Of course." The loyalty in Patrick's voice was like a muscle that's gone flabby but is still strong; it was loyalty for her, not Dolores, and it both flattered and troubled her. "It's probably time for me to check in anyway. Who knows where she is now. Spiritually and emotionally, I mean."

Margot thought of something Dolores had once told her. They had been sitting at the kitchen table, drinking sweet coffee and smoking. "When Patrick was a baby, I used to do this really mean thing to him," said Dolores. "He was just learning how to walk. All by himself, he'd struggle to his feet with this earnest frown and start slowly fighting his way forward with his little hands balled. He'd be in this nightgown our mom used to put him in, and it would trail out behind him. I'd follow along and I'd let him get so far and then I'd step on his gown and he'd fall over with this cute little 'oof.'" Dolores drew on her cigarette and left a wet red lipstick mark on it. "The funny thing is, he never cried. He'd just set his little face and slowly get up and toddle on. Sometimes I did it just 'cause it was so cool to see him get up again."

Patrick was saying that while he had enjoyed being a psychopharm, he was tired of it now and was looking for a way out. With this end in mind, he was working on a CD-ROM about depression, in which psychiatrists would appear on a tiny screen to explain to viewers what depression is and how to get treatment. "It's going to be complex and layered," he said. "Like performance art."

Margot agreed to meet him for dinner that weekend, even though she wasn't sure she wanted to. Their conversation had made her feel passive and nonplussed. When they hung up, she sat for a while and stared at the spray of greasy salt scattered across her plate, at the tidy little snarl of chicken bones and the minute pistil of broccoli. Her tabletop was red Formica. On the table she had a salt shaker in the shape of a mournful sheep and Magic Markers in a row and a dish of colored rocks mixed with cheap jewelry she'd worn when she was a kid. She liked her things, but now the sight of them made her sad. She always had arrangements of bright little things on her walls and furniture. Roberta had made fun of them, mildly at first.

Late one night, a woman Patrick didn't know had called him and asked if she could come over. He told her that she could, but when she got there he didn't like the way she looked, so he made her tea, conversed for as long as he felt etiquette required, and then asked her to leave. Margot had been asleep and, to her regret, had not seen the girl. She was fascinated by this story and by the casual way Patrick told it at breakfast; without knowing why, she found herself imagining, repeatedly and in varying ways, the girl's face when Patrick told her to leave. She could not imagine calling anyone and asking if she could come over late at night, no matter how much she wanted them, nor could she imagine letting a person who made such a call come to her home.

She and Dolores had analyzed the incident at length, sitting on Dolores's big bed in a flood of sunlight, eating from a box of dimestore chocolates. "Patrick has always had these things with women," said Dolores moodily. "And being a guy, he can't help but take advantage of them. Like, that girl put herself in a situation where he might tell her to go home, you know? What do you expect if you call up strangers in the middle of the night?"

Margot supposed it was true. "But still, something seems gross about it. Like, maybe he could've told her that he might ask her to leave."

"Oh, come on, how could he have done that? That would really have been gross." Dolores took an open package of cigarettes and a silver lighter from her bedside table; she manipulated the small objects with the grand, suppressed languor of a person moving underwater. "In his own way, Patrick is an old-fashioned gentleman," she said. "He likes things to have a certain decorum, a certain . . . gracious style. He's a romantic."

Dolores's hands were crossed at the wrist, a fresh cigarette inserted between two slightly puffy fingers. Margot wondered if the medication she took made her hands puffy. "But it doesn't seem gentlemanly to let a stranger come over," Margot persisted. "I mean, he was allowing a situation that would probably not be very gracious, whether she stayed or left. Don't you think?"

"But the thing is, she probably really wanted to come over. She probably had extremity in her voice, and any extremity is potentially very romantic." She brought the cigarette to her lips and Margot noticed that her hand trembled. "People often want something from Patrick, and he has a hard time saying no. It's our family and this awful boundary crap. Our mom was all over Patrick, physically and every other way. She let him get away with anything because he was beautiful, but then there were all these other ways she had him by the balls. She was obsessed with him. The sick old bitch. She called him 'my orchid.' " Dolores imitated her mother with fine, slippery malice. "My orchid."

They sat in silence for a moment. Dolores's bed was covered with an old quilt made of meticulously color-coordinated shapes sewn together with the pretty humor of a child. A strip of pink cloth decorated with abstract roses was sewn next to a triangle of blue and white stripes next to a lavender oblong with green and yellow polka dots on it. At the head of the bed were Dolores's pillows, in faded yellow slipcovers. She had lace curtains on her windows. Her room did not look like the room of someone who had recently torn the hair from her head.

"People get fixated on Patrick," said Dolores. "When he was in high school he actually had a female fan club. It was embarrassing. He encourages stuff like that because it flatters him, but in another way, he knows it's not about him at all. I think he's pretty lonely, actually."

"Yeah," said Margot. "I can see that." Thoughtfully, she ate a caramel; it was slightly, sensuously stale, and she chewed it with contented vigor.

Work the next day was like running a relay race through a rabbit warren while pranksters blew horns, banged cymbals, and set off sirens. The morning began with the arrival of a mother and son who had come in on an emergency basis because the son, a sixteen-year-old who attended a school for the gifted, had pierced his nose and inserted a ring through it. His father had committed suicide when the kid was ten, and his mother was convinced that the nose piercing was an indication of "suicidal ideation." It took an hour to convince her otherwise, which made Margot an hour late for her appointment with a family that had just been successfully "reunited." The daughter in this family _was_ having suicidal ideation, and Margot scarcely blamed her. Her father beat her up and her mother, a hot-wired piece of bone and muscle with a face-lift, complained constantly that the kid wasn't happy.

"I mean, I know he shouldn't hit her, but just look at her!" She gesticulated at her drooping child, a pale fifteen-year-old with dyed black hair and black lipstick. "I don't mind the black thing and the tattoos; we did stuff like that too. But we were happy! We did things! The people we knew were cream of the crop, the best and the brightest! She just lumps around with losers and doesn't care about anything."

"I think Lalena cares about her poetry," said Margot.

"Yeah—it's all about suicide!"

"But I see a lot of intensity in her poems," said Margot. "Even if they are about suicide, they feel intensely alive and fierce. They aren't fierce the way you are. But she's a different person."

The mother started and blinked. The girl glanced at Margot. Margot met her eye and held her. With an abrupt emotional cramp, she remembered Patrick sitting in the diner, holding her with his eyes.

All her morning sessions ran late, and Margot had only ten minutes for lunch. She ate her dried apricots and pecans out of a Baggie in the ladies' lounge, where she paced before the smeared mirror, furtively abusing her clients. "You wonder why she's writing suicide poems?" she muttered. "Take a look in the mirror, you deranged cow."

She looked at herself and remembered something Roberta had said. "You're a stereotype of a social worker!" she'd yelled. "You go in there like you're healing the world, and you're just as screwed up as they are! You're really trying to heal yourself, and it's not working, Margot!"

Near the end of the semester, she'd met an astonishing girl, a freshman named Chiquita. She was a giggly little thing, who painted her fingernails with a different color on each short, chewed nail and who, at the end of orgasm, would reach greedily between her legs with both hands, sighing and twisting her head as Margot's tongue played over her fingers. Margot would return home with light, bright eyes, and sometimes Patrick would see her and his eyes would light in response. She would talk about her date, and he would listen with an avid regard that felt almost like love. His voice lost the teasing, seductive quality that had so flummoxed her, and he would look at her as if she were an especially honorable enemy soldier meeting with him in an established neutral zone, a place where, unencumbered by the need for strategy, he could see her as a person and have a moment of expansive feeling that was indirectly erotic.

"When you talk about her, you get this look on your face that's just exquisite," he said. "It's so brittle and tentative. It's like you think you might be almost happy, but you're afraid to trust it."

"Patrick," she said, "the girl's got nipples you could hang shit on; of course I'm scared."

They were walking to the Brown Jug. The spring day was an exclamation point of radiant abundance. Vulgar little flowers burst from the ground like bright hiccups. Crabgrass was everywhere. Patrick wore a tan beret at a sideways angle that made his beauty a silly exaggeration.

"What about you?" she said. "Don't you ever feel that way about girls?"

"Oh, all the time. I'm always afraid to trust love and happiness. And that feeling of not quite trusting but at the same time trying to trust is the best."

The words had sounded ludicrous in his affected voice, and Margot slapped him on the butt. But now, as she stood in the ladies' lounge at work, it occurred to her that the first part of it, at least, had been true.

In mere months, Chiquita had dumped her for a particularly tedious law student. Stupid with grief, she had gone upstairs to Patrick's room. He sat up and opened his arms without a word. She stayed outside his blankets, safe in her ugly flannel gown, but he held her close and stroked her hair. His tenderness was like a secret thing he had always craved to show her. It was open, raw, almost female, but there was a boy's spirit in it, sparkling, resilient, almost cutting in its resolve. She imagined Patrick the baby, falling down with a little "oof" and getting up again. She looked up at him; his eyes were clear and deep, as if he were looking at her all the way from the bottom and, even more, inviting her to look in.

The bus home was crowded, but she was able to sit, quietly enjoying the animal comfort of proximity to strangers that she didn't have to talk to. As the bus roared forward, its machinery gave off a freakish, surging whine that, for a piercing moment, Margot heard as a smothered soprano chorus singing desperately through a distorted medium from very far away.

On the evening of her dinner with Patrick, she found that she was looking forward to seeing him; she was disappointed when he canceled. He was worn out, he said, from overwork and romantic problems. He'd broken up with Rhoda and begun seeing Tricia, the masochistic phlebotomist, again. It was all so exhausting he didn't even want to talk about it. "So," he concluded, "how was your week?"

"Well," said Margot, "I don't have girlfriend problems, but one of my clients just tried to castrate himself. Do you think that counts?"

"No!"

"I guess technically he was just indulging in a little erotic cutting. But he damn near took the whole head off. The emergency room report says that after they stitched him up, he woke and immediately started whackin' the ham."

"So debased. Just so sad and debased."

"He's just one of the people you're, um, helping. The guy's got Haldol coming out his ears."

"Margot, are you pissed at me for canceling on you? First you talk about castration, and then—"

"Patrick, not everything is about you. Anyway, you know what I did when I heard the whacking-off part? I punched the air and said, 'Yes!' Because for that guy, it was like a triumphant cry. It was beating off in the face of adversity, goddammit."

Patrick giggled.

"No, really," said Margot. "You know how sometimes you see something that looks really gross or stupid? Like a big fat guy walking down the street wearing a shirt that says 'I Like It Doggy Style'? Or a forty-five-year-old woman in a bouffant wig and purple eye shadow and it actually looks pretty good? It's that person's way of saying, 'Here I am.' Or you go into a really bad immigrant neighborhood at Christmas—these people just got here, everything's against them, they don't totally know what's going on. But you'll always see a few houses covered in lights and crèches and reindeer—they're giving it everything they have. It's a triumphant cry. And beating off after he damn near lost it—in that guy's cosmology, it was a triumphant cry."

The long silence flickered with invisible movement. "Margot," said Patrick, "I love you." The movement shimmered in his voice.

The next morning Margot woke at six o'clock, riven by the half memory of Patrick on a damp gray day, holding his rough old coat about his bare neck, his full lips parted, dry granules of skin at one corner of his mouth. She couldn't remember his eyes.

She rolled to one side of her bed and tried to comfort herself by putting her palm and face against the warm place where she had been lying. Her memory surged voluptuously: he'd held her against his chest and she'd cried about Chiquita. She rested in and was upheld by his strength and his glandular boy's resolve. She put her palm against his chest. He covered it with his hand. "I've thought about us," he said.

She opened her eyes. The artificial quality of his voice was pleasing in the way a song on a grocery store sound system can be pleasing. But it was not what she wanted.

"Basically, I could take it or leave it," he said.

She sat up and stared at him. She got off the bed. "Then you can leave it," she'd said.

Now she rolled onto her back and pulled the blankets up to her chin. She remembered Roberta getting up to go to work one morning, pulling away from Margot's embrace as she rolled naked from the bed. She'd yawned as she walked across the floor, swinging her slim hips. "Then you can leave it," Margot said aloud.

After that night, Margot had tried to act normal with Patrick, but it didn't work. He was stilted and polite. When she asked him out for coffee, he couldn't come. Breakfast conversations that should've been casual took sharp turns; innocuous comments seemed to have complicated, unseen meanings. Dolores and Donald looked on with sidelong glances. It seemed to her that Patrick had made her feel rejected for absolutely no reason when she couldn't afford to feel that way. This idea made her indignant, and her indignation mounted with each odd conversational moment, finally rearing up to its full height one morning while Patrick was telling the household about his disastrous encounter with two sisters, both of whom had briefly been lovers of his. There had been screaming, tears, awful accusations.

"The absurd thing is, I like both of them a lot," said Patrick. "But I didn't really want to have sex with either one. All this could've been avoided if—"

"Patrick," said Margot, "if you didn't want to have sex with them, then why did you?"

He tipped his chair back and looked at her with insouciant tension. "Because they wanted to, mostly."

"That is not an answer."

Patrick shrugged and eased his chair back onto its four legs.

As Margot left the room, she'd heard Donald say, "Isn't she, like, supposed to be a lesbian?"

They made plans for another dinner date, but Patrick canceled it because he had to fly to Los Angeles to tie up business related to his CD-ROM. The whole project was driving him crazy, he said. The psychiatrists were hell to work with; they were all deluded egomaniacs. And things were not going well with Tricia, who was being stalked by a biker with whom she'd had a one-night stand. His first urge of course was to protect her, but he was also disgusted with her for allowing such a situation to come about. "I mean, for so long, she was really living straight, you know? And I respected her for it. And now—"

"Patrick," said Margot abruptly, "how's Dolores? Did you get her number for me?"

"Oh, damn," he said. "I forgot about that. I'm sorry. It's hard for me to think about her, it's so sad. But I'll get it."

When Margot got off the phone she felt that she didn't want to talk to Patrick again, let alone see him. "What an asshole," she said to her darkened hallway. Hours later, preparing for bed, she spat diluted toothpaste into the sink, looked at herself in the mirror, and said it again. Her hair was held back in a ratty terry-cloth band, and her features were stark, inturned, and convictionless.

Once, on a brilliant spring day sixteen years before, she had come home just in time to see Patrick burst from their rented house with an enormous bundle in his arms. It was swathed in Dolores's quilt, and it was apparently very heavy. Without speaking, he hurried past. He had put the bundle in his car and slammed the door before she realized that he had been carrying Dolores and that she was unconscious.

Patrick hadn't come back to the house until evening. From her room she'd heard him open the refrigerator, close it, and then go upstairs to his room. She stood at her door for an irresolute moment, then she followed him. He opened the door before she knocked. They sat on his bed, and he lay his head on her shoulder, hunching his body as if he were smaller than she. She stroked his head and neck. His pulse was fluxing like an electrical current. Dolores had tried to kill herself with the Valium their mother had sent him. He'd found her on the bathroom floor.

Dolores came back from the hospital much the same as she had been before she left. She sat at the breakfast table for hours, affixing and polishing her false nails. Patrick slouched in the sun, and sometimes his attention touched his sister like a traveling drop of light.

He was supposed to call her during the next week to make another dinner appointment, but he didn't. She didn't call him, either, and as one week passed and then another, she thought of him less and less. She would've said that she'd forgotten him, except that occasionally his image would come to her, attached to thoughts or events that had no apparent relation to him, and inside her, a little tongue of feeling would fly up.

One day at work, when she was on an intake phone shift, she received another phone call from the young man who believed he was being stalked.

Margot didn't tell him they'd already spoken, and he went into his story at a full gallop.

"She keeps writing these fucked-up letters, and I don't answer, _except just to be polite_ I sent her this form letter I send all my friends, just to let everybody know what's going on. And she called me and left this hysterical message on my machine, going on about how much I mean to her, and wanting to read me some poem—"

"Tell me as clearly as you can," said Margot. "What would you like me to do?"

"—and when I called her back, she said she'd called because I'd answered her letter, but I didn't! It was a computer-generated form letter; I didn't even sign it! Hers were all personal, all handwritten! And they were sick! She's going on about how she once drew a picture of me—I've never drawn a picture of anyone since I was, like, ten!"

Margot held the phone away from her ear for a moment. The little tongue flew up. She shook her head and returned the receiver to her ear.

"—and I said, 'Oh, you _like_ me, well, that's very nice, why don't you start a fan club?' "

"Perhaps," said Margot, "you might want to make an appointment to discuss this further with a psychiatrist. Other than that, I don't—"

He hung up.

Several days later Patrick telephoned to invite her to dinner and afterward to view his CD-ROM. She said yes.

He arrived at her apartment an hour and a half late. He was driving a new car, so elaborately appointed that sitting in it made her feel like a vegetable in a velvet box. He was dressed in an elegant suit that was an announcement of competence and public force. He wore a scent that had mixed with his sweat, and the smell of it made her imagine him naked and private, carefully daubing it on his neck, his stomach, his inner wrist. The contrast made him seem vulnerable and strangely innocent. He looked at her and smiled giddily. She thought, Orchid.

"Did you notice?" he asked. "I've lost six pounds."

She hadn't.

He drove to an Italian restaurant housed in a thrusting edifice of steel and reflective glass.

"I'm not dressed for this," she said.

"Oh, come on. It's Seattle, and anyway you look great."

They ordered tasty, oily little pieces of food on large plates. Margot had wine in a deep glass. As she drank, her thoughts leapt this way and that in reaction to this curious sound, to that burst of light.

Patrick talked about depression, about how people were ashamed of it, how some people didn't even know they had it because they thought it was a mental illness, which it wasn't. "That's a very unusual position for a pyschopharm to take, I know. But the kind of common, low-level depression that almost everyone seems to—"

"If it isn't a mental illness," said Margot, "why do you treat it with medicine?"

"It's not medicine, in the usual sense. It's a consciousness-altering drug, and it's an appropriate modality considering the nature of what's happening—I mean, the rate of flux! Everything's in turnaround all around us, all the time! We aren't organically equipped to deal. We just aren't. I take it sometimes. Just every now and then." He ate a morsel of eggplant. "I was going to suggest that you try a very light dosage of, say, Zoloft. Not because I think there's anything wrong with you. It's just that you seem a little . . . I mean, with Roberta and the stressful job, you know."

He talked about people whose lives had been changed by medication, and his voice was compassionate, as if he were putting a blanket over them. His compassion tickled like a blade of grass drawn slyly across her wrist and woke her memory of the solicitous condescension she had once resisted. He talked as if other people's pain was one great, sore intimacy that he had seen and comprehended—and yet, Margot was suddenly irritated to think, it seemed he had never really looked at it. She had a cold swallow of ice water. It gave the tannic wine taste an arresting ache.

After Dolores returned from the hospital, she and Margot had gone on a long walk together. It had been a lovely, tender day. Dolores smoked cigarette after cigarette. She walked very slowly, as if she were pushing against something that didn't want to let her through. "Just a minute," she said. She paused before somebody's newly planted vegetable garden and dug around in her purse for another cigarette. The fresh-turned dirt of the garden was dressed in a pretty grid of Popsicle sticks and string.

"My dad came to visit in the hospital," she said. "It was the first time I'd seen him for two years."

"Yeah?"

Dolores found a cigarette and lit it. "He sat on my bed and asked me how I was. I said, 'Daddy, I want you to kill me.' " She flicked the match onto the garden, and they continued walking.

"What did he say?" asked Margot.

"Nothing. He just sat there and licked his lips like a nervous dog."

Margot wanted to ask Patrick if Dolores had ever told him about this. Instead, she talked about Roberta and the elaborate meditation exercises she had done when she was depressed. Patrick nodded vigorously. "That can work," he said. His agreement made her irritated again. But the irritation immediately cooled and went sticky. How had her light, heartless, lovely bête noire become this silly man? The raw, breathing spirit of his youthful conceit had gone stiff and perfunctory; whether from neglect or the wear of age, she couldn't tell. His light voice made her sleepy. The play of movement in the restaurant was a slow, tired fugue of decor and manners. She wanted to go home.

As they walked to his car, a beggar looked at them with wistful half-resentment, as if the sight of them confirmed for him that at least some people were getting what they wanted: dates, restaurants, conversation in low tones.

"A coincidence," said Patrick. "The same week I saw you I ran into my best girlfriend, Tamara, who I haven't seen for months."

"Your best girlfriend? I'm surprised you haven't mentioned her before now. I mean, you've talked so much about Tricia and the other one."

"Well, Tamara didn't affect me on an emotional level the way Rhoda and Tricia do. But she was my best girlfriend pound for pound, okay? She was beautiful by anyone's standard, she was wealthy, and she had a cool job. She wired me flowers from France on Valentine's Day, you know?"

Her sarcastic thoughts were very loud, but he didn't hear them.

"Tricia used to stalk me when I went on dates with Tamara," he said. "She'd sit outside restaurants in her car and watch us through the window. Isn't that sick?"

"Of whom?"

Their footsteps counterpointed his wiry little silence. He opened the car door for her, and she sat in the stifling plushness. He got in on the other side and sealed them in with a slam. "Her," he said. "Who else?"

They drove in silence for some moments. She felt something hard in him, something little and gristly. Something that had heard her sarcastic thoughts and strove against them. But then she felt something else, which was generous, flexible, and full of movement. She felt it as surely as if he'd touched her. She'd irritated him, but still he wanted to like her, and that made her want to like him, in spite of everything. When he asked if she wanted to see his CD-ROM, she said that she would.

His apartment was an expensive oblong with a vast, sad view of the city. A large old movie projector stood in one corner. An antique couch, its mauve cushions worn soft and forbearing, was a luxuriant ribbon in the stark room. They sat on it and had cognac in fancy glasses. She noticed a necklace made of huge red beads hanging from a doorknob behind the couch.

"Oh," he said, "that's from a long time ago." With a supple twist, he arched his back and reached for the beads with a long finger. An enshadowed vein showed on his extended neck. He dropped the beads in her lap. She handled them; the startling chunks of red were humorous and stately.

He sipped from his drink with a dainty beaklike gesture. "A minor director who liked me gave it to me," he said. "It seemed like a welcoming present from the world. We were out drinking one night, and she said a person who could wear this necklace could walk into any room and feel like he belonged there."

Margot thought of Patrick looking at the director with the same bare, needy eyes she had seen. She thought of the director wanting to console this look, to welcome it. "What a lovely thing to say," she said.

He frowned. "I don't know what happened to her," he said. "I guess her career didn't go anywhere, either." There was a beat of silence like a held breath. He turned abruptly and looked at her. She was startled by the intense look on his face. "Do you think I could wear those beads now?" he said hopefully. "Or would I look silly?"

She pictured him entering a room, wearing the red necklace over a cowl-necked shirt, regally flaunting his middle age. "I think you could wear them," she said. "You'd have to wear the right top. But you could do it. It could look very cool."

"Yeah?" He looked doubtful. Then he brightened. "Let's look at that CD-ROM." He stood and regarded her with a faint seignorial expression so absurd it was endearing. "We have to go in the bedroom, if that's okay."

He kept his computer beside his bed. "I don't sleep well," he explained. "Sometimes, if I wake up, I like to just put on my robe and get some work done without leaving the bed." They sat awkwardly sideways on the bed, so they could look at the small screen. Patrick crossed his legs and slouched, pecking at the keys with an expectant air as if he were still delighted by the complicated little machine.

All his files came up in pastel boxes. One of them was called Mad Money, another Nostalgia. He produced a little candy-wafer disk and tucked it in. A purple oblong with a tiny hourglass in it appeared on the screen. "This is going to change my career," he said. The purple vanished, piece by jerky piece, revealing a cartoon of a man with a big pink head, trying to climb over a locked wall to get to a garden of flowers. The word DEPRESSION appeared over the picture. Then another oblong, with a woman's face in it, bloomed on the screen. She was an attractive blonde in her mid-thirties, but she looked out of her oblong with the alarmed face of a horse in a burning barn.

"Millions of Americans are suffering from depression!" she announced. "Yet the sufferers feel terribly alone!"

"She looks like a lunatic," said Margot.

"What do you expect? She's a psychiatrist."

"Depression is often accompanied by feelings of shame, of failure, of not-rightness." The psychiatrist paused; her expression flared wildly.

"If I saw this woman at a party, I'd avoid her," said Margot. "I'd cross the room."

"You should've seen the other psychs I interviewed. I mean, yikes."

"In the past, depression was seen as an incurable personal flaw, a distasteful matter to be borne in silence." The psychiatrist furrowed her brow and pursed her lips. "But not now. Now there's help." She batted her eyelashes and pushed out her lips as she spoke the *h* of "help."

"Oh, God," said Margot.

"Come on, she's good-looking and she's warm, sort of. Most people like her."

"Now you don't have to be depressed!"

"Why didn't *you* read the script?" asked Margot. "You used to act."

"Isn't it obvious?"

"Now," said the psychiatrist, "you can be part of life again!"

"I'm not visually appealing enough," said Patrick.

"I'd rather look at you than her."

Patrick said thank you, but he hardened in his cross-legged slouch. Margot could tell that she had made him anxious. She tried to feel remorseful, but instead she felt righteous. She remembered a party she had attended in Ann Arbor, right after she'd moved away from the house she'd shared with Patrick and Dolores. She had casually entered a conversation among three girls who were telling stories about some ridiculous guy. It was a minute before she realized that they were talking about Patrick.

"But do you want to hear about the really awful thing?" The girl who asked had a plain face and a busy, bossy humor.

"Tell them," urged her friend.

"He said I ought to just lick his balls while he jerked off."

Everybody went "Oooh" or "Gross!" The plain girl stared at Margot, her speculative gaze a light tease. Margot blushed.

"Tragically, many people who are depressed don't realize it," the psychiatrist was saying. "Luckily, there are symptoms."

"Okay," said Patrick. "Let's click on that."

The psychiatrist, froze, with her mouth open. A box materialized over her, and then a man in a suit within the box. "Hello," he said. "I'm here to discuss key symptoms of depression." He projected out of his box like an enthusiastic dog on a tight leash.

"Patrick," said Margot, "this is absurd."

"Most common is lethargy," said the man. "You are lethargic if—"

Patrick hit a button, and the man froze with his mouth open. "All right," he said. "Tell me why you think that."

"For starters, it's condescending. You reinforce people's feelings of passivity when you encourage them to think they don't even know what they're feeling and that somebody has to tell them. And it's mechanical—"

"But a lot of people _don't_ know. I'm surprised at you, Margot, that you—"

"Do you actually think this abstract thing is going to help people? It's so detached and . . . it's just like the shrinks at work who give out meds instead of trying to connect on a human level."

"Oh, barf."

"It's barf, all right. Patrick, you can't even deal with your own sister—what the hell are you doing?"

He sat silently, in profile, staring at the static gray psychiatrist. "I can't help my sister," he said. "I've tried." There was a tiny electrical hum in the room.

"Patrick," she said. "I'm sorry."

He didn't answer.

"I was out of line."

He didn't say anything. He seemed trapped in his cross-legged position. Margot put her hand on his knee. He reached forward and ejected the CD-ROM. "It's okay," he said. "I should've known: it's not your kind of thing."

He turned to face her; he was smiling.

"I know it doesn't have anything to do with Dolores," she said. "But it seems . . ."

Still smiling, he extended his legs to the side of her. He took her hand and pulled her toward him. She went. She lay against him and put her hand on his chest. He felt sparkling and agitated, like someone who is trying so hard to tell you what he means that he is almost incoherent. She looked up at him. His face was smiling, but his eyes were tired and sad. Still, his expression was clear and deep—as if he was looking at her all the way from the bottom and, even more, inviting her to look in. He bent to kiss her.

"Patrick," she said, "we don't have that kind of—"

"Yes, we do."

"What do you mean? We—"

He pulled her close. She pushed away. Too heavily, he stroked her hair and her face; his touch would've seemed imperious had it not felt so needy.

"Patrick," she said, "stop."

"I just want to hold you, okay? Please, just let me—"

"Don't!" She sat up and put her hands over her ears. "Don't," she said again.

He lay back. She felt him take distance. "Okay," he said.

She put her hands in her lap. They looked at each other in silence. His face looked strange to her. His forehead was heavy, almost oppressive; it seemed weighted with information that the rest of his face didn't know about. His eyes and nose were arrogant and ignorant, his mouth was sensual and nervous, wanting to please. But his forehead was powerful, discerning, and strange. She felt she was looking at something very familiar and very unfamiliar at once. He reached for her carefully. He stroked her cheek with the back of his hand, barely touching her. His expression deepened a shade. The unfamiliar thing eclipsed the familiar. She could sense it more than see it. He was trying to show himself to her, to explain something. He didn't have the means, but he was trying, silently, with his eyes. And she was trying too. It was as if they were signaling each other from different planets, too far away to read the signals but just able to register that a signal was being sent. They sat and looked at each other, their youth and beauty gone, their selves more bare and at the same time more hidden.

Gently, Patrick took the tips of her two forefingers. "I'll drive you home," he said.

The
Blanket

Valerie had been celibate for two years when she met Michael, and sex with Michael was like a solid left hook; she reeled and cartoon stars burst about her head. The second time he came to her San Francisco apartment, he walked in with two plastic bags of fruit, extending a fat red tomato in one outstretched hand, his smile leaping off his face. "I brought you things," he said. "I brought you fruit to put on your windowsill, and this." He handed her the tomato and said, "I'm a provider." His voice was full of ridiculous happiness. He was wearing shorts, and one of his graceful legs was scuffed at the knee. He was twenty-four years old.

Valerie was thirty-six. Michael couldn't actually provide for her, but she didn't need him to do that. She loved that he'd gone to the grocery store and roamed the aisles of abundant, slightly tatty and unripe fruit so that he could bring her bags of it. His impulse seemed both generous and slightly inept, which she found sweeter than generosity straight.

Michael himself was a little surprised by his beneficent urges, surprised and pleased by their novelty. It occurred to him that it had something to do with her physicality, although he didn't know quite what. Valerie was pretty, but she was not beautiful. Her arms and neck were fine-boned and elegant, while her hips and legs were curvy, fatty, almost crudely female. She embraced him confidently, but her fingers sought his more delicate places—the base of his head, the knobs of his spine—with a tactile urgency that was needy and uncertain. After their first time together, on the floor of her living room, she'd put on her underpants and stood over him, posing with her hands on her hips, chin lifted, one hip tilted bossily—but she held her legs close together, and her one bent inturned knee had the tremulous look of a cowed animal. "Woman of the year," he'd said, and he'd meant it.

It was only their second time together when she suggested that they "role-play." "You know," she said. "Act out fantasies."

"*Fantasies?*" The idea was a little embarrassing, yet it also intrigued him; under the cheesy assurance of it, he felt her vulnerability, hidden and palpitant. Besides, the fantasies were fun. She would be a slutty teenager who's secretly hoping for love, and he would be the smug prick who exploits her. He would be the coarse little gym teacher trying to persuade the svelte English teacher to let him go down on her after the PTA cocktail party. She would be a rude girl with no panties flaunting herself before an anxious student in the library. Feverishly, they'd nose around in each situational nuance before giving in to dumb physicality. Then she'd make them a dinner of meat and salad and a pot of grains, and they'd eat it with their feet on the table.

When he left her apartment, Michael felt as if the entire world loved him. He walked down the street, experiencing everything—scraps of trash, traffic, trotting pets, complex, lumbering pedestrians—as a kind of visual embrace. Once, immediately after leaving her, he went into a bookstore and sat down on a little stepladder to peruse a book, and he was assailed with a carnal memory so pungent that he opened his mouth and dropped a wrinkled wad of gray chewing gum on the page. He stared at it, embarrassed and excited by his foolishness. Then he closed the book on the wad.

For the first week she wouldn't let him spend the night with her, because that was too intimate for her. But he would get in bed with her and hold her, cupping her head against his chest and stroking the invisible little hairs at the base of her spine. "My girlfriend," he would say. "My girlfriend." His chest was big and solid, but under her ear, his heart beat with naked, helpless enthusiasm.

When he held her that way, she felt so happy that it disturbed her. After he left, it would take her hours to fall asleep, and then when she woke up she would feel another onrush of agitated happiness, which was a lot like panic. She wished she could grab the happiness and mash it into a ball and hoard it and gloat over it, but she couldn't. It just ran around all over the place, disrupting everything.

Valerie made a fair living illustrating book jackets, which meant she worked at home, which meant she was pretty susceptible to disruptions anyway. When Michael appeared she had just started a jacket for a novel by a well-known hack, which required that she draw prowling leopards. It should've been an easy job, but she could not bring her sensory apparatus to bear on the leopards. She would draw for minutes and then spend nearly an hour pacing around, listening to overblown love music or obnoxious sex music. Her thoughts were fragmented. Her feelings buzzed and swarmed. She remembered sitting on the edge of the couch, him kneeling on the floor, her underpants dangling from the tip of her high-heeled foot. Finally, the gym teacher had gotten the English teacher to come across! Aggression surged between them in bursts, but he'd paused to bend and press his cheek against her thigh.

The kitchen table became littered with partial leopards.

"It's like I'm so happy I can't feel it," she said to her friend Tanya. "It's just sex, really; I mean, he's too young for us to actually get involved. But the enthusiasm of him—I mean, he's just right there."

"How can he be right there if you're not really involved?"

"We are involved, in a profound, sexually spiritual way. But we're not going to be boyfriend and girlfriend."

"But you like it when he calls you his girlfriend."

"I do." Valerie paused, thinking how she could best explain this apparent contradiction. "It's like another version of the slutty-teenager fantasy. It's real, but only in the erotic realm. I mean, we have feelings for each other, but they can't be permanent."

Michael was a bartender, but he also played bass guitar in a band. The band was a ramshackle affair, perpetuated by the dour perseverance of the lead singer and animated by the disproportionate loudness of the sound system. They were usually just a warm-up act in a good-natured dive, but Valerie was enchanted to think of Michael onstage with his guitar, one hip slung out insouciantly. "I think all twenty-four-year-old boys should play in bands," she said.

It was a condescending thing to say, but he didn't mind. He sensed that the luxury of such minor arrogance was new to her, and that she was trying it out, with a certain brittle excitement, just to see what it felt like. He would imagine her watching him from the audience as he turned away from them all, in private communion with his guitar, aloof and mysterious and secretly delighted in his role of admired object.

During the second weekend of their affair, the band went up to Seattle to play. Valerie thought she'd spend the weekend retrieving her equilibrium, but just hours after he left, she discovered one of his sweaty T-shirts balled up at the bottom of her bed and found she had to listen to loud music while she paced around with the shirt pressed to her cheek.

That evening he called her from the pay phone of a gas station while the rest of the band peed and raided the candy machine.

"I had to tell you this," he said. "When we were driving through Oregon we went past this cornfield, and I was just staring at it and I saw this little white cat walking between the rows. It so much made me think of you. The way it walked was so intrepid and fine."

He heard a quick intake of breath, followed by a soft, tremulous silence. He closed his eyes and took a long, ecstatic drink of grape pop.

Later that night, a beautiful girl threw herself at him. He was standing at the bar after the band's last set, wiping his face with a wet cocktail napkin, when she emerged from the ambient murk. She had long black hair and a fancy little strut that suggested uncomplicated, competent sex. They made out against the wall, and she nonchalantly pressed her pubic bone against him. He was going to suggest that they go to her place, but realized, in the midst of speculating about what she might have in the way of food, that to do so would only increase his longing for Valerie. The girl stuck her hand inside his shirt and circled the rim of his navel with one cold finger. "I can't do this," he said. "I'm in love with this girl in San Francisco." The irritated hoyden slunk off, and he slid to the floor, free to wallow in the thrilling abjection of his love.

The next day he called Valerie and told her what had happened.

"You shouldn't have done that," she said mildly. "That girl was probably really hurt."

"Oh, she was just a groupie," he said. "The point is, I didn't care how beautiful she was. I wanted you."

When they got off the phone, Valerie buried her face in the T-shirt, rubbing it across her lips and cheeks, helplessly nipping at it with her teeth.

His return was a festival of romantic lewdness. At four in the morning, as they lay on the rug in the irradiant caress of the television light, she invited him to sleep with her. At six in the morning, Michael slept like a healthy animal while she lay in a grim ball, tormented by overstimulation. The joy of the previous day seemed unreal, and even if it wasn't, the outsize quality of it was bound to heighten the desolation she would surely feel when the affair was over. Valerie had not had many good experiences with men in her life, and as the sad sacks and malefactors of the past assembled for her mental review, her excitement over this boy began to seem pathetic. But each time she was about to sink into a restful misery, boisterous optimism surged up and kicked her into wakefulness.

When they got up, they had mugs of tea with spoonfuls of honey in them, and then Michael pretended to be a sleazy boss dropping in on an unsuspecting housewife just after her naive husband has left for work. The boss was a terrible malefactor, but in the haven of fantasy, he was safely confined to her script. There was great drama as the poor housewife struggled to resist him, but to no avail: Valerie opened her eyes just in time to be a little startled by the look of almost demented malice on Michael's young face as he ejaculated across her mouth and nose.

They lay in each other's arms for a long time. Then Valerie got up and put on a tape of piano jazz and made them a big pancake breakfast. They ate it on a rickety table on her back porch. It was nice, except the sauciness of the jazz suddenly sounded so self-satisfied that she had to go in and turn it off. "I'm sorry," she said when she came back out. "That music was making me feel like an asshole." Michael laughed. He sat in his boxer shorts, with his long legs spread, exuding succulent boyness just faintly shaded with dim, inchoate cruelty.

They went for a genteel walk, up and down the hills of the Castro and Noe Valley. They admired the flowers with which residents had planted their yards. Michael told her that he had been fat in junior high and that other kids had made fun of him. Then he had lost weight in a dramatic growth spurt during the summer before high school and had returned to school eagerly anticipating what he assumed would be his new social status, only to have the same mean kids call him "Pig Dick" again.

"It made me think that people would just do that to me all my life, no matter what I did," he said. "After the end of that day, I went into a deserted classroom and cried. I mean, I really cried."

Valerie emitted a tender moo and embraced his hips with one arm. "I wish I could've come to you as a visitation from the future," she said. "I would've held you and told you you were handsome."

Michael stopped walking and hugged her against his chest. His heart beat like a proudly flying flag.

They went back to the apartment and had sex while imagining a heartless scene between Michael and the Seattle girl he'd rejected. About halfway through the fantasy, Valerie stopped being a bystander and became the poor girl. She pleaded with him to fuck her, but when he did, she felt a terrible rush of emotional pain that shocked her into tears. Mistaking her shudders for excitement, he became too rough, and she cried out for him to stop. They separated and Valerie turned on her side, just in time to see Michael's expression of impersonal cruelty devolve into confusion and injury. He clasped her wet face in his hands. "Oh," he said, "I didn't mean . . . I didn't mean it . . . " They started again and she cried more, but she didn't want to stop.

When they finished, they separated and stared at each other, disoriented and almost shamed. "Well," said Valerie, "and this is only the third week."

"Holy shit," said Michael. "You're right."

Again he spent the night. He slept curled around her from behind, his forehead butting against her shoulder blades, one hand on her breast. She lay wide awake, withstanding surges of happiness and fear.

The next day she was too physically sensitive for sex. Half joking, he pawed and cajoled her. His aggression ran in a giddy zigzag that grabbed her up and pulled her along, which was fun except that she didn't feel like going anywhere. Like the sleazy boss, he mauled and grabbed, and under his clownishness she sensed the vicious look she had glimpsed the day before. Another time, the look might've excited her, but now it felt like an unfriendly finger poking a tender spot. "I need to be by myself," she said. "Like, for several days."

After he left, it occurred to her that he saw her withdrawal as a squeamish flinch from his carnal might, and that idea so irritated her that she walked around muttering sarcastically for several minutes. She was older than he was! Their fantasy life was her idea! She remembered that she had cried, but the memory seemed to be about someone else; the image of her weeping face was static, as if it were an abstract signifier of something just beyond her vision. She remembered Michael's expression, as it went from malice to tenderness, with a piercing, secretive poignancy that was like a sore tooth. She felt like squirming.

She sat down to finish a jacket cover illustrated with the leafy branches of trees.

He called her the next day. The band had suddenly gotten an out-of-town gig, which meant he would be leaving town for a few days, starting tomorrow. "I know we're having a moratorium," he said. "But I can't go that long without seeing you, and also we have this big cool car that we rented for the trip. We could go for a fun drive in it."

She told him she wanted to see him but that she didn't want to have sex. "I just can't do it now," she said. "I feel too sensitive. Can you respect that?"

He paused, as if savoring an elaborate and slightly absurd delicacy. In a soft voice, he said yes.

"Are you sure? Because I don't want to have some ridiculous scene."

He swallowed voluptuously. "I'm sure."

She noticed his condescension, but it felt to her like another version of his expression, caught between malice and unspeakable tenderness. It felt secret and sweet.

When he got to her house, they cuddled on the couch. They told each other about their lives. Valerie talked about leaving home when she was sixteen. She told him about panhandling and selling jewelry on the street. She described her shiftless older boyfriend, whom she had supported by working as a waitress.

"It sounds rough," ventured Michael.

"Mostly not," she said. "Mostly it was banal. And sometimes it was fun. I would do stuff like go to Las Vegas for a weekend with some guy I'd just met. Even ordinary stuff was fun. Like when I got a job painting and lettering signs at a circus in Montreal. I thought that was really cool."

"That *is* cool," he said admiringly.

"Some bad stuff happened, though. I was raped by this asshole once."

Michael sat up and smiled. "Yeah? What happened? What did he make you do?"

Valerie felt startled, then she realized she wasn't really startled at all. "Are you reacting that way because I had sort of a smiley look on my face when I told you I was raped?"

His smile snagged and lapsed.

"That smile was left over on my face because I'd just told you this other nice stuff. I wasn't smiling about being raped."

He looked down. "I don't know why I did that. I know rape is horrible, but it's the horribleness that gives it a charge. It's like the fantasy thing. Like, right now, some guy is making some girl do something really gross. It's weird."

"Yeah, but I'm not some girl." She spoke gently, not angrily; she felt very aware that she was older than he was. "It wasn't a fantasy. I tried to fight him, and he punched me in the face. It was really bad."

He put his hand on her forearm. "I'm sorry," he said.

"It's okay," she said. "Sometimes I tell people really awful stuff like it's a joke. I don't know why. I'm trying not to do that anymore."

He put his arms around her. "I'm sorry anything bad ever happened to you," he said. His embrace was soft, but muscular underneath. She lay in it, feeling the immense relief she might feel on finally explaining herself to someone who for years had refused to hear her out. She felt upheld by his youth and strength. She felt this even though she knew Michael still didn't quite grasp that she wasn't talking about a fantasy. Even though, really, she hardly knew him at all.

He wished he could roll her up in a ball and hold her. When she'd said, "I'm trying not to do that anymore," it had provoked a storm of monstrous pathos in him. It was the kind of pathos that felt so good he wanted to make it go on forever. It shocked him that someone had hit her, but following close upon the shock was an overwhelming tenderness that made the shock seem like an insignificant segue. He remembered fucking her while she was crying, her legs all the way open; it made him think of eating sweet vanilla pudding while he watched TV.

"Let's go for our drive," he said.

He drove them to the Marina and across the Golden Gate Bridge into Marin County. The fog was heavy and wet.

"Right after I moved here, I had a dream," said Valerie. "I dreamed me and my high school boyfriend were lying on a beach in California. The sun was so bright and the sand was like a giant, breathing body. In the dream it was like, finally, I was getting to do the stuff that everybody else did—I was lying on the beach with my boyfriend!"

Distractedly he patted her leg. He was staring helplessly at the inside of his head, at images of Valerie, openmouthed and victimized, her face tear-stained and humiliated and very dear. He thought of the sounds she sometimes made when he was way inside her, deep sounds that came out ragged, like they'd been torn off. On a whim, he took a Mill Valley exit. Without the light from the freeway traffic, it was suddenly very dark.

"Why're you going to Mill Valley?" asked Valerie.

"No reason. Just driving."

"Oh. Anyway, when I woke up I thought at first I'd dreamed about an actual memory, that me and my boyfriend _had_ gone to a beach. Then I realized there weren't any beaches where we grew up; it was just a dream. I felt somehow cheated."

He didn't say anything. He was driving up a warren of narrow streets wound around a steep hill. The glimpses of people puttering about behind their windows was soothing to her.

"It probably sounds strange that I felt cheated," she said. "I think it's because since I left home so early, I didn't really have boyfriends my own age. They were always a lot older, and I didn't go on normal dates or to proms or anything."

"That's kind of sad," he said.

"I don't know. I thought proms seemed pretty horrible, actually."

Maybe, he thought, he could bend her over the seat back and pull her pants down. Maybe she would make a lot of those noises. Maybe she would cry again. If she did, he would hold her against his chest and stroke her hair until she breathed gently and evenly. He turned abruptly down a dirt road. She thought it was a very long driveway at first, but then she saw there was no house at the end of it. "Michael," she said, "what are you doing?"

He pulled over and stopped the car. He turned sideways in his seat and leaned against the car door.

He didn't answer her. She remembered the way he had held her and said he was sorry anything bad had ever happened to her. In the dark, she couldn't see his face. "Michael?" she said.

He didn't answer her.

"Michael?"

She was suddenly so scared she couldn't think. She felt her weakness like a burst of nausea; if he wanted to hurt her, there was nothing she could do about it. Indignation rose up against her helplessness, but it was like the voice of a child crying, "But you said! But you said!" over and over again. Her fear took on the flat urgency of a trance. She put her hand in her purse so that she could find the heavy chain necklace she had been meaning to take to the jewelers. She found it and wrapped it around her fist, then carefully withdrew her fist from the bag. He leaned forward. She turned to face him and retracted her fist. Her voice came out in a hoarse growl. "Don't come near me," she said.

His retreat was like a sudden frown. "Valerie?" he said. "What's wrong?"

"Don't come closer."

"Valerie?" There was a short, vibrant silence. "Are you afraid of me?"

His puzzled voice cracked her trance. She relaxed her fist and put the chain back in her purse. "Start the car," she said. "I want to go home."

"Wait a minute—"

"Start the fucking car. I mean now."

He muttered as he pulled out of the dirt road and negotiated the dainty lanes. It dawned on him that if he took his hands off the steering wheel they'd be shaking. "Valerie," he said, "are you really mad at me?"

She didn't answer. He glanced at her. Her profile had the bristling intensity of a trapped rodent. "Shit," he said. "This is really bad."

"You must be a moron," she said flatly. "For three weeks I've been doing it with a moron."

He smarted as though from a blow across the bridge of his nose. "How could you say that to me?" he said.

"I don't want to talk. I just want to go home."

The rest of the drive was an abstract of misery. When he pulled up in front of her apartment they sat in private misery for some moments. "I don't think I can see you anymore," said Valerie finally. "This was just too awful."

"Too awful? What was too awful? Nothing happened! I was only playing, I wasn't going to do anything if you didn't want it."

"You already did something I didn't want." She shoved open the car door and stepped out onto the pavement, then spun back on the first step. "What do you think? You spoiled, stupid, ignorant little shit! I tell you I don't want to fuck, I tell you about being raped, and you set up a rape fantasy? What's wrong with you!"

"I was just doing what we do all the time."

"It's not the same!" But his quiet, injured voice had interrupted her anger, and besides, what he said was true. She sat in the car and stared at the sidewalk. She abandoned her anger. "You were disrespecting me," she said quietly. "For real."

Her small voice and her words hinted at the wonderful pathos that had so gripped him. Again it made him want to roll her in a ball, to see her cry, to split her open, to comfort her. He tried to think of how he might explain this to her. He couldn't. "It wasn't disrespect," he said. "It wasn't."

Her silence was like a tiny, pale feather falling a long distance. For a moment he thought she might put her head on his shoulder. If she did that, everything would be okay.

"The problem is, you're a kid," she said. "Everything's like TV to you. You don't really know anything."

He looked out the window. His cheeks burned. "Valerie," he said. "If you don't say something nice to me, this is going to be really bad."

"Something *nice* to you?"

"Please. Say something nice to me."

His plaintive tone pierced her. Without the anger, her emotions were like blunt, blind, vying shapes, each blotting the others out before she could tell what they were. The fragmentation dazed her, almost hurt her.

"I love you," she said.

He sat up and drew back. "You don't mean that."

"I don't know." Her bewilderment increased. "I think I do."

"You love me?" His voice was astounded and fluting. "You love me!" He opened the car door, bounded out, and jumped up and down in the street, yelling.

It's true, she thought, astounded herself. It's true.

He flew around the car, into the shelter of her open door, and knelt, his arms about her waist. "I love you too," he said. "And I'm going to respect you. I'll sleep here all night and I won't try to do anything."

"Sleep here?" She took his face in her hands and rubbed her nose the length of his. "No way. You'll be after me all night, and I'll never get any sleep."

"I'm not leaving," he said. "If I leave, it'll ruin everything. I'm going away for a week tomorrow, and I've got to stay with you."

"See, you're doing it again. You're not respecting my wishes." But her voice was full of shy delight.

"I'll sleep on the floor!" he said. "In the living room!"

"That's ridiculous. It would be much too uncomfortable." She paused. "You can sleep on the bed, but you have to wear your clothes and stay outside the blankets." She felt like a little girl with a rhinestone tiara on her head. She waved her plastic scepter. "You have to promise."

All night, he shivered against her warm, blanketed body. In the light from the window, her sleeping face appeared concentrated and intent. Once she twitched, and the tiny, urgent movement seemed the result of a fierce, private effort she was making deep in her head. He turned away from her so that he could look out the window, his back firmly against hers. His thoughts went forward, then backward, then he fanned them out laterally: a phone call to his mother, a quarrel with the drummer, a newscast about a raped and murdered teenage baby-sitter, the kitchen of that dump in Seattle where he ate hot french fries out of the fryer basket and listened to the cook talk shit about some girl. He imagined scooping up sleeping Valerie and placing her in the middle of his thoughts. He imagined her waking in the thriving garden of his thoughts, confused and possibly frightened. Then he imagined her realizing what he'd done; she put her hands on her hips, she tapped her foot, she fixed him with a fussing eye.

He was cold to the bone by now, but he didn't move even to shut the window. He was respecting her.

"Michael?" She turned and gently groped his back. "What's wrong? You're shaking so—oh, you're cold! Come under the blanket!"

"It's all right. I said I would stay outside the blanket, and I will."

"Don't be silly. Come under the covers." She lifted the blankets, greeting him with her warmth and smell. "Come on. You'll get sick or something."

He hesitated, drawing out the moment.

"Don't you . . . " She faltered. "Don't you want to?"

"Yes," he said. "I want to." And he did.

Comfort

Daniel sat in his San Francisco apartment on a big, mushy pillow, with his black rubber drum pad on his lap. He stretched his legs and pushed the coffee table on which he and Jacquie had just eaten dinner into the middle of the room at a cockeyed angle. Jacquie sat on the bed, coiled in a blanket, holding an Edith Wharton novel in her small, stubby hands. As she read, her gold-brown eyes moved intently back and forth, giving off a spark of private frisson. Half hidden under her lowered lids, the movement of her eyes reminded him of an animal glimpsed as it slips quietly through the underbrush. With loose-wristed strokes, Daniel cheerfully swatted his pad. The phone rang.

"Probably somebody we don't want to talk to," said Jacquie.

Daniel rolled his eyes. It was his brother, Albert, calling from Iowa.

"Dan," said Albert. "Something bad happened."

"What?"

"Mom had a car crash. She's alive, but she's really hurt. She's broken her neck and smashed her pelvis." He paused, breathing heavily. "And she also broke some ribs."

Daniel made an involuntary noise. Jacquie's quick glance was almost sharp. The drumsticks fell to the floor and rolled.

The evening became a terrible melding of misery and sensual tenderness. Jacquie held his head against her breast and stroked him as pain moved through him in slow, even waves. At moments, the pain seemed to blur with the contours of Jacquie's body, to align itself with her warmth and care, as if by soothing it, she actually made it greater. He stared at their dirty dinner plates, shocked by their brute ordinariness: tiny bones, hunks of torn-up lemon, mashed fish skin.

Late at night, they lay without sleeping on their narrow bed. Jacquie held him from behind, one strong arm firmly around his chest, her dry feet pressed against his. She spoke against his back, her voice muffled, her breath a warm puff against his skin. "Your family gets in a lot of car crashes, don't they?"

He opened his eyes. "Yes," he said. "So do a lot of people. There's car crashes all over America all the time."

"Well, there was the one with the whole family in it when you were a little kid, and then the one when your father drove into the fence, and then the one where your mother got hit in the parking lot, and now this. That seems like a lot for one family."

"What are you trying to say?"

"I'm not trying to say anything. I just noticed it."

"My mother's lying in the hospital with half her bones broken, and you just noticed that."

Jacquie took her arm from him and turned the other way.

There is something wrong with her, he thought. They had been together for two years; this was not the first time he had had this thought.

He flew to Iowa the following day.

He had not been in his brother's suburban house before; he found it bland and characterless, and he was glad of that. A more decoratively expressive home might've waked his sensibility and made him feel worse.

Albert was a pharmacist. Together, he and his wife, Rose, reminded Daniel of two colored building blocks made to illustrate solidity, squareness, and rectangularity for children, the kind of blocks that, when picked up, turn out to be practically weightless and not solid at all. Apart from Rose, Albert became heavier, more sullen. His problems expressed themselves in his heavy brows. His hands took on a morose, defensive character. The brothers were eight years apart. They had never been close, and they had become less close in adulthood.

On the night of Daniel's arrival, they sat at the kitchen table, eating Mexican takeout and trying to comfort each other. Their words were difficult and, on the surface, not especially comforting. Their halting conversation would've been small talk but for the emotional current moving under it, sometimes rising to fill whole strings of words with mysterious feeling, then subsiding to a barely felt pulse. Rose sat forward attentively, as though she were silently monitoring the unspoken current. When they got up from the table, Albert hugged Daniel as though part of him wanted the embrace and part of him wanted to get it over with. When his face came away, Daniel saw Albert's left eye staring over Daniel's shoulder, wild, bright, and oddly furtive.

All night, he lay awake in his hard little guest bed, thinking about his mother. He remembered her serving dishes of yogurt and cut fruit for dessert. He remembered her sitting with her feet up on the couch, painting her false fingernails pink. She was wearing her nightgown, and he could see that her knees were rough and that veins had flowered on her legs. Her hair was a manic knot of curls. She looked at her watch often. He could see all these images, but he could not feel them. He turned them this way and that, trying to feel his mother. She used to sit across the table from their father, working her jaws stiffly and minutely. "Daniel," she said. "I want you to ask your father where he was last night." For five years preceding the divorce, his mother and father had addressed each other primarily through their children, although when things got truly ugly, his mother would drop the act and scream at her husband straight on. Daniel brought his hard guest pillow to his si   ˈˈˈˈoged it. "Mother," he said.

The next day they drove to the hospital. Danie' dow, and the winter air drew his cigarette ghost. He saw square porches, bricked-in fl black lampposts standing before each entrance walk; the familiar landscape soothed the itch of memory. He hoped they would pass the church with the stained-glass windows he and his friends had smashed with rocks when they were in the sixth grade. The day after they'd done it, he'd heard his mother on the phone, discussing the incident, which had destroyed thousands of dollars' worth of stained glass. She had speculated, as had the papers, about the rise in juvenile crime and what it meant.

"You must've been very angry," Jacquie had said when he told her about it.

"I was just being a kid," he'd returned.

"A very angry kid."

He'd rolled his eyes.

The ugliness of the hospital pleased him; it seemed appropriate. The lounge was furnished with smudged plastic chairs, a vinyl couch with a strip of duct tape on it, and a candy machine. People sat in various attitudes of unhappiness. Daniel looked at them. One man looked back. His hair was standing up, and his hands appeared numb. He looked as though he might say something hostile. Daniel looked away.

A girl with a bitter mouth and blue eye shadow that deepened violently in the crease of her lids handed them purple guest passes. A female voice, enlarged and blurred by a loudspeaker, clouded the hall. The elevator bore them up. They entered a room. Daniel saw a person he didn't identify as his mother until Albert said, "Mom?"

Tufts of pale, silken hair floated from her partially shaved head. Blue veins lined her scalp. The skin on her face and neck was lax, but it looked stiff as old papier-mâché. A ghostly array of bottles hung from metal poles around the bed. Little rubber tubes were taped against her arms. A thick rubber hose protruded from her distended mouth like a visual bray of anger. She was held erect by a brace at her back. It was a minute before he noticed that holes had been drilled into the frontal bone on either side of her forehead and metal rods had been driven into the holes. Her head was suspended in a netal hoop centered by the rods. Her eyes were closed. Her breath ᵉd. Daniel thought, Frankenstein. He began to sweat.

"You can talk to her, Dan," said Rose. "She's sedated, but she understands."

Albert sat in a chair beside the bed and touched the papery arm. "We brought Daniel, Mom. He's here from California."

Her eyes opened.

Daniel's ears were suddenly filled with internal noise. A tremulous black fuzz blocked his vision. "I'll be right back," he said. "I have to go to the bathroom." He stumbled out, palming the bumpy wall of the hallway. He banged his shins on a bench and sat on it, dropping his head between his knees. The fuzz parted to reveal an expanse of gold-flecked tile.

"Daniel?" Rose's voice. "Are you all right?"

When they got back from the hospital, their father called. He invited Daniel out to dinner, without Albert and Rose. He preferred taking his sons to dinner one at a time, a preference neither brother questioned.

Before hanging up, his father said he was involved in a new business. His last venture, importing tropical fish, had lasted two months.

"It's some weird thing to do with informational videos," said Albert. "Some crap for tourists in hotel rooms."

"That sounds viable," said Daniel.

"I doubt it," said Albert.

The comment annoyed Daniel, and he changed the subject. "Has he seen Mom?"

"Yeah," said Albert. "He's been good that way." He sighed and stiffly stretched in a hard, ungiving little chair. "He was there the first night they brought her in. All Mom's family were there, and I guess it was a bad scene. It might've been better if Rose and I were there, but we didn't arrive until after."

With a sort of angry relish, Albert told his second-hand version of the story. When their father arrived in the waiting room, no one in the family could tell him what exactly had happened to their mother, what condition she was in or where she was, apparently because they had been given inadequate information by the hospital staff and were too timid to press for more. Their father roared around the waiting room, cursing and calling them all sheep. Aunt Pauline wept and Uncle Jimmy called their father a bastard. A nurse came out of her station and told their father what he needed to know, and everybody shut up.

"Once again, Dad does the thing everybody wants done but no one will do," said Daniel.

"Yep," said Albert. A smile of unhappy vindication made his dull eyes glint. "Later, after we got there, Grandpa came up to Dad and tried to make up, but Dad told him to fuck off."

"Oh, man." But Daniel felt a sneaking little triumph for his father.

Albert half looked away, as if he knew what Daniel felt and didn't want to think about it. Instead of saying anything, he got up and went to the refrigerator to get a drink from his water jar. He was only thirty-five, and already he walked like an exhausted man in late middle age.

Daniel and his father went to an expensive mall restaurant with a railroad theme. Booths were tricked out to look like the seats in trains, and there were framed pictures of trains on the walls. Waitpeople dressed like porters had their names affixed to their jackets on plastic cards. Daniel never went to restaurants like this in San Francisco, but he secretly loved them; they made such an effort.

His father sat away from the table, his long legs crossed, a cigarette lax in his fingers. He was very handsome. He wore an expensive suit. His eyes were harsh and watchful, his thin mouth downwardly taut. Daniel admired him.

As they ate, his father described his new project, producing instructional videos for people who have to stand in line, at the post office or the DMV or anyplace where lines are formed.

"I was thinking maybe you could represent us in San Francisco." His father's eyes shifted up. "If you're interested."

"I've never done that kind of work before."

"That doesn't matter. You'd be a natural." His father speared a slice of lobster meat with a tiny aluminum pick. "The next time you start worrying about your career as a musician, I want you to do this: Just put on your best suit, then go stand in front of a full-length mirror and take a good look at yourself. Just see what a good impression you make. You'll always have that. Whatever happens, with your music or anything else, you can always sell." He drew on his cigarette, his eye wrinkles tensing. "Although you would have to cut your hair."

No matter how thoroughly his father failed, Daniel saw him as a suave, sneering gambler who might win at any time. The ridiculous tropical fish business, the trips to South America, the drunken squabbles with surly young girlfriends in motel restaurants, the seedy hotel rooms, the dirty socks that surely accumulated under the beds of the wifeless—it all merely added to his allure. Even the vision of his father rising from a badly scrambled bed in a box-shaped motel room and staggering into the bathroom to vomit gave Daniel a pang of admiration and love. When he was a teenager, his father had said to him, "You're the son I don't worry about at all. You're a cat that lands on its feet. You could be stuck in the middle of the desert and you'd find your way." He loved his father for saying that to him.

"How did your mother look when you saw her?"

"Well . . ." Daniel hesitated and, to his dismay, smiled. "It was horrible. I almost fainted." His smile was watery, his lips felt weak— why was he smiling at all? He had exposed a tender spot. "I had to leave the room."

"It is horrible." His father vigorously uncrossed his legs. "Horrible and unfair." He meticulously separated some lobster meat from its shell, then lost interest in it. "You know we had a bad relationship. That marriage was ruined by her family. But your mother and I are still close in a way I've never been with another woman. We're still man and wife, even if we never speak to each other again." He chewed rapidly and lightly, then swallowed. "Marriage means something to me, and so does family."

"Me too," said Daniel.

His father looked up. "I still can't believe that idiot family of hers. Sitting there letting nurses tell them what to do." He snorted and poked his tongue around in his mouth. "Probably all doped out on Prozac."

Daniel noticed a red-haired girl with large sweatered breasts at the next table. Her mouth was darkened with bad lipstick gone awry, but she handled her utensils very gracefully.

"How is Ray?" he asked. "Do you still see her?"

"Sometimes." His father smiled, a little harshly. "She's crazy as always. Last time I saw her, we went to some restaurant, pretty late at night. She had coffee and she poured about four sugars into it. I told her it wasn't a good idea to eat so much sugar, and she went nuts. She said, 'Everybody hates guys like you. What the fuck do you know about health, you alcoholic asshole?'" His father snorted mildly and shook his head, his mouth a rude line.

Then he noticed the redhead too.

It was late when they left the restaurant. The night cold reached in through Daniel's nose and seized his lungs. Buildings and cars looked stunned and abandoned in the intense cold. His father's big car shuddered in the wind. Its rusted, corrugated ass end stuck out beyond the other cars, proud and devastated. They got in the car and sat silently for several minutes while his father worked to make the engine turn over, grunting slightly as if he were lifting a heavy object. In the small, cold enclosure, Daniel felt his father intensely, felt him trying really hard.

Jacquie had never liked his father. "He's a handsome prick," she'd said once. "But he's a prick."

"Don't call my dad a prick," said Daniel. "You don't know what you're talking about."

They tried to scoot to the far sides of the bed, but it was so mushy in the center that they rolled together anyway.

When he got home he called Jacquie. She was glad to hear from him; she had thought he was still mad at her. "I realized I must've sounded cold," she said, "but that's not how I meant it."

"It's okay. You were just freaked out." He imagined Jacquie sitting invisible in the car with him and his father, feeling his father. He pictured an expression of understanding slowly altering her face. If they knew each other as he knew them individually, he thought, they would love each other.

"I was thinking about this thing that happened when I was a kid," she said. "I mean, in relation to what I said to you about the accident."

He thought of being with her on their bed, massaging the little ribs between her breasts. These bones were spare, and they gave slightly if he pressed hard. She loved to have them rubbed, especially the places in between the bones.

"We were going to the ice cream social at my school," she said, "which naturally I liked because it meant a ton of ice cream and cake. But as we were pulling out of the driveway, we ran over our cat, Midnight. She was up under the wheel, and she didn't get out in time. It was awful, because when we got out we saw her hips were crushed but she was still moving reflexively, trying to get up."

He listened, alert and puzzled.

"I said, 'Look, she's still alive,' and my mother said, 'No, it's just reflex,' and my sisters immediately began to sob. But I didn't."

"Do you think you were shocked?"

"I don't know. I don't think so. I think I just wanted to go get ice cream. We went to the ice cream social, and I sat there and packed it in. My sisters were too upset to eat, but not me. My mother said, 'Why aren't you crying?' I just shrugged, but later I felt guilty about it."

"Well, it's kind of weird, don't you think?"

"No. And neither does my therapist."

"What did your therapist say?"

"That I was probably not as oriented toward the sensate as my sisters. That I was probably a cerebral child and that plain death didn't seem terrible to me. Like, the cat's dead, there's nothing we can do, so let's go have our ice cream."

"But it's normal to care about pets."

"It wasn't that I didn't care. I just had a different set of responses than the conventional one."

He sighed and stuck his feet in front of a furnace vent made of metal strips and dark, heat-breathing slits.

"Actually I remember getting more upset about Midnight's brother, Walnut. He was obviously very distraught when he saw her body. He walked around the house for days, looking for her and meowing. That did seem sad to me. Partly because he didn't understand what had happened and we couldn't explain it to him."

He got off the phone feeling okay. But later that night he lay in bed, wide awake and furious at Jacquie.

He visited his mother every day during the ten days he stayed in Iowa. He got used to the thin hoop haloing her impaled head. The tube came out of her mouth, and her eyes began to show expression—usually a dull and cantankerous one. Cards and flowers proliferated in her room. Daniel noticed with irritation that nothing had come from Jacquie.

Finally she was able to talk. "How is Jacquie?" she asked.

"Pretty good."

"That's good. She's a nice girl." Her voice was devoid of inflection, flat and invulnerable. There was an undercurrent of grudging bitterness in it, as if she had concluded some time ago that there was no hope for her but was willing to pretend otherwise so that you wouldn't feel depressed, even though the pretense was a nuisance. Daniel realized with discomfort that she had talked like this for years. His mother's eyes shifted vaguely around the room. "She is a nice girl," she repeated. Her hand began to twitch on the rumpled bedsheet. He put his hand out to still it. It felt like an injured and panicking bird. His hand sweated, and he wondered if it repelled her. No, he thought. Just hold her hand.

"Has Harry been to see you?" he asked. Harry was a talkative gynecologist whom she had been dating for the last three months.

"Oh, yes. Several times. I think he's afraid of running into your father."

"How is he?"

"Oh, he's Harry. He's incredibly Harry." She smiled, and her eyes wrinkled elfishly. He saw for a second the pert little girl that smiled at him from old black-and-white photos in the family album. "Tell me about your music," she said.

He told her about his one steady job, in a dark little bar with a crippled neon sign that blinked "Free Crabs—Funk Nite." He told her about playing in the park and being chased by cops. He told her about the time the famous piano player had told him he was "the death." He wasn't sure what it meant to her. It could seem seedy and pathetic.

He finished talking, and they were quiet. She whispered. "Honey, I'm so glad you're here. Let's just sit quietly together now."

The flat rasp of her voice made the endearment strangely poignant to him. He shifted his sweating fingers, stretched them to air them out, and then took her hand again. The room was a lulling beige-and-cream terrain permeated by the muted hum of the building. He listened to it and became aimlessly thoughtful. He thought of Mrs. Harris, whose son had been killed in an amusement park accident several years before. He had liked the son, and yet, when confronted with the weeping Mrs. Harris, he'd been embarrassed and hadn't known what to do. He wished he could see Mrs. Harris again, so that he could hold her and console her.

His mother opened her eyes. "I've never felt so much pain before in my life," she said. "It's unbelievable." She closed her eyes again.

Daniel stroked the length of her arm with his hand. When he was little and he had a headache, his father would put his hands on either side of his head and say, "I'm drawing the pain out of your head and into my hands." He would stand over Daniel with his hands firm on the boy's skull, a terrible look of concentration on his face. Then he would step away and say, "Now your headache is gone." Daniel would still have a headache, but it didn't matter. He loved it when his father came to take the headache away.

He held his mother's shoulders, watching her face for signs of relief. Her cheeks sagged, her eyes were peevishly closed. It struck him that this was only an extreme form of her habitual expression. She always seemed to be suffering in some remote, frozen way. He had been so used to it that he hadn't recognized it as suffering. He didn't think she did, either. It seemed to be her natural state. It seemed natural in part because of her courage, which was also habitual. He thought of her driving on the highway, dressed in her checked business suit, drumming her fingers on the wheel and moving her lips in silent conversation with herself.

The door opened. A dark-haired nurse with a still face came in, pushing a small metal machine. His mother poked one eye open and regarded the nurse like an animal from within a lair. The nurse told her she had to do a test, extract something. "It won't be painful," she said.

"Bullshit," snapped his mother.

Awake at four in the morning, Daniel thought of calling Jacquie again. But he was still mad at her about the cat story and half afraid that if he called she'd say something else that would piss him off. He sat alone at the kitchen table, swatting his drum pad. He felt he was learning something important, something to do with families and with himself that he needed to sort out.

But Jacquie had a thing about families; in the abstract, the subject almost always made her scornful and antagonistic, especially toward parents. She was the kind of person who saw child abuse everywhere. When she went to visit a married friend, her friend's daughter, who was three, brought home painted Easter eggs she'd done at day care. The kid had wanted to eat them, and her father had said no, because he didn't think they were free-range chicken eggs. The child cried and threw an egg on the floor. Her father spanked her and made her clean it up. Daniel didn't think that sounded so bad, but Jacquie was furious. She was even madder at their neighbors, who she said "mocked" their children.

"Ercie will run up to him to show him something she's found, and he'll say, in baby talk, 'Oh, look what Ercie has.' And then he'll look over her head at me and sneer and say, 'Really interesting, huh?' And she looks crestfallen."

"Maybe he's embarrassed to be talking baby talk in front of you. Like you'll think he's uncool or something."

"That's no excuse. She's going to grow up and have all kinds of problems with men, and nobody will understand why. Not even her."

"I don't know, Jacquie. It doesn't sound that bad to me. Kids are okay as long as you love them, basically."

"But what's called love in most families is inadequate shit."

"Loving doesn't mean being perfect."

"I'm not talking about perfect. I'm just talking about respect and kindness for your own kids."

He didn't understand her when she talked this way. Jacquie was a strong girl. She had square shoulders and a muscular butt. She took karate classes. Competence and spirit seemed built right into her. Most of the time he could see her spirit in the animal vibrance of her gold eyes. But sometimes her eyes would reflect a sense of stubborn injury that he could not quite locate. It was an expression that seemed to regard competence and spirit as contrivances that, while they kept her going, had nothing to do with who she really was.

He felt the look in a different way when they had sex. They would embrace, and he'd feel her engage him from the surface of her skin to the wet muscularity of her hidden organs. But there always came a moment when he stopped feeling her. She held him close, but she was somewhere else. He would look at her face and see it twisted away from him, her eyes closed as if she were looking at the inside of her own head in horror and fascination and need. There would be a moment of tension like a fishing line pulled taut, and then he would feel her slowly return. She would open her eyes and look at him and clasp his hand, her ardent palm open against his, her expression fierce and triumphant.

He decided to call her, even though it was two o'clock in San Francisco. There were four rings and a laborious click; his recorded voice asked him to leave a message. He hung up. He wondered where she was.

He sat back in his chair and remembered her naked, kneeling over the low coffee table with her thighs open wide. "If I fucked you in the ass I would own you," he'd said.

She turned over quickly. "No, you wouldn't. What a ridiculous thing to say."

An hour later he called again, but she wasn't home then, either.

The last time Daniel went to see his mother, he went with his father. In spite of what his father had said in the restaurant about how close he was with Daniel's mother, there was a sense of overwhelming discomfort between them. It was clear that they were both sad, but they seemed to be sad in separate, restricted ways, as though they were hoarding it. His mother's mouth was sarcastic, as if she found it ridiculous to be suffering before her ex-husband. His father was gentle, but the gentleness was excruciating. He didn't say anything to her about his new business. They didn't refer to the past or to her family. They talked about the accident, about Albert and Rose, and a little about the country club they had once belonged to. When Daniel talked, he felt that he was, in a more advanced and subtle form, serving the same function he had when they relayed messages through him.

They had been in the room for about half an hour when two

interns came in. They said they needed to do a brief examination. One of them asked, "Are you Mr. Belmont?" Daniel's father said yes. "And you're the son. Then you can stay if you want. This will only take a few minutes." Then, with gestures that would have seemed rapacious had they been less efficient, they stripped the sheet from Daniel's mother, jerking up her gown to expose her lower body. Her pelvic bones stuck out. Her pubic hair was thin and snarled. Gross metal pins attached her at the joints. "Whoops, sorry," said an intern. He pulled down her gown and absently patted her belly. "All in the family."

Jesus Christ, thought Daniel.

His mother smiled like a bitter doll. "Oh, doctors, hello. You might be interested to know that Mr. Belmont and I have not been married for ten years."

His father didn't say anything.

The next day he flew back to San Francisco. Jacquie made him a special chicken dinner, and they ate it on the low coffee table. He told her about how difficult it had been to see his mother that first time and how he had almost fainted. He told her about his father and how he had routed the relatives in the hospital waiting room. He told her how his mother had said "bullshit" to the nurse. She listened attentively; he had the impression that she didn't know what to say. She worked on her sweet potato with inordinate delicacy. Her gold eyes subtly glimmered. He wanted to tell her about the moment he'd had with his father in the car, but it was too far away from him now.

"Could you tell me again why your grandparents hate your father?" she asked. "I know you've told me, but I can't remember exactly."

"Mostly because my father is more adventurous than they are. When my father worked for my grandfather, he had a lot of ideas. He wanted to expand the business into something bigger than this little local thing, and my grandfather just wanted to keep it the way it was. They were arguing about it, and then my grandfather found out that my father was expanding certain lines without telling him. So he fired him."

"Really? I thought it was something different. I thought you told me that your father lost the company money, and that's why he fired him."

"I told you that's what Grandpa said. You weren't listening to me." She tilted her head toward her plate in a vaguely deferential way. "I always wondered how your father could possibly be angry at them."

Daniel pushed the little table away. "Because they tried to emasculate him. What they did would've really fucked up another man. But not my father. That waiting room incident is a perfect example of the difference between them. He was the one who took control of the situation, he made things happen, and they just sat there like jerks."

She looked at him as though she was coming to a new conclusion about him; it seemed that pity was part of the conclusion. He fought an urge to strike her.

"I want to ask you something," he said. "Why didn't you send my mother a card?"

She blinked. "Well, from what you said, I thought she'd be too bad off to read it or even know about it. Actually I looked at some cards today, but they were all really ugly. I'll look at a better store tomorrow."

"You think she cares what the card looks like?"

"If I'm going to send a card, I want it to be a good one."

"You don't understand at all." He stood. "You're just thinking about yourself and about the impression you're going to make. The point isn't a cute card and a cute comment inside it. You're right, of course, she's too bad off to look at it. She can hardly fucking move."

"It wasn't about making an impression." Jacquie's voice was going high and stricken. "Sending cards isn't something I usually ever do. I was going to send one to your mom because what else am I going to do? But it's a stupid, inadequate way of saying anything to anybody."

"That's not the point. The point of all those stupid cards on her table is one thing. They're all signed 'Love.' That's it. Every time she sees another card signed 'Love,' she knows somebody else is behind her, caring about her. That's what counts. And last week was the time to send it. Of course it's inadequate. It's still better than nothing. Do you know how much pain she's in? They've got her so sedated she can hardly talk, and she's still in pain. And you don't send her a card?"

She hovered between emotions, then went into an afflicted flinch. She covered her face with her hands, and he knew she was crying. This was what he had wanted to see, but now he felt sorry, even though she wasn't crying much.

"It's not that I don't care about your mother. I just didn't want to send a card that didn't mean anything. I hate cards. I wanted to send her a letter, but I knew she couldn't read it." She wiped her face, lifted her head, and faced him. "I was going to send her a book after she gets better. I have it picked out. It's not that I wasn't thinking of her."

He sat down next to her and put his arm across her shoulders. "I know," he said. He paused. "You've just never been in this kind of situation before, and you don't know how to respond." Her quivering slowed, and he felt her listening. "I used to be like that. Something like this is so awful that you don't know how to react, and part of you is worried about how you're going to look. But the important thing is just to say that you care, somehow. It doesn't matter if it's not exactly right. You just do it."

She looked up at him. "But I can't think that way, Daniel. If I make a gesture, I want it to be real. Especially if the situation is really bad. It seems insulting to act out of convention. It's like saying 'Have a nice day.' It isn't connected to anything."

He dropped his arm from her shoulder and turned away. There was a stretched-out silence with nothing in it.

He separated into two pieces. Part of him sat square in the middle of pain and held on, knowing that he could endure, knowing that his mother could endure and his father too. But another part of him was extended in darkness, reaching for something without knowing what it was.

"Daniel?" She embraced him from behind. "I'm sorry," she said. Her heart moved in loud, hyperextended beats against his back.

He turned into her embrace and held her head against his chest, locking his legs around her hips. He felt her intensely in the solidity of her little body, felt who she was under her words. She was good inside. She just didn't know how to show it. She didn't know how to look outside herself. He wanted to care for her.

She shifted in his arms and reached up to hold his face in her hands. "You're so cute," she said.

She disengaged herself, got up, and went into the bathroom. He heard the dull ruffle of toilet paper unraveling from its roll, the hiss and squish of a nose blow. She emerged into the room again, moving with familiar authority. But her face, half turned away from him, was strained, diminished, and searching for something that he didn't know, something that had nothing to do with him, nothing at all.

The
Girl
on
the
Plane

John Morton came down the aisle of the plane, banging his luggage into people's knees and sweating angrily under his suit. He had just run through the corridors of the airport, cursing and struggling with his luggage, slipping and flailing in front of the vapid brat at the seat assignment desk. Too winded to speak, he thrust his ticket at the boy and readjusted his luggage in his sticky hands. "You're a little late for a seat assignment," said the kid snottily. "I hope you can get on board before it pulls away."

He took his boarding pass and said, "Thanks, you little prick." The boy's discomfiture was made more obvious by his pretense of hauteur; it both soothed and fed John's anger.

At least he was able to stuff his bags into the compartment above the first seat he found. He sat down, grunting territorially, and his body slowly eased into a normal dull pulse and ebb. He looked at his watch; desk attendant to the contrary, the plane was sitting stupidly still, twenty minutes after takeoff time. He had the pleasing fantasy of punching the little bastard's face.

He was always just barely making his flight. His wife had read in one of her magazines that habitual lateness meant lack of interest in life or depression or something. Well, who could blame him for lack of interest in the crap he was dealing with?

He glanced at the guy a seat away from him on the left, an alco-holic-looking old shark in an expensive suit, who sat staring fixedly at a magazine photograph of a grinning blonde in a white jumpsuit. The plane continued to sit there, while stewardesses fiddled with compartments and women rolled up and down the aisles on trips to the bathroom. They were even boarding a passenger; a woman had just entered, flushed and vigorously banging along the aisle with her luggage. She was very pretty, and he watched her, his body still fee-bly sending off alarm signals in response to its forced run.

"Hi," she said. "I'm in the middle there."

"By all means." The force of his anger entered his magnanimity and swelled it hugely; he pinched his ankles together to let her by. She put her bag under the seat in front of her, sat down, and rested her booted feet on its pale leather. The old shark by the window glanced appraisingly at her breasts through her open coat. He looked up at her face and made smile movements. The stewardess did her parody of a suffocating person reaching for an air mask, the pilot mumbled, the plane prepared to assert its unnatural presence in nature.

"They said I'd missed my flight by fifteen minutes," she said. "But I knew I'd make it. They're never on time." Her voice was unexpect-edly small, with a rough, gravelly undertone that was seedy and schoolgirlish at once.

"It's bullshit," he said. "Well, what can you do?" She had large hazel eyes.

She smiled a tight, rueful smile that he associated with women who'd been fucked too many times and which he found sexy. She cuddled more deeply into her seat, produced a *People* magazine, and intently read it. He liked her profile—which was an interesting com-bination of soft (forehead, chin) and sharp (nose, cheekbones)—her shoulder-length, pale-brown hair, and her soft Mediterranean skin. He liked the coarse quality in the subtle downturn of her lips, and the heavy way her lids sat on her eyes. She was older than he'd origi-nally thought, probably in her early thirties.

Who did she remind him of? A girl from a long time ago, an older version of some date or crush or screw. Or love, he thought gamely.

The pilot said they would be leaving the ground shortly. She was now reading a feature that appeared to be about the wedding of two people who had AIDS. He thought of his wife, at home in Minneapolis, at the stove poking at something, in the living room reading, the fuzzy pink of her favorite sweater. The plane charged and tore a hole in the air.

He reviewed his mental file of girls he'd known before his wife and paused at the memory of Andrea, the girl who'd made an asshole of him. It had been twelve years, and only now could he say that phrase to himself, the only phrase that accurately described the situation. With stale resentment, he regarded her: a pale, long-legged thing with huge gray eyes, a small mouth, long red hair, and the helpless manner of a pampered pet let loose in the wilderness.

The woman next to him was hurriedly flipping the pages of *People*, presumably looking for something as engrossing as the AIDS wedding. When she didn't find it, she closed the magazine and turned to him in a way that invited conversation.

She said she'd lived in L.A. for eight years and that she liked it, even though it was "gross."

"I've never been to L.A.," he said. "I picture it being like *L.A. Law.* Is it like that?"

"I don't know. I've never seen *L.A. Law.* I don't watch TV. I don't own one."

He had never known a person who didn't own a TV, not even an old high school friend who lived in a slum and got food stamps. "You must read the newspapers a lot."

"No. I don't read them much at all."

He was incredulous. "How do you connect with the rest of the world? How do you know anything?"

"I'm part of the world. I know a lot of things."

He expelled a snort of laughter. "That's an awfully small perspective you've got there."

She shrugged and turned her head, and he was sorry he'd been rude. He glanced at her profile to read her expression and—of course; she reminded him of Patty LaForge, poor Patty.

He had met Patty at Meadow Community College in Coate, Minnesota. He was in his last semester; she had just entered. They worked in the student union cafeteria, preparing, serving, and snacking on denatured food. She was a slim, curvy person with dark-blond hair, hazel eyes, and remarkable legs and hips. Her beauty was spoiled by the aggressive resignation that held her features in a fixed position and made all her expressions stiff. Her full mouth had a bitter downturn, and her voice was quick, low, self-deprecating, and sarcastic. She presented her beautiful body statically, as if it were a shield, and the effort of this presentation seemed to be the source of her animation.

Most of the people he knew at Meadow were kids he'd gone to high school and even junior high with. They still lived at home and still drove their cars around together at night, drank in the small bars of Coate, adventured in Minneapolis, and made love to each other. This late-adolescent camaraderie gave their time at Meadow a fraught emotional quality that was like the shimmering fullness of a bead of water before it falls. They were all about to scatter and become different from one another, and this made them exult in their closeness and alikeness.

The woman on the plane was flying to Kentucky to visit her parents and stopping over in Cincinnati.

"Did you grow up in Kentucky?" he asked. He imagined her as a big-eyed child in a cotton shift, playing in some dusty, sunny alley, some rural Kentucky-like place. Funny she had grown up to be this wan little bun with too much makeup in black creases under her eyes.

"No. I was born there, but I grew up mostly in Minnesota, near Minneapolis."

He turned away, registered the little shock of coincidence, and turned back. The situation compounded: she had gone to Redford Community College in Thorold, a suburb much like Coate. She had grown up in Thorold, like Patty. The only reason Patty had gone to Meadow was that Redford didn't exist yet.

He felt a surge of commonality. He imagined that she had experienced his adolescence, and this made him experience it for a moment. He had loved walking the small, neat walkways of the campus through the stiffly banked hedges of snow and harsh morning austerity, entering the close, food-smelling student union with the hard winter air popping off his skin. He would see his friends standing in a conspiratorial huddle, warming their hands on cheap cups of coffee; he always remembered the face of a particular girl, Layla, turning to greet him, looking over her frail sloped shoulder, her hair a bunched dark tangle, her round eyes ringed with green pencil, her perfectly ordinary face compelling in its configurations of girlish curiosity, maternal license, sexual knowledge, forgiveness, and femininity. A familiar mystery he had meant to explore sometime and never did, except when he grabbed her butt at a Halloween party and she smiled like a mother of four who worked as a porn model on the side. He loved driving with his friends to the Red Owl to buy alcohol and bagged salty snacks, which they consumed as they drove around Coate playing the tape deck and yelling at each other, the beautiful ordinary landscape unpeeling before them, revealing the essential strangeness of its shadows and night movements. He loved driving with girls to the deserted housing development they called "the Spot," loved the blurred memories of the girls in the back seat with their naked legs curled up to their chests, their shirts bunched about their necks, their eyes wide with ardor and alcohol, beer and potato chips spilled on the floor of the car, the tape deck singing of love and triumph. He getting out of the car for a triumphant piss, while the girl daintily replaced her pants. In the morning his mother would make him "cowboy eggs," eggs fried on top of bacon, and he would go through the cold to Meadow, to sit in a fluorescent classroom and dream.

"Did you like growing up in that area?" she asked.

"Like it? It was the greatest time of my life." Some extremity in his voice made her look away, and as she did, he looked more fully at her profile. She didn't look that much like Patty; she wasn't even blond. But the small physical resemblance was augmented by a less tangible affinity, a telling similarity of speech and movement.

Patty belonged to a different crowd at Meadow. They were rougher than the Coate people, but the two groups were friendly. Patty was a strange, still presence within her group, with her hip thrust out and a cigarette always bleeding smoke from her hand. She was loose even by seventies standards; she had a dirty sense of humor, and she wore pants so tight you could see the swollen outline of her genitals. She was also shy. When she talked she pawed the ground with her foot and pulled her hair over her mouth; she looked away from you and then snuck a look back to see what you thought of her. She was accepted by the Thorold people the way you accept what you've always known. The stiffness of her face and body contradicting her loose reputation, her coarse language expressed in her timid voice and shy manners, her beauty and her ordinariness, all gave her a disconnected sexiness that was aggravating.

But he liked her. They were often a team at work, and he enjoyed having her next to him, her golden-haired arms plunged in greasy black dishwater or flecked with garbage as she plucked silverware from vile plates on their way to the dishwasher. She spooned out quivering red Jell-O or drew long bland snakes of soft ice cream from the stainless-steel machine, she smoked, wiped her nose, and muttered about a fight with her mother or a bad date. Her movements were resigned and bitter, yet her eyes and her nasty humor peeked impishly from under this weight. There was something pleasing in this combination, something congruent with her spoiled beauty.

It was a long time before he realized she had a crush on him. All her conversation was braided together with a fly strip of different boys she had been with or was involved with, and she talked of all of them with the same tone of fondness and resentment. He thought nothing of it when she followed him outside to the field behind the union, where they would walk along the narrow wet ditch, smoking pot and talking. It was early spring; dark, naked trees pressed intensely against the horizon, wet weeds clung to their jeans, and her small voice bobbed assertively on the vibrant air. The cold wind gave her lips a swollen raw look and made her young skin grainy and bleached. "So why do you let him treat you like that?" "Ah, I get back at him. It's not really him, you know, I'm just fixated on him. I'm working out something through him. Besides, he's a great lay." He never noticed how often she came up behind him to walk him to class or sat on the edge of his chair as he lounged in the union. Then one day she missed work, and a buddy of his said, "Hey, where's your little puppy dog today?" and he knew.

"Did you like Thorold?" he asked the girl next to him.

"No, I didn't." She turned toward him, her face a staccato burst of candor. "I didn't know what I was doing, and I was a practicing alcoholic. I kept trying to fit in and I couldn't."

"That doesn't sound good." He smiled. How like Patty to answer a polite question from a stranger with this emotional nakedness, this urgent excess of information. She was always doing that, especially after the job at the cafeteria ended. He'd see her in a hallway or the union lounge, where normal life was happening all around them, and she'd swoop into a compressed communication, intently twining her hair around her finger as she quickly muttered that she'd had the strangest dream about this guy David, in which a nuclear war was going on, and he, John, was in it too, and—

"What did you do after Redford?" he asked the girl next to him.

"Screwed around, basically. I went to New York pretty soon after that and did the same things I was doing in Thorold. Except I was trying to be a singer."

"Yeah?" He felt buoyed by her ambition. He pictured her in a tight black dress, lips parted, eyes closed, bathed in cheap, sexy stage light. "Didja ever do anything with it?"

"Not much." She abruptly changed expression, as though she'd just remembered not to put herself down. "Well, some stuff. I had a good band once, we played the club circuit in L.A. for a while six years ago." She paused. "But I'm mostly a paralegal now."

"Well, that's not bad, either. Do you ever sing now?"

"I haven't for a long time. But I was thinking of trying again." Just like Patty, she looked away and quickly looked back as if to check his reaction. "I've been auditioning. Even though . . . I don't know."

"It sounds great to me," he said. "At least you're trying. It sounds better than what I do." His self-deprecation annoyed him, and he bulled his way through an explanation of what he did, making it sound more interesting than selling software.

A stewardess with a small pink face asked if they'd like anything to drink, and he ordered two little bottles of Jack Daniel's. Patty's shadow had a compressed can of orange juice and an unsavory packet of nuts; their silent companion by the window had vodka straight. He thought of asking her if she was married, but he bet the answer was no, and he didn't want to make her admit her loneliness. Of course, not every single person was lonely, but he guessed that she was. She seemed in need of comfort and care, like a stray animal that gets fed by various kindly people but never held.

"Will you get some mothering while you're at home?" he asked.

"Oh, yes. My mother will make things I like to eat and . . . stuff like that."

He thought of telling her that she reminded him of someone he'd known in Coate, but he didn't. He sat silently, knocking back his whiskey and watching her roll a greasy peanut between two fingers.

Out in the field, they were sitting on a fallen branch, sharing a wet stub of pot. "I don't usually say stuff like this," said Patty. "I know you think I do, because of the way I talk, but I don't. But I'm really attracted to you, John." The wind blew a piece of hair across her cheek, and its texture contrasted acutely with her cold-bleached skin.

"Yeah, I was beginning to notice."

"I guess it was kind of obvious, huh?" She looked down and drew her curtain of hair. "And I've been getting these mixed signals from you. I can't tell if you're attracted to me or not." She paused. "But I guess you're not, huh?"

Her humility embarrassed and touched him. "Well, I am attracted to you. Sort of. I mean, you're beautiful and everything. I'm just not attracted enough to do anything. Besides, there's Susan."

"Oh. I thought you didn't like her that much." She sniffed and dropped the roach on the raw grass; her lipstick had congealed into little chapped bumps on her lower lip. "Well, I'm really disappointed. I thought you liked me."

"I do like you, Patty."

"You know what I meant." Pause. "I'm more attracted to you than I've been to anybody for two years. Since Paul."

A flattered giggle escaped him.

"Well, I hope we can be friends," she said. "We can still talk and stuff, can't we?"

"Patty LaForge? I wouldn't touch her, man. The smell alone."

He was driving around with a carload of drunk boys who were filled with a tangle of goodwill and aggression.

"Ah, LaForge is okay."

He was indignant for Patty, but he laughed anyway.

"Were you really an alcoholic when you lived in Thorold?" he asked.

"I still am, I just don't drink now. But then I did. Yeah."

He had stepped into a conversation that had looked nice and solid, and his foot had gone through the floor and into the basement. But he couldn't stop. "I guess I drank too much then too. But it wasn't a problem. We just had a lot of fun."

She smiled with tight, terse mystery.

"How come you told me that about yourself? It seems kind of personal." He attached his gaze to hers as he said this; sometimes women said personal things to you as a way of coming on.

But instead of becoming soft and encouraging, her expression turned proper and institutional, like a kid about to recite. "If I'm going to admit it to other alcoholics in the program, I can admit it in regular life too. It humbles you, sort of."

What a bunch of shit, he thought.

He was drinking with some guys at the Winners Circle, a rough pickup bar, when suddenly Patty walked up to him, really drunk.

"John," she gasped. "John, John, John." She lurched at him and attached her nail-bitten little claws to his jacket. "John, this guy over there really wants to fuck me, and I was going to go with him, but I don't want him, I want you, I want you." Her voice wrinkled into a squeak, her face looked like you could smear it with your hand.

"Patty," he mumbled, "you're drunk."

"That's not why. I always feel like this." Her nose and eyelashes and lips touched his cheek in an alcoholic caress. "Just let me kiss you. Just hold me."

He put his hands on her shoulders. "C'mon, stop it."

"It doesn't have to mean anything. You don't have to love me. I love you enough for both of us."

He felt the presence of his smirking friends. "Patty, these guys are laughing at you. I'll see you later." He tried to push her away.

"I don't care. I love you, John. I mean it." She pressed her taut body against his, one sweaty hand under his shirt, and arched her neck until he could see the small veins and bones. "Please. Just be with me. Please." Her hand stroked him, groped between his legs. He took her shoulders and shoved her harder than he had meant to. She staggered back, fell against a table, knocked down a chair, and almost fell again. She straightened and looked at him as if she'd known him and hated him all her life.

He leaned back in his seat and closed his eyes, an overweight, prematurely balding salesman getting drunk on an airplane.

"Look at the clouds," said the girl next to him. "Aren't they beautiful?"

He opened his eyes and silently looked.

Shrewdness glimmered under her gaze.

"What's your name?" he asked.

"Lorraine."

"I'm John." He extended his hand and she took it, her eyes unreadable, her hand exuding sweet feminine sweat.

"Why do you want to talk about your alcoholism publicly? I mean, if nobody asks or anything?"

Her eyes were steadfast, but her body was hesitant. "Well, I didn't have to just now. It's just the first thing I thought of when you asked me about Thorold. In general, it's to remind me. It's easy to bullshit yourself that you don't have a problem."

He thought of the rows and rows of people in swivel chairs on talk-show stages, admitting their problems. Wife beaters, child abusers, dominatrixes, porn stars. In the past it probably was a humbling experience to stand up and tell people you were an alcoholic. Now it was just something else to talk about. He remembered Patty tottering through a crowded party on smudged red high heels, bragging about what great blow jobs she gave. Some girl rolled her eyes and said, "Oh, no, not again." Patty disappeared into a bedroom with a bottle of vodka and Jack Spannos.

He remembered a conversation with his wife before he married her, a conversation about his bachelor party. "It was no women allowed," he'd told her. "Unless they wanted to give blow jobs."

"Couldn't they just jump naked out of a cake?" she asked.

"Nope. Blow jobs for everybody."

They were at a festive restaurant, drinking margaritas. Nervously, she touched her tiny straws. "Wouldn't that be embarrassing? In front of each other? I can't imagine Henry doing that in front of you all."

He smiled at the mention of his shy friend in this context. "Yeah," he said. "It probably would be embarrassing. Group sex is for teenagers."

Her face rose away from her glass in a kind of excited alarm, her lips parted. "You had group sex when you were a teenager?"

"Oh. Not really. Just a gang bang once."

She looked like an antelope testing the wind with its nose in the air, ready to fly. "It wasn't rape," she said.

"Oh, no, no." Her body relaxed and released a warm, sensual curiosity, like a cat against his leg. "The girl liked it."

"Are you sure?"

"Yeah. She liked having sex with a lot of guys. We all knew her, she knew us."

He felt her shiver inwardly, shocked and fascinated by this dangerous pack-animal aspect of his masculinity.

"What was it like?" she asked.

He shrugged. "It was a good time with the guys. It was a bunch of guys standing around in their socks and underwear."

Some kid he didn't know walked up and put his arm around him while he was talking to a girl named Chrissie. The kid's eyes were boyish and drunkenly enthusiastic, his face heavy and porous. He whispered something about Patty in John's ear and said, "C'mon."

The girl's expression subtly withdrew.

"What?" said John.

"Come on," said the kid.

"Bye-bye," said Chrissie, with a gingerly wag of her fingers.

He followed the guy through the room, seizing glimpses of hips and tits sheathed in bright, cheap cloth, girls doing wiggly dances with guys who jogged helplessly from foot to foot, holding their chests proudly aloof from their lower bodies. On the TV, a pretty girl gyrated in her black bra, sending a clean bolt of sex into the room. The music made his organs want to leap in and out of his body in time. His friends were all around him.

A door opened and closed behind him, muffling the music. The kid who'd brought him in sat in an armchair, smiling. Patty lay on a bed with her skirt pulled up to her waist and a guy with his pants down straddling her face. Without knowing why, he laughed. Patty twisted her legs about and bucked slightly. For a moment he felt frightened that this was against her will—but no, she would have screamed. He recognized the boy on her as Pete Kopiekin, who was thrusting his flat, hairy butt in the same dogged, earnest, woeful manner with which he played football. His heart was pounding.

Kopiekin got off her and the other guy got on; between them he saw her chin sticking up from her sprawled body, pivoting to and fro on her neck while she muttered and groped blindly up and down her body. Kopiekin opened the door to leave, and a fist of music punched the room. John's body jumped in shocked response, and the door shut. The guy on top of Patty was talking to her; to John's amazement, he seemed to be using love words. "You're so beautiful, baby." He saw Patty's hips moving. She wasn't being raped, he thought. When the guy finished, he stood and poured the rest of his beer in her face.

"Hey," said John lamely, "hey."

"Oh, man, don't tell me that. I've known her a long time."

When the guy left, he thought of wiping her face, but he didn't. She sighed fitfully and rolled on her side, as if there was something under the mattress, disturbing her sleep, but she was too tired to remove it. His thoughts spiraled inward, and he let them be chopped up by muffled guitar chords. He sat awhile, watching guys swarm over Patty and talking to the ones waiting. Music sliced in and out of the room. Then some guy wanted to pour maple syrup on her, and

John said, "No, I didn't go yet." He sat on the bed and, for the first time, looked at her, expecting to see the sheepish bitter look he knew. He didn't recognize her. Her rigid face was weirdly slack; her eyes fluttered open, rolled, and closed; a mix of half-formed expressions flew across her face like swarming ghosts. "Patty," he said, "hey." He shook her shoulder. Her eyes opened, her gaze raked his face. He saw tenderness, he thought. He lay on her and tried to embrace her. Her body was leaden and floppy. She muttered and moved, but in ways he didn't understand. He massaged her breasts; they felt like they could come off and she wouldn't notice.

He lay there, supporting himself on his elbows, and felt the deep breath in her lower body meeting his own breath. Subtly, he felt her come to life. She lifted her head and said something; he heard his name. He kissed her on the lips. Her tongue touched his, gently, her sleeping hands woke. He held her and stroked her pale, beautiful face.

He got up in such a good mood that he slapped the guy coming in with the maple syrup a high five, something he thought was stupid and usually never did.

The next time he saw Patty was at a Foreigner concert in Minneapolis; he saw her holding hands with Pete Kopiekin.

Well, now she could probably be on a talk show about date rape. It was a confusing thing. She may have wanted to kiss him or to give Jack Spannos a blow job, but she probably didn't want maple syrup poured on her. Really, though, if you were going to get blind drunk and let everybody fuck you, you had to expect some nasty stuff. On the talk shows they always said it was low self-esteem that made them do it. If he had low self-esteem, he sure wouldn't try to cure it like that. His eyes rested on Lorraine's hands; she was wadding the empty nut package and stuffing it in her empty plastic cup.

"Hey," he said, "what did you mean when you said you kept trying to fit in and you couldn't? When you were in Thorold?"

"Oh, you know." She seemed impatient. "Acting the part of the pretty, sexy girl."

"When in fact you were not a pretty, sexy girl?"

She started to smile, then caught his expression and gestured dismissively. "It was complicated."

It was seductive, the way she drew him in and then shut him out. She picked up her magazine again. Her slight arm movement released a tiny cloud of sweat and deodorant, which evaporated as soon as he inhaled it. He breathed in deeply, hoping to smell her again. Sunlight pressed in with viral intensity and exaggerated the lovely contours of her face, the fine lines, the stray cosmetic flecks, the marvelous profusion of her pores. He thought of the stories he'd read in sex magazines about strangers on airplanes having sex in the bathroom or masturbating each other under blankets.

The stewardess made a sweep with a gaping white garbage bag and cleared their trays of bottles and cups.

She put down the magazine. "You've probably had the same experience yourself," she said. Her face was curiously determined, as if it were very important that she make herself understood. "I mean doing stuff for other people's expectations or just to feel you have a social identity because you're so convinced who you are isn't right."

"You mean low self-esteem?"

"Well, yeah, but more than that." He sensed her inner tension and felt an empathic twitch.

"It's just that you get so many projections onto yourself of who and what you're supposed to be that if you don't have a strong support system it's hard to process it."

"Yeah," he said. "I know what you mean. I've had that experience. I don't know how you can't have it when you're young. There's so much crap in the world." He felt embarrassed, but he kept talking, wanting to tell her something about himself, to return her candor. "I've done lots of things I wish I hadn't done, I've made mistakes. But you can't let it rule your life."

She smiled again, with her mouth only. "Once, a few years ago, my father asked me what I believed to be the worst mistakes in my life. This is how he thinks, this is his favorite kind of question. Anyway, it was really hard to say, because I don't know from this vantage point what would've happened if I'd done otherwise in most situations. Finally, I came up with two things: my relationship with this guy named Jerry and the time I turned down an offer to work with this really awful band that became famous. He was totally bewildered. He was expecting me to say 'dropping out of college.' "

"You didn't make a mistake dropping out of college." The vehemence in his voice almost made him blush; then nameless urgency swelled forth and quelled embarrassment. "That wasn't a mistake," he repeated.

"Well, yeah, I know."

"Excuse me." The silent business shark to their left rose in majestic self-containment and moved awkwardly past their knees, looking at John with pointed irony as he did so. Fuck you, thought John.

"And about that relationship," he went on. "That wasn't your loss. It was his." He had meant these words to sound light and playfully gallant, but they had the awful intensity of a maudlin personal confession. He reached out to gently pat her hand, to reassure her that he wasn't a nut, but instead he grabbed it and held it. "If you want to talk about mistakes—shit, I raped somebody. Somebody I liked."

Their gaze met in a conflagration of reaction. She was so close he could smell her sweating, but at the speed of light she was falling away, deep into herself where he couldn't follow. She was struggling to free her hand.

"No," he said, "it wasn't a real rape. It was what you were talking about—it was complicated."

She wrenched her hand free and held it protectively close to her chest. "Don't touch me again." She turned tautly forward. He imagined her heart beating in alarm. His body felt so stiff he could barely feel his own heart. Furiously, he wondered if the people around them had heard any of this. Staring ahead of him, he hissed, "Do you think I was dying to hear about your alcoholism? You were the one who started this crazy conversation."

He felt her consider this. "It's not the same thing," she hissed back.

"But it wasn't really a rape." He struggled to say what it was. He recalled Patty that night at the Winners Circle, her neck arched and exposed, her feelings extended and flailing the air where she expected his feelings to be.

"You don't understand," he finished lamely.

She was silent. He thought he dimly felt her body relax, emitting some possibility of forgiveness. But he couldn't tell. He closed his eyes. He thought of Patty's splayed body, her half-conscious kiss. He thought of his wife, her compact scrappy body, her tough-looking

135

flat nose and chipped nail polish, her smile, her smell, her embrace, which was both soft and fierce. He imagined the hotel room he would sleep in tonight, its stifling grid of rectangles, oblongs, and windows that wouldn't open. He leaned back and closed his eyes.

The pilot roused him with a command to fasten his seat belt. He sat up and blinked. Nothing had changed. The woman at his side was sitting slightly hunched, with her hands resolutely clasped.

"God, I'll be glad when we're on the ground," he said.

She sniffed in reply.

They descended, ears popping. They landed with a flurry of baggage-grabbing. He stood, bumped his head, and tried to get into the aisle to escape, but it was too crowded. He sat back down. Not being able to leave made him feel that he had to say something else. "Look, don't be upset. What I said came out wrong."

"I don't want to talk."

Neither do I, he thought. But he felt disoriented and depressed amid these shifting, lunging, grabbing people from all over the country, who had been in his life for hours and were now about to disappear, taking their personal items and habits with them.

"Excuse me." She butted her way past him and into the aisle. He watched a round, vulnerable piece of her head move between the obstructions of shoulders and arms. She glanced backward, possibly to see if he was going to try to follow her. The sideways movement of her hazel iris prickled him. They burst from the plane and scattered, people picking up speed as they bore down on their destination. He caught up with her as they entered the terminal. "I'm sorry," he said to the back of her head. She moved farther away, into memory and beyond.

The
Dentist

In Jill's neighborhood there was a giant billboard advertisement for a perfume called Obsession. It was mounted over the chain grocery store at which she shopped, and so she glanced at it several times a week. It was a close-up black-and-white photograph of an exquisite girl with the fingers of one hand pressed against her open lips. Her eyes were fixated, wounded, deprived. At the same time, her eyes were flat. Her body was slender, almost starved, giving her delicate beauty the strange, arrested sensuality of unsatisfied want. But her fleshy lips and enormous eyes were sumptuously, even grossly abundant. The photograph loomed over the toiling shoppers like a totem of sexualized pathology, a vision of feeling and unfeeling chafing together. It was a picture made for people who can't bear to feel and yet still need to feel. It was a picture by people sophisticated enough to fetishize their disability publicly. It was a very good advertisement for a product called Obsession.

At least this is what Jill thought about it, but Jill was an essayist who wrote primarily for magazines, and she was prone to extravagant mental tangents that were based on very little. She had to be, in order to keep thinking of things to write about. Besides, she was perhaps hypersensitive to the idea of obsession, as she had just become obsessed with someone. He was a mild, pale, middle-aged man who did not return her ardor, and what should've been a pinprick disappointment had swollen into a great live wound that throbbed at night and deprived her of sleep, of thought, even of normal physical sensation.

"Drop it," said her friend Pamela. "Don't even, as they say, think about it. He sounds really fucked up, and not in an interesting way. There wouldn't be any satisfaction for you. It would be like jerking off forever and not coming."

It was. She would lie curled on her bed, making sounds of animal pain, dry even of tears, as thoughts of the loved one so feverishly inflated her desire that she could not fit it into a fantasy which she could then make end in at least rote physical satisfaction.

The odd thing was that the object of her inflated feelings was her dentist.

The terrible situation had begun when she had gone to have a wisdom tooth removed. Jill was thirty-seven, and her one remaining wisdom tooth had had ample opportunity to grow where it didn't belong, for example, around her jawbone. Neither she nor the dentist had realized this at the onset of the operation, and he had, in a professionally somnolent voice, assured her that the ordeal would probably be over in fifteen minutes. An hour later, the as yet mercifully unsexualized dentist was still gripping her jaw with enough force (as it turned out) to bruise her, perspiring and even grunting slightly as he tore her tooth out bit by tiny bit.

"It became almost comic," she said later. "He kept heaving back, sort of panting with exertion, and he'd say, in that voice of inhuman dentist calm, 'Just a little more; we're going to move it around in there just a little bit more, and then I think we've got it.' It got to the point where I could smell him sweating, and a certain indecorous tone crept up under that professional voice, a sort of hysteria straining at the borders. Finally, when he started to give me the speech one last time, I snapped, 'I just want the fucking thing out.' And he snarled back, 'Okay,' totally ripping the lid off the calm facade, which is probably pretty hard-core for a dentist."

"And that's when you got excited?" asked Pamela.

"No. No, I felt united with him in disbelief and disgust at the whole thing, but I was certainly not excited. That didn't happen until later."

A few days after the tooth came out, there were complications. She developed an infection and had to return to the dentist's office twice. She had an allergic reaction to the pain medication he prescribed for her, and to make up for the unpleasantness, he gave her free medication out of his closet. The gift pills didn't make her itch, but they made her pulse lunge and her mind twist, so that she was too disoriented to write a commissioned piece for a fashion magazine on the torment of having small lips. With a great effort, she decided not to become discouraged and instead sat down to type a long handwritten draft of a two-part series on whether or not people's memories of being abused as children are real. She had typed the first line when her word processor collapsed.

Her word processor was so old and primitive that no local repair company would service it, and it would take weeks for the whimsical midwestern manufacturer to do it, what with shipping and all. No computer she could rent, borrow, or buy could read the old monster's disks. Besides, she couldn't afford to buy another machine, and since she had recently moved to San Francisco from Boston, she did not know any writers from whom she could borrow one, and she was not confident about her ability to use a new one anyway. Right about then her jaw started to throb through the pain medication. "I'm tearing my hair out," she said to Pamela, and it was close to the truth. She couldn't pay that month's rent, she was lonely, she had bad dreams, she was worried about losing her looks, and her jaw hurt like hell.

There is nothing like physical pain for enlarging and enhancing free-floating emotional pain. As she walked to the dentist's office, Jill began to feel desperate. She was maddened by the noise and motion of the street, she was irritated by the sweet spring air. A burst of purple flowers on a dirty white wall shocked her with their brightness and lulled her with their low whisper of the deep earth, making her feel pulled in two directions and unable to go in either.

"Well, you've got a dry socket," said the dentist, drawing back from her with a mournful, empathic air. "It's something that *can* happen sometimes, and it's nothing to worry about, although it *can* be quite painful. We'll just increase the pain medication and pack the area nice and tight. Then it's up to you to keep off that sensitive area." He paused. "I'm sorry you've had to walk around with it hurting so much. With that exposed bone, I frankly don't know how you stood it."

"I *can't* stand it," she said. She hesitated, fearing that she was perhaps tastelessly spewing into the dentist's vast spaces of professional calm. Then she decided that with all that vastness, he could afford it, and she spewed hard. "It's not just the tooth. It's everything. I can't sleep. I can't talk to anybody. I'm going broke and I can't write my articles because I'm in a drug haze. I can't even type an article, because my stupid word processor broke and I can't afford another one. And now you're telling me it's going to keep being like this for days more. I don't know what to do. I don't know what to do."

"I can loan you my laptop," he said. "No problem."

She paused to adjust to the sudden shift in terrain. "I don't know how to use a computer."

"It's easy," he said. "I'll teach you."

She looked into his gray eyes. They were opaque with dutiful kindliness. He wants to be my friend, she thought. Probably he's not thinking sex; he's not the type. I'll just have to be friendly with him, which is a pain, but if I can type that article, the activity will make me less hysterical.

"I could bring it by tomorrow evening," he offered. "It's no trouble at all." His voice was like a stream of lukewarm water running over her wrist.

"All right," she said slowly.

"And he did it," she said to Pamela. This was much later, after the grueling drama had erupted. "He did exactly what he said. I felt sort of guarded when he first came in, but I saw right away it wasn't necessary. He set the thing up, showed me how to work it, and *left*. He was like a UPS man or an electrician. I think even the cat was impressed with his discretion."

"Was he friendly?"

"More like beneficent. Actually it was this combination of beneficence and self-conscious goofiness. He carried the computer to my desk with this proud little outthrust of his chest in front and this silly little outthrust of his butt in back. Like he was performing a skit he'd done a thousand times before and was still just bemused enough to do again."

Pamela uttered a cautious, noncommittal sound. She lived in New York and, as Jill's oldest friend, had stood by her through many grueling dramas. But Jill hadn't gotten involved in anything *too* ridiculous for a few years, and Pamela seemed to find this recidivism depressing.

"When he left he said I could call him at any time of the day or night. If he was at work, his beeper would go off and he'd call me back."

"Well, his behavior is strange," said Pamela. "Because he certainly gave you every reason to believe he was interested."

The dentist's rigorous and polite reliability impressed Jill, who had not often seen such behavior in men. She had left home at sixteen to live with a commercial artist almost fifteen years older than she was, and although the affair only lasted three years, she left it in a state of unfortunate attunement to the kind of refined, convoluted fellow who likes to make a very fancy mess. She had put herself through school with five years of work in various strip bars and go-go joints, and, at the age of twenty-six, had entered into journalism with the publication of an essay about down-and-out jazz musicians in a trendy men's magazine. Because of the unusual career segue, she had few professional acquaintances and almost no experience with the sort of mundane camaraderie that makes up the common social staple; thus her baseline emotional life had consisted mainly of going from one loud mess to the next. To her, the dentist's simple and undemanding generosity looked like a shining piece of integrity, which aroused first her surprise and then her admiration. Admiration didn't develop into love right away, though, and the first time she called him, she did so reluctantly. It was, after all, one in the morning, but the computer had disobeyed her at a decisive moment, and he *had* said anytime.

He greeted her as if he had been waiting alertly for her call. As he solved her problem, their conversation dipped and bumped along easily. He complained mildly about difficulty he was having with a lab he used. He told her about an old movie he had seen on TV that

evening, called *Hot Rods to Hell*, in which a father (played by Dana
Andrews) is terrorized and humiliated by sexy youths but eventually
triumphs over the youths. The dentist compared it favorably to
newer humiliation/triumph-based movies he'd seen recently. His
disembodied voice was gentle and authoritative, and had an undertone that sounded thwarted, feisty, and playful at once. She pictured
him in an apartment made up of utilitarian oblongs, gray shadows,
gleaming limbs of furniture, and an entertainment center, all alone
with his thwarted feistiness.

"George?" she asked. "Are you happy?"

"Pretty much," he answered. "Why wouldn't I be?"

She hung up feeling enveloped and upheld by his "Why wouldn't
I be?" His tone seemed to acknowledge all that might threaten happiness—"It's something that *can* happen sometimes and it's nothing
to worry about"—and then to shoulder it aside as if the important
thing was to get through life somehow, to extract teeth, to follow the
schedule, to do what you said you would do. This was a new point of
view for Jill, and it affected her profoundly. She finished her article
quickly and went to bed feeling an unfamiliar species of warmth and
comfort. She woke imagining the dentist holding her from behind,
and she prolonged the image, allowing it to become a thought.

That day she sent her article to the magazine that had commissioned it and, since her jaw was feeling better, arranged to have dinner with her friend Joshua. Joshua was a frustrated musician. He was
frustrated mostly by himself. He had achieved a modest success in
Boston and then come to San Francisco to pursue a hopeless infatua-
tion with a lesbian who didn't even like him as a person. He claimed
the experience had damaged his "voice," and now he worked as a
cabdriver, occasionally managing a sit-in gig for some obscure band.
Joshua was very intelligent and very dear, and like many people who
have difficulty managing their own lives, his opinions and advice
were often excellent. They went to a cheap Thai place in the Mis-
sion. Jill told the story of the dentist as if it were a funny joke.

"He's a total nerd," she finished. "He's the kind of guy who says
'All righty' at the end of conversations. Of course, I'm not really
attracted to him. But it's funny that the thought even crossed my
mind, don't you think?"

"I don't know," said Joshua thoughtfully. "I can see it, actually."

"See what? What's there to see?"

"Well, it's like—remember when those weird thieves broke into my apartment?"

He was referring to the time a spectacularly eccentric thief or thieves had broken into the house he shared with three other people and apparently meandered through it, stealing a scarf, two pairs of pants, an address book, a Sonic Youth tape, and the contents of the mailbox.

"They took my unemployment check, and I had to go through this ordeal of getting it canceled, which meant I had to officially sign up for benefits again. Which meant standing in line at the unemployment office and explaining my situation and being told I was in the wrong line—it went on all day, and still it wasn't fixed. And that's the kind of thing that drives me crazy."

Jill murmured sympathetically.

"So I had to come back the next day and wait in yet another line. I was almost at the end of my rope when this woman who worked there overheard me talking to another clerk about it, and she said, 'Come over here, I'll help you.' And not only did she help me, but she turned the whole experience into this really nice exchange."

"Was she good-looking?" asked Jill.

"Not especially. She was a middle-aged woman with a smart haircut. She had on a nice blouse with tiny polka dots, which I always like. But what really made me respond to her was that when these people just behind me in her line started bitching, she yelled out this funny comment off one of their complaints and made them laugh. That opened up the experience and made it okay to be standing there in line. I felt really attracted to her because she could do that."

"Enough to ask her out?"

He shrugged. "It was more ephemeral than that. Sort of like what you're describing. But it was a great little moment."

"Yeah," she said. "It is like me and the dentist. You and I are so inept at practical details that when the practical details are, like, exploding in your face, and suddenly there's someone who can not only straighten it out for you but who seems to embody a whole universe where these disasters are just taken in stride, you're going to be incredibly grateful. Like, yes, there is an emotional hell that can't be fixed, but on the other hand, there's the dentist and the unemployment lady working away making things go smoothly at least on some level."

"And who also acknowledge the emotional hell," said Joshua. "Like the polka-dot lady with her joke."

"Yes! Exactly."

"What's interesting about the dentist, though . . ." Joshua paused, and his face became uncharacteristically sly. "He's solved your problems, but he also caused them to a certain extent. I mean, he hurt you."

They finished dinner and relocated to a dark little bar. They sat in a booth with sticky wooden seats and steadily drank. Joshua described a TV show he'd seen, about an experimental program being conducted by some prison systems that enabled victims and their families to confront the criminals who had victimized them. He described the emotional scene between a thief and the clerk he'd shot, each of them telling the other what the robbery had been like for him—the clerk refraining, "Why did you do that to me?" until the robber apologized and they embraced with a great deal of emotion.

Jill was interested, but as she settled more comfortably into drunkenness, she found it hard to concentrate on the story; she was distracted by the memory of the dentist's disembodied voice issuing instructions over the phone. "I want you to press 'alt,'" he said inside her head. "Good. Now I want you to go to file."

"But the last confrontation was pretty nasty," continued Joshua. "It was between a woman whose daughter had been raped and murdered and the guy who did it. The mother was religious, apparently, and she kept trying to appeal to the guy on those terms. He seemed to have respect for religion, and a couple of times he said he was sorry for raping and killing the daughter. But he said it with this odd kind of reserve, this detached compassion for the poor old mom, and that just seemed to drive her crazy. She kept saying she wanted to know exactly what it had felt like to rape and strangle her daughter, and after a while he started to look at her like, 'Hey, lady, who's the freak here?' And I have to say he had a point. But he couldn't remember anything about the murder or the rape, because he'd blacked out—which he also apologized for. The mom got more and more frustrated, and in this kind of masochistic frenzy she blurted out, 'I know I should get down on my hands and knees and thank you for not torturing my baby.' And a look of utter shock flashed in the killer's eyes, like two live wires had just been touched together inside him. He just stared at her. Like he *recognized* her. It was way creepy." Joshua paused. "The girl's father was there too. But he didn't say anything. He just sat there with his head down."

The next evening she called the dentist. She pretended to have a question about the computer, and he said, "I want you to press 'alt.' " The banality, the politeness, and the harmless hint of command were all accentuated by the abstracted context and took interesting forms in her imagination. Happily, she visualized all kinds of things he might want her to do.

When he finished instructing her, she asked him questions about himself. He told her that before dental school he had studied theater and film. He had done his undergraduate thesis on lesbianism among strippers—which, he confidently assured her, was quite high, at least in Scranton, Pennsylvania.

"Really," said Jill. She felt slightly nonplussed without quite knowing why. "What kind of show did they do?"

"Show?"

"You know, when they stripped."

He told her that he had only interviewed the strippers and had not watched them perform.

"Why not?" she asked. "I mean, weren't you curious?"

No, he wasn't.

"That should've been your first hint," said Pamela. "A twenty-some-year-old guy who's not interested in watching strippers but who wants to establish their lesbianism? He's either a pervert or he's pathologically frightened or he hates women. Or all three."

"I don't know," said Jill. "I thought it might be something else with him. I was pretty surprised when he said it, but I thought maybe he was trying to be a feminist or something."

When she finished her project, he brought her his printer.

"I must take you to dinner," she said. "You've been so incredibly kind."

He demurred, making the expected mutterings about the least he could do. "Besides," he said, "I like to help creative people."

They went to an Italian place in North Beach. They stared at their menus with ritual concentration. In the public setting, the dentist looked like a stranger, and that unnerved her; vainly she tried to revive the mysterious frisson that had arisen over the phone. He was wearing a loose-fitting turquoise sweater and faded corduroy pants, the casualness of which gave him a rumpled, little-boy sensuality that was pleasing but overly sweet for her tastes.

"How old were you when you did your thesis on lesbian strippers?" she asked.

"Twenty-two. Why?"

"It's very unusual for a man that age to be so uninterested in watching women take off their clothes and gyrate. Especially if you were interested in whether or not they were dykes."

"Have you ever been in one of those places, Jill? They're pathetic and—"

"I used to work in one, actually." She paused so that he could say "Really?" but he just sat there and blinked. Maybe, she thought, he had read it in a magazine bio note. "I didn't think of it as pathetic, personally. Some of the women were worth seeing, I thought."

"It wasn't the women who were pathetic; it was the men." A certain professorial tone had crept into his voice. "Sitting there slavering over women who were really lesbians anyway."

"I'd just think . . . out of curiosity, if nothing else—"

"Look, during my second year of college I worked as an assistant cameraman for a low-grade porn company, and I wasn't interested in seeing any more naked women."

"Oh," she said. "Well. That's—"

"And I was disgusted by the way the women were treated. Really bad."

She pictured the young dentist standing in a nondescript basement holding camera equipment while all about him nondescript naked women assumed lewd poses. He was wearing the same beneficent, self-consciously goofy expression he'd worn when he'd first arrived at her home with his computer.

"But a strip show isn't necessarily the same as porn," she said. "At least not when I did it. It's more about watching someone's fantasy of themselves." She paused. "Unless of course you're gay."

"No, I'm not."

"Well, then—"

"Jill, I'm shy."

"The funny thing was, when he said the thing about not wanting to watch strippers? It made me feel slighted, almost demeaned." Jill was stationed on her bed in extended phone call position, bolstered by pillows, wrapped in a quilt, legs tensely curled into her chest. "When he said he wasn't interested in seeing any more naked women, it was almost like he'd slapped me," she said.

Joshua was silent for a moment. "That's a very unusual reaction," he said.

"I know it doesn't make sense," she said. "But I felt the same way when he talked about how terrible the porn people were. What he said seemed nice and even moral, but there was something . . . hostile in it."

"Are you sure?"

"No, of course not. But I can't shake the feeling. It's infuriating. He's trying to put himself in this superior position. Like, here's these strippers, doing their all, and he's sitting there going tut-tut. Unlike the gross, pathetic men who *are* interested, he's scrutinizing it with a purely scientific eye, in order to ascertain exactly how many lesbians there are per strip joint. And if he's so disgusted by porn, what was he doing there? He was feeling superior, the smug fuck."

"So I guess you don't like him anymore."

"He told me he didn't like strip shows because he's shy," she went on excitedly. "But I don't buy that. Strip shows exist for shy men."

"I don't know about that," said Joshua. "I'd be shy about going to a strip show. I mean, I could picture some huge, leering stripper putting her underpants over my face while brutish guys laugh."

"Oh, come on, Joshua. You know it wouldn't be that good."

But later that night, his plaintive joke had its effect. She lay in bed, fantasizing about the dentist lording it over a grinding stripper, then interposing it with another fantasy, in which he trembled in fear before her. Each image was affecting in its own way; together, they were dramatic and moving. The dentist was complicated and unusual, she thought, yet decent. Like her, he had done things not everyone could understand, and he was perhaps not sure what he felt about it all. She went into sleep imagining that she was leading the dentist up a gentle, grassy hill over which a primary-colored rainbow stoutly arched.

She woke the next day feeling very emotional. She decided she was going after the dentist whether he was a ridiculous love object or not. She went for a long walk, during which she brooded, toiling uphill and down, on how to best declare herself.

"I got him some flowers," she reported to Lila, her hairdresser. "And I brought them to his office."

"That's so sweet," said Lila as she moved efficiently about Jill's perched, enrobed frame. "How did he respond?"

"Well, I was planning to just drop them off with his secretary, but he happened to be standing there by her desk when I walked in with them. He just gave me this glassy-eyed stare. His face looked frozen, like he was suppressing insane rage. And then he looked normal and flustered." Just beyond the dentist's shoulder, Jill had glimpsed the profile of a woman's head lying on the headrest of the reclining dental chair; her open mouth made her look stunned and victimized. "He said thanks, I shouldn't have, and that he had to get back to work. He took them and just wandered off to some back room, while his secretary beamed. I figured, okay, he's not into it. But then he called that night and asked me to the movies."

In fact, he had asked if she wanted to go to a body-piercing exhibition. She was surprised, as she would not have thought piercing was the dentist's kind of thing—it certainly wasn't hers, at least not as it would occur in the gaudy vacuum of a public exhibit. She said she'd rather see a movie, and they decided on an art film about a drug-addicted police officer who sexually abuses young girls.

The dentist arrived at her apartment an hour early, which was awkward as Jill had just emerged from the shower and had to answer the door in her bathrobe. Still, she chattered enthusiastically all the way to the theater, in spite of her crude, unkind thoughts when the dentist proudly described his car as "the smallest in the world."

She had hoped the vaunted sex scenes in the movie would provide a delicious cocoon of titillation and embarrassment that they could inhabit together. But she just felt embarrassed.

"I hated it," she declared as they left the theater. "I thought it was pretentious and boring, except for that one jerk-off scene. I have to admit, that wasn't bad."

"I thought that went on a little long—for what it was," said the dentist judiciously. "And it was very unrealistic that the nuns they raped were all so good-looking."

They went to a restaurant and talked about random minor subjects. Neither one of them, it seemed, was at ease. The dentist's facial skin appeared strangely immobile, and although he looked at her, his eyes seemed shut from the inside. As if in reaction to his stillness, Jill's voice leapt and darted with an animation that embarrassed her and could not be restrained. She ordered glass after glass of wine. Her animation felt increasingly like a sharp object with which she vainly poked the dentist. What a boring person, she thought. I definitely don't want to have sex with him. This thought calmed her, and as they sailed back to her apartment in the smallest car in the world, she felt so calm that she wanted to put her head in his lap.

"Would you like to come in for a little bit?" she asked as he pulled up to the curb.

"I can't," he said. "I have to feed the dog."

She took a deep breath and exhaled. "Could you please come in for just a minute? It'll make me feel safer."

"And that's exactly what he did," she told Lila. "He came in for a minute. He stood there while I fed the cat, and then he said, 'Had fun. I'll call you,' and left."

"This guy really likes you," said Lila.

"You think so?"

"Yeah." Lila gazed at Jill's hair in the mirror, meditatively cupping its new shape with both hands. "I think he likes you a lot."

For the next week her octopus imagination wound itself about the dentist, experimentally turning him this way and that. But he remained obdurate and glassy-eyed in its sinuous grip, and eventually she released him with an exasperation that became forgetfulness.

She didn't even notice when he failed to call her; partly because of an emotional fight with an editor named Alex, which made her rage about the apartment, angrily talking to herself for days. Alex, with whom she had cultivated a rather tender friendship, had wanted her to write something about her sexual experiences, even though she hadn't had any for over a year. She was offended because she thought he was being exploitative, which offended him because he thought she was being judgmental and hypocritical as well—hadn't she, after all, written about being a stripper two years earlier? "That was different," she huffily explained to Joshua. "That wasn't about stripping; that was about power struggles in relationships. Stripping was just the motif."

Then her word processor returned, looking small and likable in its Styrofoam nest, and she was offered an unusual job writing text for a book of photographs by an artistic photographer, which would require her to travel to Los Angeles. The photographs would all be of a famous model known for her risqué public persona, and the model wanted some of them to be taken in a strip bar with a real stripper.

"We want a thousand words on illusion and transformation," said the editor. "We want your real-life take on it."

Jill arrived at the strip joint at eight in the morning. Various assistants, looking tired and hungover, worked at arranging elaborate camera equipment or stood with an air of taxed authority over portable tables of makeup. The model was sequestered in her trailer, and the famous photographer was shooting the stripper as she walked on a table. The photographer told the stripper she was beautiful. She wasn't, and she appeared to know it, but the photographer said she was again and again until she finally, shyly, began to carry herself as if she were. The owner of the place sat behind the bar, nursing an early cocktail and desultorily jeering his employee. "Take it off!" he weakly cried.

"She doesn't have to take anything off." The photographer spoke in the proud tone of a mother. "She's perfect just as she is."

"The big star," muttered the owner.

"Shut up, Nelson," said the stripper. "If she says I'm beautiful, then I'm beautiful."

"Silly bitch," he replied.

The photographer turned sharply. "Don't call her a bitch," she snapped.

"It's okay," said the stripper mildly. "I am a bitch."

The model entered in the full splendor of her great height and conferred glamour. "Wow, there she is!" bawled the stripper. "Yeah!"

As the model and the stripper posed together, Jill drank coffee with a set of superfluous assistants, listening while the model asked the stripper about her life. For example, did her boyfriend object to what she did for a living?

"Boy, that light sure is hell on the old cellulite," said Jill.

"We were just saying the same thing," responded an assistant.

During a break, Jill questioned the model about why she wanted to pose in a strip joint.

"These women are so interesting to me," she said. "Their lives are totally degrading—but are they really so different from us? I'm saying, Look, let's have some compassion."

Jill remarked that she had not felt degraded when she was a stripper, which seemed to surprise the model.

"Well," she said, "there's a lot of denial. There has to be, in order to survive."

The crew was still engaged in a disorderly departure when the bar opened for business. The lone customer did not seem to notice the harried people carrying camera equipment. He just sat there with a drink in his hand and stared at the stripper, who had taken off her G-string and was bending over to look between her legs at him. He looked completely uninterested, but still he sat there and stared. When the song was over, he handed the girl two dollars. She came off the stage, holding the two dollars and griping about the lousy tip. There was humiliation in her griping, but there was also feistiness, and the combination was lovable. Jill tried to figure out why it was lovable and couldn't, except that it was an interesting combination of collapse and ascendancy. Jill thought the dentist might really like the stripper. She was, after all, a lot like him, yet he could feel superior to her.

On the plane back to San Francisco, she imagined talking with the dentist about the experience. She didn't imagine anything more than a conversation, but she so layered this conversation with the pleasure of understanding and being understood that it became a fantasy of mental sensuality: She and the dentist would rub their brains together. Together, they would pick apart each strand of the model's show of compassion and daring juxtaposed with the stripper's humiliation and guts juxtaposed with the customer's bland compulsive staring and the editor's relentless practicality. It was a cornucopia of contrasts and bursts of personality and slithering emotional undercurrent, from which they could select the strands that made their inmost strands vibrate and hum. And they would feel the vibrating and humming in their voices, deep under their ordinary words. For days she cherished this fantasy, even as it faded like a favorite rough spot on the inside of her mouth.

Then he called her. Her impulse to vibrate and hum was pretty well exhausted by then, but still his voice aroused it, even though his voice was jocular and empty. It was fun to talk about the stripper and the model. He loved the stripper's saying, "I am a bitch," and he liked the part where she bent over in the guy's face. He didn't say he liked it, but his voice became warm and friendly, as though he were being rubbed. Jill got stuck for a moment on the complexity of it; was he responding that way because he was enjoying the idea of someone in a degrading situation or was he too feeling the lovable feistiness bleeding through the story? Both of them enjoyed condemning the model and the vulgarity of the project. Jill complained about being forced to write something charming about such a false and manipulated experience, and she infused her complaints with a flirtatious petulance that invited him to compare her to the undertipped stripper. She wallowed in a sense of voluptuous connection through mutually acknowledged degradation, and she thought he did too. He said he was very busy but that he'd call her sometime and they could go to a movie.

That night she thought of the dentist again. She wanted her thoughts to be tender and kind, like they had been the first time she'd thought of him. But they weren't. Try as she might, she could not imagine him touching her, or even being close to her. She couldn't imagine him going away, either. Whichever way she turned, his face and his eyes stayed before her, staring with a masklike fixity that was both intense and detached. There was a hint of contempt and a hint of fascination in his face, except that, in her mind's eye, those feelings were too stilted to properly be called feelings. The image made her both desperate and numb, and, under that, other feelings oscillated too rapidly for her to identify them.

By the morning, she was sick of the dentist. Grimly, she directed her thoughts at the essay she was supposed to write; when they moved elsewhere, she supervised them sternly. But whatever they touched upon, she felt the dentist lurking beneath. She remembered Joshua's story about the mother confronting her daughter's rapist and killer. She imagined the incoherent weeping mother and the killer sealed away in his politeness. She imagined the killer's eyes sparking with recognition as the mother stepped out of her territory and onto his. She imagined telling the dentist about it, over and over again.

Every night during the next week the dentist stared at her from inside her head. Eventually, she got used to it and slept through it, the way one can learn to sleep through a persistent noise. Any day, she thought, he would call and they would talk and their words would gradually diffuse the potency of the image. But he didn't call, and his absence polarized his imaginary presence, making it both more vague and more powerful, so that it seeped through all her thoughts and feelings whether or not she visualized him at night.

She tried to remember what she had liked about him. She had thought he was kind and discreet. His kindness still seemed real, but it was mixed with elements she wasn't sure of. His discretion now seemed like a remoteness so intense it was almost fierce. To receive kindness combined with such remove was like receiving an anonymous caress while blindfolded.

She went on a magazine assignment to see a performance piece by a masochist who tortured himself onstage in various complex and aesthetically pleasing devices of his own making, while he made jokes and talked about his childhood. His childhood was significant in that he had cystic fibrosis and thus experienced pain, frustration, and social humiliation very early on, which, he felt, had prepared him for a life of masochism—and for which he was therefore grateful. "It's not about anger or self-hate for me," he said. "It's like a kind of spiritual jujitsu. It's like, you give me pain? I'll take it to the hundredth power." He was a vulnerable and compelling person, desiccated, scarred, and rather luminous in spite of being quite puffy from cortisone shots. Several people in the audience were so moved by him that they wept. When he drove a nail through his penis, one man passed out.

That night, she dreamed about a tattooed man whose face and body had been ornamentally pierced many times over. They walked up a hill, on a beautiful wooded path. The man was naked to the waist, and he had the masochist's slim, starved, scarred torso. His face was hollow, and the hollowness invited her in. Their entire conversation consisted of him pretending to want to touch her and then backing away. She eventually became angry. "Oh," he said. "But you are very special to me." And, as if to illustrate that sentiment, he opened his mouth and a bird flew out. It hung in the air, frozen like an iconic carving.

She decided to see a therapist, even though she would have to put it on a credit card. The therapist was a small, stylish person with coiffed white hair and a wardrobe of sleek suits. She thought the dentist sounded shy and that Jill should encourage him to, as she put it, "come out and play."

"But something about him feels off," said Jill. "Like maybe he's a pervert of some kind."

"Why do you interpret his behavior as in some way perverted?"

"Because . . . well, I don't think it's conscious. But it's like he's being apparently nice to me, and then when I respond he pulls away. Only it's more complicated. First he seems like one thing, and then like the other." She paused. "I can't explain it. I just feel it. There's something funny going on."

The therapist said that "in the culture," many people had not been confirmed enough so that they could extend themselves to other people with "the full capacity of their being," because "the culture" was in a state of spiritual lassitude that enforced a level of blandness as the only acceptable way of relating. Underneath, she continued, was a great longing for free, unconvoluted expression, in which beings could be fully present with one another. She thought Jill's dream was about this desire in herself, that the man on the path was her unintegrated male side, who was providing her with an opportunity to "take the initiative" and thus integrate her maleness. Why not just call him, she suggested, and tell him she would be delighted to get to know him in an unguarded way?

Jill liked the sound of this, although she wasn't sure it had any thing to do with the dentist. She discussed it further with her friend Doreen.

"I don't know," said Doreen. "He just sounds like a prick to me."

"Why? I mean, an actual prick?"

"Look, he's fucking with your mind. He does all this stuff for you, which usually would mean he wants to do it with you, and when you get interested he's not there. 'Feed the dog'? What's that? All this crap about saying he'll call and then he doesn't? I'd say your instincts are right on."

Doreen was a former backup singer Jill had met through Joshua. She was forty-two. She lived in a tiny basement room in a house that she shared with several people, all of whom were on minimal government support for ex-drug addicts. The house was an odd mix of squalor, comfort, and mundane beauty. In the small, sorry yard giant roses grew, the petals almost fleshy in their dense unfolding, swollen with failing beauty. Adults, children, and animals lived together in the house, all scrambling after their divergent, yet interwoven, lives. The TV was usually on. They ate awful food and snacked hideously from pails of discount ice cream and bowls of candy. Doreen thought one of the little girls was being molested in day care, but the mother, who suspected Doreen of secret drug use and was trying to get her thrown out of the house, thought Doreen was dramatizing.

Doreen kept to herself in the basement, where she could smoke. She had covered the walls with paintings depicting horrible scenes from her childhood and posters of rock stars. Every time they talked, Doreen told the same stories about her abusive mother and her experiences with bands and coke dealers. They talked of other things too, but variations of these stories always ran through the weave. Jill had heard them many times, but she still liked the way

Doreen told them: as sad and absurd as they were, she brought them out as if they were exquisite silk prints that she fluttered before Jill's eyes and then lovingly folded away. It was as if, in preserving and keeping the stories present, she was somehow preserving herself, even though the stories were often about situations that had hurt her and led to her decline. Doreen was sick with hepatitis C, which would probably kill her one day. Even in this state her face had a strong, bitter beauty. Her full lips were well defined and richly striated, so that they resembled thick, fleshy petals. When she listened to Jill, she kept her lips open in a tense oval, which made her look dramatically receptive.

Doreen thought the dentist sounded like a speed freak ex-boyfriend of hers, who had cruelly manipulated her and stolen drugs from her besides. Jill thought it was an odd comparison. But as she sat there amid Doreen's paintings, watching her put her cigarette between her dry, beautifully striated lips, she imagined the strange, staring night face she had given the dentist, his actual stilted calm, his jovial, seducing phone voice, all in contrast to Doreen's wounded, still-potent femaleness. Again, she thought of the killer and the weeping mother who willfully drew near him.

Which made no sense, she thought. Surely the dentist was not a killer. She walked up the steep hill to her apartment, the cool wind making her dried sweat feel matte and almost grainy on her skin. It was night, and the slim branches of flower bushes swayed against the city light of the sky, their silhouettes trembling eerily. She remembered the dentist at his office with his hands in her mouth. She was aroused, and the ridiculousness of her arousal embarrassed her. But that wasn't the dentist's fault, was it?

During the next two weeks she called him twice. He seemed delighted to hear from her. He asked her how "that tooth" was doing. He talked about his work. His tone was jolly and defeated, as if Jill naturally understood—as if anybody would understand—that defeat and boredom were inevitable, and there was something jolly and comforting about that. Jill told him about the masochistic performance artist, how he had suffered as a child and how that had informed his masochism. The dentist seemed interested. He said he liked "freak shows," the old-style carnival ones. "A good geek is hard to find," he said. Jill said that she didn't think this particular masochist was about a geek thing.

"He encourages people to relate to him," she said, "to see how his masochism is just a different way of dealing with pain that everybody has."

"Yeah, well, I—"

"I mean, look at the flap about recovered memories of sex abuse," she chattered. "As a subject, sex abuse had become a metaphor for a lot of different kinds of pain. The problem is—"

"But sex abuse isn't a metaphor, it's—"

"What I mean is, I think many people with these recovered memories are really describing psychic abuse when they say they were molested, only they don't have the language to describe that even to themselves. Lots and lots of people have experienced some severe neglect or emotional disregard as children. So when their therapists give them these suggestions of sexual violation, it rings true to them. Even though they may not have been literally violated."

"But that's shit," blurted the dentist. "Families are being destroyed over these accusations, because somebody thinks they didn't get enough attention when they were five?"

Excited by this thrilling friction, Jill shoved forward. "I don't know how you were raised, George. But in this culture, in lots of families the level of emotional vibrancy is so low and so bland, and there's so much emphasis on conformity—"

"I hate it when people talk about this culture as if it's worse than anywhere else," he said.

"Well, maybe other places are like that too; I don't know. I'm just saying that for really bright, open kids, that denial of depth and intensity—it's like having their arms and legs chopped off. It *is* violent. Besides, a lot of people are literally molested, and a lot of them do forget it."

"But they've done studies that show that kids almost never forget traumatic experiences. The more traumatic and painful it is, the more likely you'll remember it."

"Well, *I* was molested when I was five and I forgot it. I remembered it when I was ten, when I was watching some old cartoons with bad animation, where the lips on the characters moved really stiff and disconnectedly from the rest of the face. I think it was because when the guy molested me, he didn't look at me while he was doing it—he kept talking about other subjects, like nothing was happening. So when I saw those weird, jerking lips I got so excited I had to go masturbate, and while I was masturbating, I remembered being molested."

There was silence on the other end of the phone. Jill had the distinct sense that the dentist had not liked hearing about her masturbating as a child but didn't feel he could say so. She felt him move away. She moved forward.

"So," she said, "I think the reason those cartoons made me remember was that the guy who molested me—his mouth and eyes were totally stiff and disconnected." She did not tell him how she had felt before she got up to masturbate, of her embarrassment, her terrible sense of vulnerability, her feeling that everyone in the room—her brother, her sister, her father—could see what she was feeling. She did not tell him that after she had finished masturbating, her embarrassment became shame, and that the shame was so intense that she had gone to hide in her parents' closet, way in the back, under her mother's coat, where she held herself tight and tried to breathe.

Silence.

"George?" she said. "Does it make you uncomfortable that I'm talking like this?"

He said no, she could talk about whatever she wanted, but he had to go now. He said he would call her, except that he might be too busy.

Jill hung up feeling a little funny that she'd talked about being molested and the resultant masturbation. But she had wanted so badly for him to see what she'd meant. Since people talked about sex abuse all the time anyway, she had thought it was okay. But in retrospect, she thought, he'd probably just felt the intensity of her want pressing upon him without knowing what it was about, while being forced to think about her genitals. It must've been pretty confusing.

Late that night, she was startled awake by sounds that she thought might've been made by someone coming in the window. The first thought that followed her fear was that the intruder was the dentist, but there wasn't anyone there at all. She lay back in bed and breathed deeply to slow her heart. It occurred to her that her feelings about the dentist were like the feelings she'd had when she'd seen those cheap, poorly done cartoons, that they were the echo of something that was not fully visible to her. Except that while the cartoons had nothing to do with her molestation, she couldn't believe that the dentist's almost morbidly bland public self had nothing to do with the increasingly alarming image she had of him. She felt she was sensing some secret part of him, something that was hurting him as well as her.

She had a lull in writing assignments. She watched TV a lot, mostly shows about crazy middle-aged women who were trying to kill the husbands who had left them for younger women, or shows about crazy perverted men who were trying to kill teenage girls who wouldn't have sex with them. After she was finished watching TV, she sometimes went to bars and drank. She woke in the afternoon with slow, heavy headaches that were almost sweet. She met Joshua for dinner and Doreen for coffee. She talked to Pamela on the phone. At night, the dentist wafted peacefully above her head, close enough to keep her company but too far away for her to beat off about. That was fine with her. When he came into her mind during the day, she regarded him as a friend. She felt they'd gone through a lot together.

It felt very natural for her to call him and leave a message on his answering machine, inviting him to come to her apartment and have a drink. It must've seemed natural for him too, because he called her back that night, sounding bright and enthusiastic, for him. He said he'd just enjoyed several martinis but that, as usual, "I don't feel a thing." She asked him if he'd like to come to her house the following evening and not feel a thing with her—that is, to have a glass of wine after work. He said yes, he'd like that.

When she described the evening to Alex, the magazine editor, she said that she'd grabbed the dentist and reached for his fly, but in truth that never happened; she was just trying to make a good story of it. Alex and she had just cautiously reconciled, after all, and she had wanted to feel close to him. He had started the conversation by telling a story about his unrequited passion for a beautiful young lap dancer, and her lie about the dentist seemed to follow naturally. "No!" said Alex. "You didn't!"

"Well, why not?" she replied testily.

"My God, Jill, you probably frightened him to death. Couldn't you have been more gentle?"

She was taken aback; she would've expected a comment like that from Joshua, but Alex was an outrageously self-confident and rather jaded fellow. "But I wanted him to know how much I liked him," she said.

"In that case, hold his hand, don't grab his dick."

"Really? You think?"

"Yes! He probably felt totally unmanned. He sounds like the type who needs to feel in control, and you took that from him."

It was a nice observation, and probably an apt one even though she'd exaggerated the events of the evening.

They had spent the first hour of their "drink" in stop-and-start conversation. They talked about Truman Capote and sexual harassment on the street. The dentist expressed outrage at the latter. Jill told him a story about a boy on the street who'd recently grabbed her breast, and how, although she'd turned around and kicked him in the butt, she actually had a certain perverse sympathy for the kid.

"Oh, Jill," said the dentist, "you think you're so perverted, but you're really not."

"I didn't mean perverted, I meant perverse. It's different."

"Even so. I've seen things you'd never even think of."

This remark so puzzled her that she disregarded it and raced ahead to describe how she could imagine that if she were a boy and she saw a pair of tits coming down the street, looming out of the dark in a skintight white shirt, she'd probably feel like grabbing one too.

"You mean that was okay with you? Somebody just grabbing your body?"

Under the propriety of the words she felt the other thing move. "George," she said, "I've got to ask you something."

The dentist stood. The expression on his face and his eyes sank inward until nothing showed. "What?"

She stood too. "Do you have sexual feelings for me?" she asked.

When she described what had followed to Joshua, she said it was as if they were from different cultures, or that each of them was so involved in projecting onto the other that they weren't actually addressing each other. But it was worse than that.

He said he had never really thought about her sexually. He said he had to spend a lot of time getting to know a person before he had sex. He said this was all very unexpected and he needed to digest it. He asked if she would like to see a movie with him next week. She understood his words. She understood the sentiments that would seem, at least, to lie behind his words. But she felt something beneath those words that she didn't understand. She said she didn't want to see a movie. She said that if they got to know each other, they probably wouldn't want to have sex. She told him that if she'd waited to get to know people before having sex, she'd probably still be a virgin. She didn't understand what moved beneath her own words. It seemed too big to be chipped off in word form, but it didn't matter; she kept talking until the dentist stepped forward and embraced her. She closed her eyes and extended her face upward, to kiss him. There was no sexual feeling in her body, and she didn't feel any in his. That made her want to press against him all the more fiercely, as if she were pinching numb flesh to feel the dull satisfaction of force without effect. Then he bent his head and kissed her on the lips. She glimpsed his face; it was infused with tentative lewdness. A thin shock of sexual feeling flew up her center. It scared her as much as if it had been a tongue of flame shooting out of thin air, and she stepped away as quickly as he did. She almost said, "George, I'm scared, I'm so scared." But she didn't.

"I've gotta go," he said.

"Wait a minute," she said. She put her hands on his shoulders and pushed him down on the couch, except the pressure she exerted wasn't enough to properly be called a push. Even so he sat, with a little affectation of imbalance; a sensualized shadow of benevolent goofiness passed over his face. It was familiar and dear, this shadow, and she couldn't have it. In truth, she probably didn't even want it, and he probably knew that. It occurred to her that he couldn't have it, either, even though "it" was him. She sat down and curled her body against his. He put his arms around her.

"Do you think this is strange?" she asked.

"Am I supposed to think it's strange?"

"I don't know. *I* think it's strange."

"Why?"

"Because you're not my type at all."

"Then why . . . ?"

"I don't know." Her voice was as false and cute as that of a ventriloquist's dummy. But her real voice wouldn't come out. She put her head against his chest. He stroked her hair. He said, "I have to go, Jill. I have to feed the dog. I'll call you. I know I always say that, but I will this time."

On his way out, he complimented her on her choice of wine.

She boiled some asparagus, poured salt on it, ate it, and watched TV. She watched a show about a crazy middle-aged woman who seduced teenage boys and then made them kill people. About halfway through it, it occurred to her that the dentist was her type after all.

She didn't think of him that night. But in the nights that followed, she did. In her thoughts they did not have sex. They did not talk or look at each other. He only touched her in order to pierce her genitals with needles. She did not look at him or talk to him or touch him.

Jill described these thoughts to her therapist. She said she wouldn't consider them problematic if the dentist had been willing to put them into practice with her, but that it had become increasingly clear that he was not. She asked the therapist why she had encouraged her to be friendly with the dentist, pointing out that everyone else she knew had warned her off him. The therapist said that what Jill had described sounded like a fairly typical man who was perhaps a little bit frightened and immature, and that she thought Jill's friends were simply "speaking out of their defenses." Jill said that even if that were true, it was clear that her attraction had devolved into a masochistic compulsion and that the dentist himself appeared to be in the grip of some ghastly, half-conscious sadism. The therapist said that just because Jill had been hurt by the dentist didn't make him a sadist, and Jill conceded that this was true.

"The thing is, I didn't want it to be about a piercing fantasy," she said. "And I don't think he wanted it to be this way, either. So I don't understand what happened."

By the end of the session, it was decided that Jill projected her fears onto the dentist and then judged him, and that the more she judged, the more fear she felt. "I'd like to encourage you to stop taking a victim stance," said the therapist. "Why don't you show some compassion?"

Pamela thought the therapist sounded like an idiot. She thought that the dentist was a secret sadist; even Joshua, who still maintained that the dentist was just "a scared guy," thought he'd acted like a jerk. Doreen said he reminded her of a guy who had raped her some years back. Jill reminded her that the dentist felt he didn't know her well enough to rape her.

"Well, this guy didn't technically rape me, either," said Doreen. "It was more of a head trip. He was like a poodle on my leg for months, even following me into my house to bug me. So finally, the last time he did that, I said, 'Look, I don't give a shit. You want it so bad, you can have it. Just do it and then get the fuck out of my life.' And I took my pants off and just lay on the bed. I thought he'd be too embarrassed to do it, but he wasn't. He fucked me."

"Did he at least get lost after that?"

"Yeah." Doreen laughed and blew smoke. "That was the good part."

She decided to write the dentist a note. She wrote that she was very confused about what had happened between them. She wrote that she had deeply appreciated the respect and kindness he had shown at the beginning of their relationship and that she didn't understand why he now disrespected her by not calling her when he said he would. If he wanted to break off contact, she understood, but she would prefer him to do so in a spirit of kindness. She went to his office and left the note with his secretary, who smiled at her conspiratorially.

"He actually called about the note," she said to Lila. "He seemed like he really wanted to talk. His voice sounded different and everything."

"Yeah?" Briskly, Lila wrapped a piece of cellophane around Jill's chemical-treated hair. "How was his voice different?"

"More feeling. Softer." Like he was having the pleasure of an emotional experience that would cost him nothing. "He said he had just been sorry that the tooth experience turned out so badly and that's why he loaned me the computer. He apologized for not communicating and said he wasn't very emotionally connected but that he liked me a lot. I said, Well, do you want to fuck or not?"

"Hah!"

"I guess it was kind of obnoxious. Anyway, he said, no, he didn't think so. He said he couldn't do it just like that. He said he was from the Midwest and that they were gentlemen there. He said he had to go but that he'd call me, which of course he didn't."

"You should've told him that gentlemen call ladies when they say they will."

"Yeah, and anyway, what does he mean, that he's too much of a gentleman to do it with me?"

"Oh, no, I doubt it. Men are just funny. You remember that Italian guy I was with? I had a totally different situation with him. It was almost all sex right from the beginning."

"Was it nice?"

"It was . . . gymnastic. And it was nice for a while, but then I began to feel like he was treating me like a whore. So I told him that. And he said, You know, you're right." Lila nodded with a satisfied equanimity that was augmented by the smart, nimble movements of her working fingers. "That was pretty much the end of the relationship, which was too bad in a way. We actually liked each other a lot. But the sex thing just went over the top."

They were silent while Lila attended to Jill's hair. Jill enjoyed being enveloped in women's voices and canned music and hair dryer noise. She loved being in a room of women engaged in personal bodily rituals meant to fulfill the need for understandable public signals. The women who worked here had a slightly beat-up, stalwart air, and there was a gallantry to their little pieces of jewelry, their inexpensive but smartly belted and accessorized outfits, their fussy fingernails, the jiggling curls one wore on either side of her face.

"Lila, you used to be in Sex and Love Addicts Anonymous, right?"

"Yeah, for a year and a half. Why?"

"My therapist suggested it. She said they make you promise to not have sex with anybody until you've known them for six months.

But I don't see how that would help. If you're going to be compulsive, it seems like you could easily drag your compulsion out for six months. I know *I* could."

"Yeah, well, frankly, I came to the same conclusion." With a graceful slouch, Lila reached for the cup of coffee amid her implements. "Although I also saw people do a lot of growing and sharing."

The last time Jill saw the dentist, she went to his office. She went when she knew he would just be finishing his office hours. She expected the secretary to be there, but she wasn't. When Jill saw her empty desk, she hesitated. A door opened and the dentist emerged. He looked at her with the same neutral calm he had worn when he was tearing her tooth out piece by piece.

"Hi," said Jill. "I was in the neighborhood and I thought I'd drop by."

He said he was glad to see her but that the automatic surveillance system was just about to go on, and if anyone was in the room besides him, it would arouse the hired security.

"That's okay," she said. "I just dropped by on my way to an early movie."

"Oh?" He sounded curious. "What are you seeing?"

"Just some silly thing this friend of mine's ex-wife is in. She wouldn't have sex with him for a year before they got divorced, and in the movie she's playing opposite her new girlfriend, who in the movie apparently fucks the shit out of her with a strap-on. You'd think her ex-husband would be jealous, but I guess he's just so proud of her for getting the part."

"Well, like I said, the system's about to go on."

"Yeah, okay. I just wanted to ask you something." She got distracted by the cup of cold coffee on the secretary's desk, its red lipstick impress weak and melancholy in the harsh office light. The dentist followed her eye, and they both stared at the cup. "The last time you were at my house, why did you say I thought I was so perverted, when I'm really not?"

"I don't remember saying that."

"You did. You said you'd seen things I couldn't even imagine, and I just wondered—"

"I don't remember, but I'm sure it didn't mean anything." He removed his white coat with such agitation he got his wrist stuck in one sleeve.

"But people usually mean—"

"I don't *mean* anything! I'm a very simple person! I'm bland and I have a low level of emotional vibrancy and I like it that way!" He wrested his wrist free, then frantically fooled with his tie.

"But—"

"Why are you always saying these strange things to me? What do you want? Why are you always talking about sex?"

"I'm not talking about sex right now. I—"

"I didn't say you were! But you—you're—I'm just trying to be—"

To her grief, she saw it was true: he was apoplectic with fear.

Oh, honey, she thought. Oh, darling.

"Call me tomorrow," he said thickly. "I can't talk anymore now."

This incident made a very funny story. Everyone laughed when Jill told it a few nights later, at a dinner with Alex the magazine editor, his friend the television producer, and an assortment of writers eager for a free dinner and an assignment. Most of the people at the table knew each other only tangentially; they had been assembled through an acquaintance of the producer's, on the grounds that they were the most interesting people in San Francisco.

"So at that point I was, like, this guy is kooky, so I just said good-bye and went to leave. And so he *follows me out* and holds the door for me and says, 'Sorry I had to kick you out. But the rules are the rules.' Referring, I suppose, to the automatic surveillance system."

"He really does sound peculiar," said Alex.

Alex and the television producer had come from New York on business. Most of the writers present were also "sex workers," although one of them, an earnest bald woman, handed out cards advertising a therapy by which to recover from sex abuse. The television producer, a melancholy person with whom Jill once had a minor telephone flirtation, confided in her that Alex had arranged this dinner in order to meet Cindy, a determined and impish woman who published a stylish sex magazine. She had apparently written an article about anal sex which had gotten under his skin and provoked a correspondence. She seemed very nice, but Jill wondered why Alex couldn't find anyone to have anal sex with in New York.

"Why do you like this guy?" Cindy asked. "Is he sexy in any way?"

"Not in the normal ways." Jill imagined the dentist standing before these people, and the bewildered looks on their faces. "Except I could feel . . . I'm convinced he's a secret pervert and that he just doesn't know it yet."

Cindy smiled appreciatively. "You think if you could just get him into a sling, he'd be fine?"

"No, I don't think he'd ever actually get into a sling, whether he wanted to or not. I think he'd just keep getting into slinglike positions in inappropriate situations." Jill had of course just described herself, but Cindy didn't know that, so she laughed. Jill wondered how Cindy would've reacted if she'd said, "Because I thought he was kind."

Several of the guests began to discuss the politics of the various strip clubs around town, one of them denouncing "those corporate strippers" who were really just middle-class girls who thought it was cool to be a sex worker. Someone else expressed disdain for those who said sex workers had all suffered child abuse and did such work as a result. Another got irritated over the negative portrayals of sex workers in the media. The woman to Jill's left was muttering darkly about her desire to infect the water supply with chemicals that would sterilize the population.

Longingly, Jill thought of the dentist at home with his entertainment center. As if reading her mind, Alex said she should've invited the dentist to the dinner this evening. "He wouldn't have come, of course. He would've driven up and down the street looking in the windows over and over again, wondering whether or not he should come in. It would've driven him crazy."

"I don't want to drive him crazy," said Jill. "He's shy, Alex."

"Nonsense. Of course you want to drive him crazy. And in the long run you will. Because you touched his fear. Every time he sees anything you've written, he'll think of you and twist a bit."

"You think?"

"Oh, yes. Why do you think I put out a magazine? So that girls I've been with will see it and twist." Alex's voice as he said this was calm, but underneath was a muffled agitation that made Jill think of the dentist wresting his wrist out of his sleeve. It made Jill want to hold Alex and stroke his head. "I wanted him to pierce my genitals with needles," she said dreamily. "It's funny. That's not something I usually fantasize about."

"Was he wearing his white coat while he pierced you?"

"No. He was just George." George with his glassy eyes, his cold lips, his jocular warmth held far away in a tiny place.

"That's the trouble with your fantasies," said Alex. "You haven't got the right clothes."

Meanwhile, someone made the argument that it would be awful if the "mainstream" ever came to truly accept whatever anybody might want to do sexually, because then sex wouldn't be shocking anymore.

"That won't ever happen," said Jill. "Sex is too complicated, it means too many things to people. It connects to the dirt within, and there's just too much dirt."

"You're wrong," said the television producer. "It's already happened, in San Francisco anyway."

Their words were such announcements, yet Jill could barely feel the life in them. She tried to fixate on the dentist, but he only came to her in faint, cold wisps of idea. The woman next to her was describing a transvestite bar to which they might go after dinner. She said that when loathsome suburban men came to her strip shows expecting to buy sex, she sent them to this place as a joke, archly informing them that "the ladies" there would be pleased "to negotiate." She was tall and full of disdain. Her long black hair was dull and fake, her eyes were made up huge and dark in her chalky face, her lips were full and dry; like a starved feral cat, she appeared both fierce and desperately unctuous, which was interesting with her disdainful affect. Jill thought she was beautiful and wanted to talk to her, but the woman's words were harsh and so full of puzzling judgments that Jill was afraid of her. She looked down at the woman's hands, which were delicate and looked strangely lost in their movements, the nails pathetically small and bitten. Jill put her own hand down on the table so that their wrists were touching. The woman let her wrist stay there, and Jill thought she could feel her through her skin. She did not feel harsh or disdainful; she felt like a tense animal, very fearful but also resourceful and curious, even rather innocent. Jill thought she could feel the woman sensing her back, as one animal sniffs another. But then she moved her hand.

Jill and Alex left at the same time. They stood on the street for some moments, chatting. He said that he had gone to a sex store to get toys in anticipation of his tryst with Cindy. He said he was going to tie her up, and he pulled a piece of black thong from his pocket, apparently thinking that Jill would want to see it. Jill thought that if she hugged him goodbye, it might generate feelings of warmth and friendship, but it only made her feel uncomfortable.

"I'm enjoying your discomfort," he said.

"I'm glad someone is," she answered.

They kissed each other goodbye. Alex got into a cab and sped away. As the evening was warm and mild, Jill decided to walk a little. Homeless people strolled about, pushing shopping carts full of hoarded things. Traffic ran and darted according to plan. She imagined the dentist driving up and down the street, staring at the restaurant, trying to glimpse the dinner party inside. She imagined his eyes moving back and forth as he turned his head away from the window and then looked back again. She was distracted by the sound of someone muttering. It was a man crouching on the sidewalk in dirty, wadded blankets. He glared at her. "If it's a man, I'll castrate him and stuff his balls in his mouth," he said. "If it's a woman, I'll stick my fist up her cunt and fuck her dead." Jill understood how he felt, but she still walked a few feet up before she stepped off the curb to hail a cab.

Kiss
and
Tell

Lesly was desperately writing a trite, boring screenplay that he could barely bring himself to face, even with a bottle of Scotch at his side and the TV companionably talking in the background. His failure in this regard was highlighted for him—he knew it was petty, but he couldn't help it—by the recent success of the woman he loved, Nicki Piastrini, who had just made her film debut in a thing called *Queen of Night* and was now being invited to glamorous parties. His normal misery over this was exacerbated by the fact that, after having wild, drunken sex with him three times, little Nicki had decided that they should just be friends.

The drunken sex and her terrible decision, expressed in a pause-strewn phone conversation, had occurred over a year ago, and he'd since been hanging around, meeting her for coffee after maddening coffee, plotting her eventual change of heart, which now seemed, in the light of her impending celebrity, unlikely. Obviously, his only hope was to sell the screenplay and become a celebrity himself, and time was running out.

Thus, fighting on through failing hope, he sat down before a hostile piece of paper every night, drunk or sober, even when exhausted by his degrading restaurant job, plowing through senseless sex, monsters, exploding heads, and the like, all to no avail.

Lesly's apartment was not an inspiring place to work, especially for someone who saw himself hanging over an abyss by his finger-nails. He'd moved in after graduating from film school. He'd per-versely dwelt on the ugliness of the place, romantically seeing himself as the alcoholic hero of some seamy detective series avail-able only in the bargain bins of used-book stores, bitterly turning his back on the world of success for mysterious reasons. He'd been forced to romanticize it; after as many fruitless interviews as his spirit could bear and one job as a gofer for the deranged producer of a tiny slasher-movie outfit, he'd sunk into the dark glamour of the "King Farouk Room," which is what he'd almost immediately named his apartment.

It was a gloomy rectangle on the ground floor of a reeking Green-wich Village tenement with smeared linoleum walls. The ceiling sagged as if it were about to cry; plaster from the crumbling walls gathered in little heaps on the uneven floor. His dresser looked like a hiding place for dismembered corpses, his throw rugs emphasized the sad state of the splintering floor, his mattress was beset by a mean snarl of blankets.

"Welcome to the more-than-Oriental splendor of the King Farouk Room," he'd debonairly sneered as he ushered Nicki in for the first time.

He'd met her at the West Village restaurant where they'd both worked. He'd been instantly taken with her unconventional beauty—her wide, long-lashed green eyes and luminous skin were the only normally pretty features on her bony, angular face. Her thin brown hair would've been mousy on another girl, but it accentuated her Botticellian frailty. Her unfashionably thin lips and eyebrows, which could've made her face too spare, instead added an arresting severity that offset her expressive eyes, giving her the piercing inten-sity of a small cat. Her body was merely pretty, but it was made beautiful by the invisible electricity that she discharged like a sweet, grainy odor as she ran from kitchen to dining hall with her hands full of plates.

He had spent a year developing the courage to ask her out, had been rejected twice, and then, as he was resigning himself to casual flirtation, she'd asked him out. They'd had dinner, during which she chatted happily, dropping silverware and flicking mustard. They saw a movie and then went to a cheerful Eurobar, where romantic music flew from the sound system in bright ribbons, and Nicki got sloppy drunk in the middle of his impressive analysis of the film. He'd thought she was joking until she brained herself opening the door to the ladies' room. This was an odd development in view of his courteous relative sobriety; he decided he'd better get her out before she keeled over.

"Listen," he said, gripping her jacket as she slid giggling down the side of the building next to the bar. "Do you realize I've been adoring you for over a year, from afar, and now here you are, falling on your face? Pull yourself together; it's idiotic."

She giggled, sighed, and put her cold fingertips on his face. Clearly, there was no choice. He bundled her into a cab and bore her off to his lair, gloating yet slightly disappointed that it had been so easy after all. At least he could put to rest his worry that her delicate sensibilities would be offended by the ambience of the King Farouk Room, as she would probably barely see it.

He was mistaken about that. As soon as they entered, her suddenly clear eyes moved alertly from crumbling wall to collapsing bookcase, and then she excused herself to go to the bathroom, where she crashed around for several minutes, peeing, running water, probably going through his medicine chest. He was thinking he'd made a mistake bringing her there and that he should take her home, when she emerged without her pants and bore down on the bed. She wore a pair of cream-colored panties over which peeped curly brown hairs.

"Well," she said, "as they say, I'm much too drunk to fuck." With that she climbed under the blankets and curled into a sleeping position.

He politely turned off the light over the bed, got a bottle of vodka, and sat down to contemplate the small bundle on his bed. Her thin shoulder in its T-shirt was exposed; it looked both winsome and pathetic in the King Farouk Room. This would be cute, he thought, if they were anywhere between eighteen and twenty-five. But they were both over thirty; they had lines under their eyes, stains on their teeth, faces that more and more showed their essential confused mildness.

He finished the bottle, then crawled into bed with his clothes on and eased into a consoling blackout with his arm around the gently breathing body of his coworker.

He woke up feeling the granules at the foot of the bed with his clammy feet; she turned into his arms and smiled with her mascara-smeared eyes. Their clothes came off. She reached between his legs and stroked him fore and aft. With sodden hands he groped her breasts and genitals; he mounted and pasted her through a pounding headache.

He made them tea, and they clawed off hunks of Italian bread to have with butter and jelly. She sat with the blanket wound about her hips, crumbs and a blob of purple jelly ranging nicely across her breasts. "I haven't done this for years," she said. "The last two people I was with were married, so they never spent the night. This is fun!"

The next date was more seemly. They had dinner at a Thai restaurant; Nicki sat erect as a fourth grader practicing penmanship and gestured with her skewered meat while talking about her most recent casting-call failures as if they were hilariously funny. He asked her how she felt about their night together. She seemed surprised; she shrugged and said she didn't know yet. He didn't want her to think he was sensitive, so he didn't pursue the subject. Instead, he listened to her talk about her therapists, psychics, and healers, and the progress she was making on all her problems, the great upswing her life was about to take. Her talk had the aggressive charm of someone who has just met you and wants to make a good impression, as well as the false candor of someone who doesn't want to reveal herself yet wants to give the impression of doing so. Hey, he wanted to say, I just fucked you. Then he was embarrassed that he'd even thought such a thing.

Still, he walked with her to her apartment for "tea." This meant roughly fifteen minutes of conversation, after which they rolled around, poking each other's faces with their tongues. It was fun, but he had not recovered from the sense of remove her dinner chatter had caused him, and besides, at this moment he didn't want to fuck Nicki. He wanted to find the vibrant girl he'd seen running around at work, but she didn't seem to be present in the body of this agreeable but somehow inaccessible person who was pulling off his pants. Watching her, he felt that he could chain her to the radiator and perform on her every obscene act possible and still not possess her.

Naturally, this made him feel he must possess her. Firmly he turned her around, pressing himself against her back and her round, dumb ass. Her body stiffened; her butt nudged him in greeting. He embraced her about the waist. Her hands splayed, her elbows poked out, he saw her crumpled, side-turned face from behind her fore-grounded haunches.

Afterward, there was a miasmic moment of separate breathing, and then, tenderly, she turned her head and kissed his hand, first with her lips, then with her hot, dry tongue. A gasp of happiness escaped him. He held her all the next morning, while the radio mut-tered about congressional scandal and she slept fitfully, discharging an innocent odor of sweat amid the musty sheets with every slight movement.

The third time was a drunken riot in the King Farouk Room, dur-ing which she ground astride him backward, showing him the rindy fat of her bunched ass—the unsuspected ugliness of which inflamed him all the more.

It was after this strenuousness that, as they lay sharing a smoke on the mattress, she told him she had been sexually molested as a child. He was so startled by this information that afterward he couldn't remember how or why it had come up; suddenly it was just there.

"It was my uncle," she said. "He and my aunt lived near us when I was nine and ten. Then they moved, and then he killed himself." She drew on her cigarette, and for an instant her lips formed an expres-sion he had seen on other women but never on Nicki: a tight down-ward sneer that was cynical and tough, yet weak and repellently vulnerable.

He felt bad for her. He wondered if this meant she was an emo-tional wreck. "Do you think it had a terrible effect on you?"

She looked thoughtful. "For a long time I tried to deny it had any impact at all. But I think it formed my sexuality a lot."

He started to ask how, then put his arms around her instead.

A week after this discussion, they had the terminating conversa-tion. He said he hoped they could still be friends. She said of course she cared for him as a friend, and they hung up. He felt dazed, as if he had suddenly found himself in a commercial for a love movie in which he had rapidly performed scenes of seduction, passion, emotional bonding—and then the commercial was over. He lay down and wondered if this development had anything to do with her story about her uncle.

Then their long, arduous friendship ground into being. They saw each other mostly at work, swimming through the slow, silly conversations of people doing jobs they don't like. At first he didn't long for her, although her abrupt ending of the affair hurt him. He wasn't sure how he felt about her, and at times he thought there was something wrong with her. His ambivalence made him receptive to her, and his receptivity gradually made him feel her charm and beauty even more potently than before. He would look at her and it would seem, even in the black anonymity of her waitress wear, even at the squalor of the break table, as if she were lounging at a casino on the deck of an ocean liner. He could not recall if she had looked that way to him before he'd fucked her, and he perplexed himself with the question of whether his perception had changed after the act to render her queenly or if she had actually become so.

Then one day he opened the door to the cold, cardboard-box-filled changing room and saw Nicki and a large blond waitress named Deirdre looking at themselves in a shard of mirror propped against the wall. Deirdre was seated, gazing dreamily at her own rosy face. Nicki stood behind her, tenderly combing the other girl's long, pale hair. Deirdre said hi to him in the mirror. Nicki turned, dropped the comb, and looked at him, her eyes so startled and fraught that his heart filled with echoes of illicit intimacy. Suddenly he felt her touch, her breath against his chest, the lithe, muscular energy of her body beneath his hands. He wanted to have her, and he couldn't.

"Deirdre is so beautiful," said Nicki later. "If I looked like her, I'd be a movie star by now."

"If I was a casting director, Deirdre wouldn't stand a chance against you," he said. "She's just another pretty blonde. You're beautiful."

She blushed and touched his hand with her cold fingers. "Thanks, Lesly," she said.

They had coffee, then began to go to dinner and the occasional movie together. He felt her slowly opening to him in a way that seemed more genuine and incrementally deeper than during their previous hectic dates—and he felt himself opening to her. He remembered their lovemaking with a poignant shudder; its brief, superficial nature seemed to have been an exquisite distillation of what he imagined could happen between them. When he looked into her beautiful, caffeine-shadowed eyes, it seemed to him that she was thinking these things too. The afternoons spent with her in coffee shops radiated a muted glow that permeated the entire week, leaking over into the next week, until every week was saturated with her presence. He saw other women occasionally, but the sight of them naked in his bed could not arouse him as Nicki did sitting fully clothed in a café window, sunlight baring the meeting of age and youth in her thirty-two-year-old face. He thought: It's only a matter of time.

This thought was nurtured by the incredible fact that, in the lengthening time since their affair, she hadn't become involved with anyone else. An expression in her eyes or a slight movement of her body toward him could make the hairs on his neck rise; he'd move forward to meet the embrace he saw coming—then she'd lean back in her chair and dive into conversation again. Still, he dreamed of her.

Then one afternoon, as he was fighting his way out of an alcoholic sleep, the Cerberus of his answering machine clicked in warning and her voice fluttered forth. "Lesly," she said, "it finally happened! I auditioned for Brian Slossman and I got it! It's going to be a real movie and he—he—he loved me!"

He lay back in his bed and croaked, "Oh, my God."

When she left for L.A. he thought she was gone forever, but she wasn't. She returned to New York often, and they would sometimes have dinner together. She would describe for him the mysterious artificial world of the movie set, with its harsh aurora borealis of lights and sounds that, by twinkling transmutation, became the magic glass that humans stepped into and mythic beings stepped out of. He liked to picture her on the set, her face covered with the sugar dust of cosmetic powder, her eyes laden with cosmetic jewels, surrounded by and bathed in lights that were like giant technological flowers.

He kept expecting her—encouraging her, even—to display the deluded self-importance he assumed all successful people harbored, and when she didn't he felt disbelief, disappointment, and respect.

He almost felt as if he were experiencing the excitement of her new life with her. He nursed the fantasy that it was still he for whom she felt the deepest affinity, that he was the one she could turn to at her most confused, when she needed to tell the truth about those Hollywood phonies. He would always be there for her—when she lost her looks, when her pictures flopped, when the tabloids went after her.

It was hard to identify the moment when talking to her began to make his life seem like a crushed ball of aluminum in an empty can. But there was a point at which he noticed her expression become vacant and polite when he laid before her even the juiciest gossip about the restaurant. Then there was the subtle change in the way she described her experiences with the director and the other actors; instead of tremulously setting out her stories like new toys she wanted to share, she now displayed them so he could see but not touch them. There would be a sudden smugness in the way she held herself aright and puffed her cigarette, but then she would turn and face him with her candid eyes and he'd shudder inwardly with the memory of her tongue licking his fingers.

When the film was over and she returned to New York, she became yet more distant. Although *Queen of Night* was not due to be released for some months, Nicki was already "hot" in Hollywood. She had an agent, who fielded film offers and laid piles of scripts at her feet. She sarcastically denounced the snotty clique of New York–based actors who wouldn't countenance talented newcomers, and then she went to their parties. She met a famous actor there—"A pig," she said—who had come on to her rudely and arrogantly. It was at this point that Lesly was startled to realize that if this famous actor had fancied her, others would too, and that not all of them would be pigs. He hurled himself at the vast emptiness of his screenplay with unprecedented ferocity.

She was visibly pleased when he told her about it. "I'd love to see it when you're done," she said. "I'll bet it's really good." But it wasn't, and he shredded it on the tenth page. After a relaxing three-day drunk, he started another script. He didn't like that one, either, but when he tore it up he didn't go on another bender. With the novel sensation that he knew what he was doing, he started another draft. He wasn't sure this one was good either, but it was fun, and he surprised himself by staying in to work on it during his nights off instead of conducting his usual drinking man's tour of lower Manhattan.

Then Nicki did the Rude Thing. He had gotten tickets for them to see a dance company she loved. On the evening they were to go, a few hours before he was to pick her up, she canceled. "A friend," she said, had phoned at the last minute; she was coming in from L.A. and Nicki had to have dinner with her. He didn't understand until she stammeringly explained. "She isn't just a friend. She's my girlfriend. I got involved with her during the shoot—she's a camerawoman—and I haven't seen her for weeks."

"You never said anything about her before," he said stiffly.

"Well, yeah, I know. It was because—I know it's silly—but I thought you might be jealous."

He snorted violently. "No, not quite. It's your business, and it's not like you and I were ever really involved anyway. I just don't like being stood up at the last minute. What am I supposed to do with your ticket?"

For several seconds after they said goodbye, he stood with the buzzing receiver in his hand, staring at the dresser that looked as if it had been made to hide dismembered bodies.

The following week they were in a bar, eating salty peanuts, drinking tequila, and being assaulted by heartlessly fashionable music. "I'm sorry you had to find out about Lana that way," she said. "I hope you don't hold it against her; it was my fault, really. But I'm glad I finally told you. I don't know why I held back. I should've known you wouldn't mind."

Grimly, he drank. He tried to comfort himself with the thought that if she was a lesbian, it could hardly be his fault that she'd dumped him, but it didn't work. Nicki began to describe Lana's subtle and dashing personal style, her strength, her tenderness, her wit. Nicki really couldn't be a lesbian, he thought. This was yet another irritating affectation, or else a symptom of her deep distrust of men, which he alone had overcome. Then Nicki started in on Lana's sexual prowess.

"Oh, really," he said.

"What?"

"I mean, I'm not one of those idiots who can't picture what two women could do together. I know there's a lot of things. I picture lots of slow, languorous . . . you know. But still, there's a limit to what—I mean, to what any two people can do."

"Well, we haven't reached ours," said Nicki. "We do everything. Even corny stuff, like she wears a suit and I wear a garter belt and stockings—"

"Excuse me," he said. "I need to use the men's room."

He stalked to the john, taunted by visions of the formidable dyke fucking garter-belt-clad Nicki. He tried seeing it as beat-off material, but he was too irked.

When he got back to the table, her face recoiled slightly.

"Lesly, are you upset?"

Of course he wasn't.

She began to talk about her anxiety about the reviews *Queen* would get. He could tell from the artificial quality of her voice that she knew something was wrong. He felt she was trying to charm him out of being upset with a display of modesty and vulnerability, and that made him even madder. He tried to tell himself he had no right to be mad, but it didn't help. The professional jealousy he had staunchly suppressed in the name of friendship rose and joined forces with romantic jealousy. While his head nodded agreement and tilted at polite angles, Nicki's conversation raced ahead, trailing a bright streamer of self-involvement. He remembered her on her knees in his bed, moaning into the sheets. He remembered another girl from the past whom he had broken up with, remembered specifically how, long after their affair had ended, he could make her blush merely by looking intensely into her eyes the way he had when he'd fucked her. If he looked at Nicki that way, he thought, she wouldn't even notice. He looked at the tense, delicate face before him, fixating on one bright, jiggling earring; a black tunnel opened before him, spanning days, maybe weeks, a tunnel filled with shadowy forms of pain and deprivation.

"And so," said Nicki, dramatically ending a story he'd heard before, "there's nothing he won't do to have me in the part. Plus he'd like to screw me, so I know he's gonna be totally nice about the script. It's pretty much up to me at this point."

"That's a little self-aggrandizing, wouldn't you say?"

She tipped back her head to release a throatful of smoke and then coolly faced him. "Yeah," she said. "It also happens to be true." There was no false vulnerability in her voice.

"Does he know you're a lesbian?"

"He probably thinks I am. A lot of people do." She jerkily tapped cigarette ash into her empty glass and then looked directly at him. "That only makes men want you more, actually."

"Nicki," he said, "why didn't you tell me you're gay?"

She lowered her eyes and shrugged. "I don't know. Because I'm not, totally. I do like men sometimes, and I hate the idea that I have to absolutely identify myself as one thing or another. It's true I generally prefer women and that men are usually more casual for me." She looked up quickly. "But I liked being with you a lot." She turned her eyes down again. "It didn't seem necessary to tell you. Until now."

For the rest of the wretched evening, he wanted only to go home, to sit in bed and drink. But when he got home he found he was too agitated to do that. He paced the King Farouk Room, thinking of every affected, self-indulgent, obnoxious thing Nicki had ever said. He reflected how his foolish love had blinded him to her offensive personality. He thought of how true it was that the pushiest, most vulgar people always rose to the top. He imagined hitting her. He imagined mashing a grapefruit in her face.

His eyes fell on his screenplay. He threw it across the room. He stood staring after it for a long moment. Had there been a movie camera trained on his face, it would have recorded an expression of pernicious ingenuity dawning, then slowly spreading from feature to feature. He sat down before his computer and began to type. He typed until three in the morning.

He was awakened the following day by the clicking answering machine and then by Nicki's voice leaving a long, scattershot message. He got up, made coffee, and returned to his computer.

A few days later she called again, but he was screening his calls. As he listened to her voice, he gave the machine a loud, farting raspberry. As if she'd heard it, she stopped calling, although there were several hang-up calls during the following week. He wasn't interested in talking to her. He had developed a much more satisfying relationship with the tiny Nicki cavorting across the pages of his new screenplay.

The screenplay had started as an exorcism of his demeaning

anger and had become, on the same night, a serious idea. Nicki was a perfect heroine: capricious, sexually manipulative, ambitious, charming, ruthless. She tripped girlishly over the hearts of maddened men while prattling quintessential nineties sentiments. She was a waitress moonlighting as a hooker until she clawed her way into the film business by sleeping with the right people. She slept with men who would enhance her profile and then cast them aside. She slept with women, leaked stories of their lingerie-clad romps to the press for titillation value, and then cast *them* aside. She capitalized on her incestuous relationship with her uncle by discussing it on talk shows until the frantic fellow shot himself. She was eventually forced to be the sex slave of the cruel editor of a scandal magazine, who was holding over her head an embarrassing kiss and tell written by one of her male victims. That was only the start of her disastrous decline, during which she repented but too late.

Factually the character bore little relationship to the real Nicki, except that he used her favorite jokes, mannerisms, and sayings, and quoted verbatim from private conversations they had had, most notably about Lana and about the pedophile uncle. He would not have thought she was recognizable. But when he finished the first draft and showed it to a friend who worked at the restaurant, the guy called him after reading the first ten pages and said, "Is this Nicki?"

He titled it *Kiss and Tell*.

He stuck it in a drawer and took it out a month later. He was shocked at how good it was. He had never written anything this good in his life. It rattled him to think his first belated triumph had sprung from sheer vindictiveness; he stuck it back in the drawer. He started another screenplay but was distracted by persistent daydreams of Nicki playing scenes from *Kiss and Tell*, particularly the one where the heroine is sodomized by the nasty magazine editor.

He didn't look at the script again until the first promotional posters for *Queen of Night* appeared. He saw them when he was returning home from work late one night; they were freshly glued to the rotting side of a cheap men's-clothing store. Nicki's face was not on it, but to him it might as well have been. He stood and stared at the poster, while the wind blew plastic bags and candy wrappers about his ankles.

The next morning he reread *Kiss and Tell* and felt a certain psychic prickling. He decided to send it to a film agent whom he'd met eight years before. As he put it in the mail, he felt the faint nausea that always accompanied his attempts to accomplish something.

Queen of Night opened. He didn't see it, but he religiously read the reviews. They were mixed about the movie but unanimous in their praise for the "incandescent" performance of "sex imp" Nicki Piastrini. He smiled in spite of himself when he read them. He wanted to call and congratulate her. He did call once but hung up when she answered. He spent an evening at a bar, trying to revive his feelings of anger toward her, and realized that he hadn't thought of her with passion for some time. He felt sad, then began to flirt with the girl behind the bar.

Early one morning his phone machine clicked on. He'd turned the volume down the night before and he was half asleep, so he was only barely aware of a voice leaving quite a long message. He dimly imagined that it was Nicki; he thought he might return her call when he got up, then he went back to sleep. When he woke and played the tape, he was stunned to hear the confident voice of the film agent. *Kiss and Tell*, he said, was wonderful. Could Lesly call him back as soon as possible?

Then he was in the agent's office. If he'd worn a hat he would've wrung it in his hands. The agent looked at him as if he respected him. In fact, he looked as if people he respected came and sat in his office every day. Lesly felt disoriented and sick. The agent sat back in his chair as if everything were okay.

"I'm not a person who gushes, typically," said the agent, "but I'll tell you honestly I haven't clicked like this with a script for a long time. I could literally see the scenes before my eyes. I could see what the actors looked like. I actually have somebody in mind for the lead. But first things first."

The next few weeks were a jumble. He couldn't sleep, he couldn't eat. He would tell people about the agent and feel his face in conflicted expressions of happiness and fright. He called Nicki three times and hung up on her machine. He called his parents, and the shocked pride in their voices almost made him weep.

The agent was right. He sold the screenplay within weeks, to a director Lesly had heard of since adolescence. Lesly went into the agent's office to sign the contract, and the agent talked to him about going to Los Angeles to meet the director. Lesly nodded dumbly.

"By the way," said the agent, "remember I mentioned to you that there's an actress who I think is perfect for the lead? I'm having a colleague of mine show her the script. Have you seen *Queen of Night?*"

He flew to Los Angeles the next day. The trip was a series of disconnected still frames out of which popped various animated heads. An escort of palm trees flanked his car trips through each different frame. Bright, winking signs called out to him, doors opened to reveal great expanses of rug and mahogany. Everywhere, people in uniforms wanted to bring him and his friends—smiling men in suits—alcohol, coffee, or snacks. He sat in the sunken tub of his hotel bathroom, drinking Scotch, listening to MTV, and thinking how odd it was to find himself an accessory to all the jokes he'd made about the grossness and vulgarity of Los Angeles. He felt a little hypocritical, but he knew Los Angeles didn't mind. It knew it was a joke and a face-lift and didn't try to hide it, and therein, he thought as he swigged, therein lay its charm. In L.A., writing a script called *Kiss and Tell* about a kiss and tell that was an honest-to-God kiss and tell was only one more kooky face appearing in one more frame, the frame of outraged Nicki reading the script, a great punch line underscored by pop music.

He flew back to New York with a terrible headache and a vague sense of guilt.

His answering machine greeted him with an urgently flashing light. He had ten messages! But they were all the irritating kind of hang-up call where the person waits for several seconds and then loudly puts the phone down. He muttered and paced as he listened to them. Well, maybe she hadn't read it yet. He became so absorbed in hanging his travel-wrinkled shirts on his tatty hangers that he jumped when the phone rang.

Her voice was so tense with politeness and repressed expression that he didn't recognize it. "So you're there," she said. "I'll be over in two minutes."

"Nicki, I—"

Click.

His first impulse was to leave the apartment, but that was too embarrassing. Besides, he wanted to see her face. Not just because of the script but because, he suddenly realized, he'd missed her; he wanted to tell her about L.A. The thing was, she probably didn't want to hear it. She was probably on her way over to punch him. He reminded himself she was only a girl, but still his hands shook. He decided that when she rang the buzzer he could make up his mind whether to let her in. She rang. He buzzed. He paced the King Farouk Room, trying to compose himself into an expression of implacable rightness. She knocked. He wiped his palms on his pants before he let her in.

Her cold face was very different from the face he had held in memory. She looked oddly diminished, ordinary, and—for the first time—unsexy. He could not picture her sitting on him backward, exposing her cellulite in her abandon.

"Hi," he said.

She stared at him. She was holding a copy of his script; she dropped it on the floor. "Why," she said, "did you do this?"

"Nicki," he said, "no one will know it's you."

"Only everybody in the restaurant. But that's not what matters."

"It isn't you, Nicki. It's an imaginary person. It's a cartoon character with some of your traits."

"A lesbian cartoon character who was molested by her uncle. Couldn't you think up anything by yourself? God, you're the cartoon character."

"You'll have to forgive me, but that sounds a little funny coming from a woman who brags about wearing lingerie and getting fucked by a dyke."

"I wasn't bragging, you idiot. I was talking to my friend, or at least I thought I was. You're a coward and a rip-off. I respected you and—"

"You never respected me. I was a fixture for your vanity."

"Spare me the masochism. I don't respect you now." She turned, manhandled the door, and walked out.

He followed her out onto the sidewalk. When she heard him she turned; he thought he saw a flicker of relief on her face before it went indignant again.

"Nicki, come on. It's not that bad. I did not rip you off."

"And what was that shit just now about me and Lana? What was that?"

"I was just responding to—"

"Let's be honest for a second. The reason you wrote that bitchy piece of junk is that I wouldn't fuck you. We both know that. You were mad at me because you ran around my heels like a little dog for months and—"

He slapped her hard, clipping her across her cheekbone and nose. She staggered and froze in disbelief. Remorse dilated his heart. The busy tableau of daytime Manhattan became a gray backdrop for the hugeness of Nicki's face and the disembodied heads of strangers turning to stare in disgust at the swine who'd struck this small, fragile woman. "Watch it, buddy," said someone. He turned with an impulse to explain himself, and then she was on him, punching his face and body, hammering his shins with her feet.

"You little piece of shit!" she screamed. "You nothing! You dare to hit me, I'll kill you!" She sprang away and ran down the street, her handbag flapping at her side.

He fled to the King Farouk Room.

That day and the next were rent with sadness. He was mortified that he'd hit her and glad she'd hit him. Perhaps he had done the wrong thing; perhaps he *had* stolen her life. Perhaps he should rewrite the screenplay, modifying her character. Then he would think, Why should he? What about artistic license? What about the way she'd led him on?

He went out and got drunk alone for the first time in weeks. On his way home he emptied his pockets of dollars, to the delight of the homeless who received them. He considered passing out on the sidewalk but went home instead.

The next day he crept out to find stabilizing carbohydrates for his listing body. He went into a coffee shop and, while he was waiting for his muffins and coffee, had the irrational wish that he'd never sold his screenplay, that he could just be sitting here among these bleary people, sharing coffee with Nicki. The sun poured through the smeared window, and a swarm of dust churned visibly in the air. A woman's eyeglasses became fierce shields of opaque reflection, an old man's hair turned inhumanly silver.

His imagination opened in a dark, fecund slice. He imagined himself five years thence, living in a sun-desiccated white bungalow in

L.A., a sought-after scriptwriter. One day he would get a call; there was renewed interest in *Kiss and Tell*. Why? Because Nicki Piastrini wanted the lead. Once the years had passed and her anger had faded, she had seen that the script was not only brilliant but the role of a lifetime, written by—basically—loving hands, for her and only for her.

He took a swallow of the cold, dirty ice water that had been placed before him, not even noticing the long black hair clinging to the lip of the glass. In his mind he heard the climactic finale of a song about doomed love, the singer crying, *"Jamais! Jamais, jamais, jamais, jamais!"*

His fantasy did not include a reunion with Nicki or even a conversation. Instead, he fast-forwarded straight to an image of himself at a preliminary screening of *Kiss and Tell*, at which Nicki was strangely absent. He sat in the plush privacy of darkness, feeling intensely replete and resolved, waiting to see the lover who had slipped away, caught in his net of words. In his fantasy the script had not been rewritten, the way scripts always are, and his words fell on him in a rain of affirmation. Nicki's huge, cinematically beautified face bloomed violently before him, sprung from some part of his psyche that was too dark for him to see. The character—his character—was a mutable androgyne wearing glittering psychic armor over its woman's form, beautiful and seemingly without substance, yet impenetrable. When she was brought low in the film, it was with fabulous erotic drama, the realization that her armor was torn and her defeat could be boundaryless. He imagined the pivotal scene, her confrontation with the magazine editor. The blood rushed to Lesly's crotch as the editor circled Nicki, her delicious look of fear increasing with each circle. The scene became sexy. Close-up: Her eyes looked into the camera, inviting penetration through the openness of her expression. His sense of triumphant possession would be mitigated only by his admiration for her acting. He inhaled and leaned forward as if to grab something in his hands—when, like an eel turning around on itself in a tiny space, his fantasy changed direction. Nicki faced the camera as the editor, seen from behind, greedily seized her. Close-up: By sensual gradations, her vulnerable expression became hard and predatory. Irrationally, the scene held static, as Nicki seemed vampirically to draw the editor's aggression from him, to make it her own. The man whom Lesly had invented to violate Nicki was alchemically subsumed by her, as she swallowed Lesly's triumph whole. Except that in his fantasy, her triumph felt like his. His grabbing hands closed on air. From inside his head, Nicki smiled at him and pinned him to his seat. Involuntarily, he smiled back; smiling, he let her go. He came back into the coffee shop as if waking up and, in doing so, releasing a dream into the world. A cloud covered the glaring sun, and someone violently blew his nose.

He did move to Los Angeles and he did write many more screenplays, some of which were actually produced. There was, however, no renewed interest in *Kiss and Tell.* Although he saw her in several films, he never saw Nicki in person again.

The
Wrong
Thing

Turgor

Today the clerk in the fancy deli next door asked me how I was, and I said, "I have deep longings that will never be satisfied." I go in there all the time, so I thought it was okay. But she frowned slightly and said, "Is it the weather that does it to you?" "No," I said, "it's just my personality." She laughed.

It's the kind of thing that I enjoy saying at the moment but that has a nasty reverb. I want it to be a joke, but I'm afraid it's not.

Last week a woman I have not spoken to for years called to tell me that someone I used to have sex with had died of a drug overdose. I was shocked to hear it, but not especially sorry. He'd had a certain fey glamour and a knack for erotic chaos that was both exhilarating and horrible, but he was essentially an absurdly cruel, absurdly unhappy person, and I thought that, in the end, he was probably quite relieved to go. I had not seen him in ten years, and our association had been pornographic, loveless, and stupid. We had had certain bright moments of camaraderie and high jinks, but none of it justified the feelings I'd had for him. Even now he occasionally appears in my dreams—loving and tender, smiling as he hands me, variously, a candy bar, a brightly striped glass ball, a strawberry-scented candle. In one dream he grew wings and flew to South America with me clinging to his back, ribbons flying from our hair and feet.

"I know he hurt you," my friend said. "But I think he hurt himself a lot more."

"Yeah," I said. "He did."

When I got off the phone, I sat still for some moments. Then I got up and dressed for the party I was about to attend. It was a birthday party for an acquaintance, a self-described pro-sex feminist who had created a public niche for herself as a pornographer and talk-show guest. I put on a see-through blouse, a black bra, a tiny black skirt, high-heeled boots, and a ratty black wig I had found in the bargain bin of a used-clothing store.

I took a taxi to the party, and the driver, whom I had engaged in conversation, commented on my clothes. "I just wondered," he said, "why you're dressed so, well, so . . . I mean . . ."

"You mean like a slut?"

"Uh, yeah." He glanced in his rearview. "Not that I'm saying anything."

"It's okay," I said. "It's because I think it's fun. It's not a big scary sex thing. It's an enthusiastic, participatory kind of thing. Besides, I'm thirty-nine, and pretty soon I won't be able to do it anymore, because I'll be an old bag."

He nodded thoughtfully. "Well, that's cool," he said. "It's just that you don't seem like the type who needs the attention."

His comment was so touching that it made me feel maudlin, and feeling maudlin made me feel belligerent. "A guy I used to be involved with used to criticize me for not dressing slutty enough," I said. "He said I wasn't much of a girl. He'd probably like what I've got on, but the little jerk is dead now." I dug around in my bag for the fare. The driver's eyes flashed urgently in his rearview.

At the party, I quickly found the bar. I was working on getting drunk when I noticed that a pretty, snooty-looking boy was staring at me, his large eyes glowing with cheap, carnivorous ardor. I found that pleasing, especially coming from someone who looked at least ten years younger than I, but there was also something a little unnerving about it. It wasn't exactly lust; it was a look of stunted idealism, a shallow romanticism that could only be disappointed at—even appalled by—the substance that lurks under any fancy facade, including mine.

"You look like a movie star," he said.

I mumbled abashedly.

"How did you get your look?"

"It's just a wig." Perplexed and embarrassed to think he might be making fun of me, I looked at the gift table, upon which guests had impishly heaped dildos, vibrators, carrots, daikons, and cucumbers. "My," I said, "look at that preponderance of elongated objects."

"*What?*"

He looked at me askance; I immediately launched a meaningless exchange of questions and answers: "Where are you from?" "How long did you live there?" "Do you like San Francisco?"

"What is this, an interview?" he snapped.

"I was hoping it was an exchange of friendly noises," I said.

"I'm going to get a drink," he said. "I'm going to get a drink now." He turned on his haughty heel. Already the substance had squished out and repelled him! Oh, well. I circulated, working hard on my drunken stupor. I was sitting with a jovial group of women when he approached me again. He had one of the impish daikons in his hand; he sat down and rapped the vegetable on the table and said, "I've got a point to make here."

I gazed into space and murmured, "I hear you."

After that we communicated more smoothly. We chatted about rock stars, haircuts, hair dye, and whether or not there is such a thing as national character. His name was Frederick. He said he had come to this party because his friend Al had given the birthday girl a computer, and he wanted Frederick, who was, it seemed, a particularly esoteric interface designer, to show her how to create her own web site. "He begged me to come," said Frederick. "He even offered to *pay* me." He sighed as if this request were a distasteful burden.

I tried to think of something to say, and while I was trying, a blond girl with a Polaroid camera came and asked us if she could take our picture. She was drunk, and she gave off a peculiar chemical shimmer that was sweet and lurid and had a seductive little suck to it. We assumed self-conscious expressions, and she took the picture. She handed it to me with a small, sharp smile and walked away.

Frederick and I decided to share a cab home. In the cab he sat very close to me, and that artificial closeness made me sense acutely how alone I would feel when I said good night and entered the long, dark hallway of my apartment. I interrupted our banal conversation by taking his hand; I was surprised when he gave me some sweet, gentle pressure.

"Frederick," I said. "Would you like to come in for a minute?"

"Sure," he said. "But I won't stay for long."

I said "Okay" very softly.

I offered him something to drink, but I only had rum and a few ounces of Jägermeister. We sat on the floor and shared the ounces.

"This is really weird," I said. "I haven't had anybody in my apartment like this for over a year." He looked skeptical. My cat came into the room. I told him I'd had her for ten years. I said I was concerned about her weight because I'd recently taken in and tamed a feral kitten, who was probably hiding under the bed, and since kittens need to eat a lot I was compelled to overfeed the cat so she wouldn't feel neglected.

"She isn't fat," Frederick said. "I think she's pretty."

Maybe he was nice after all. I raised one of my booted feet and coquettishly poked my pointed heel into his stomach. His face underwent a funny shift of expression. He kissed me. We lay on the floor, and I mauled him, pausing to gently touch my nose against his face, neck, and slight chest. He told me he was twenty-six. I told him I was thirty-nine. I said I hoped that my age didn't bother him. I said that sometimes it bothered me and other times I looked forward to old-bagness, when I could stop worrying about sex and be like a kid again. I sat on him and lightly bounced. He said he thought I was a very interesting person and that he would like to see me in another context; he asked if I thought I'd like to "hang out" with someone so much younger. "I don't know," I said. "I might feel self-conscious, and besides, we might not like each other." I bent and kissed him again, cupping his head the way I would hold a baby's head to keep it from falling. "Before we left the party, Darleen told me something about you," I said. "She said you were really good but that you wouldn't call me the next day or the day after that or the day after that."

"And that was all right with you?"

"Yeah," I said. "It was."

He stared at me.

We rolled around some more. He felt very different from the way he talked. He felt fragile and tentative, but with a muscular hot streak running up his center. He vacillated between full presence and no presence at all; his present moments were animal and nervous, his absence was like a snake that you can feel, but not see, moving past you. He made me feel submissive and high-handed at the same time. "Man," I said, "you are so sweet."

In response, he kissed me, and then pulled back so that my mouth was left open; he moved in again as if he were going to kiss me, and then, when I responded, pulled away again. Through slit eyes I noted his smirk. I recalled that my last boyfriend, who was also in his twenties, had told me that he sometimes liked to pull out of a kiss so that the girl's tongue would be sticking out and looking funny. Fondly and fairly hard, I bit Frederick's lips. He sat up and, out of nowhere, began to talk mean shit about a girl who had been at the party.

"She's nothing but a dog," he said. "She likes to be ordered around. Like, go into the corner, sit up, stay, wait, beg."

"Yeah, well, there's a lot of that going around," I said. I paused, looking up at him. "How do you know that about her?" I asked. "Did you screw her?"

His smirk wobbled uncertainly. "Uh, no. But that's what all her performances are about. Didn't you notice those pictures of her on the wall tonight? With the whips?"

"No. I'm surprised. I would've thought emotional pain was more her thing." I took him by his shoulders and put him on his back again. I wondered if he had brought up this girl's dogness in order to indirectly implicate me in it. I felt hurt for a second and then decided that I didn't care; it seemed the evening could sustain some dog influence. "Actually, I don't know about this whole San Francisco S-M yoga-class crap," I said. "Like, watch me up on stage getting my butt whipped. I mean, it's so schematic or something." I lay on top of him and rubbed my lower lip gently against the grain of his left eyebrow. He stroked my back and my head. He found my lips with his hand and insinuated his finger into my mouth.

I sat up and straddled him. "People are fucking crazy," I said.

"This girl I know once had a thing with this guy through E-mail. Finally, they met, and she went home with him. He made out with her and did all kinds of stuff, and then he just rolled over and went to sleep, except he had a big hard-on. The next night the same thing happened. After that she never heard from him. Then she ran into him and he called her a cunt."

His expression as I told this story became soft, even humane. He also looked as if I'd called him on something—which perhaps, in some muddled way, I had. He put his hands on my hips and said, "I like you." He looked into the air with that strange, tender face. "But I'm not sure why."

"I like you too," I said, reaching for his belt buckle. "And I know what you mean about not knowing why. Actually, you remind me of a real prick I used to be involved with about ten years ago—not that you're a prick or anything. He was weird in a lot of ways. He was the only man I've ever known who didn't like blow jobs."

"I don't like them much, either," Frederick said. "Because most girls aren't any good at them. Except the last girl—and I think that was a guy."

"What about if you're in love?" I asked.

"The love thing—that's different," he said. "That doesn't have anything to do with technique."

"For me it does. If I'm in love, I'm pretty much going to like what the person does. But I guess men are different." I was beginning to think he *might* be a prick, but his prickness seemed minor key and strangely weightless; I didn't think he would hurt me. So I sucked his dick. When I stopped he said he liked my tongue. "It's a pointy little guy," I said. "Probably from constantly reaching out for, um, things."

"Really?" He looked mortified.

"Uh-huh." I ran one hand down his front, then his thigh. "You're so frail," I murmured. "But you have this nice masculine turgor thing happening too."

"You keep using words I don't know."

"Oh, 'turgor'? I just learned that myself. It means the tension inside plants that gives them form. It's nice, don't you think?"

He sat up. "What do you do for a living?"

"I teach at Berkeley. I teach poetry."

I imagined myself as I would be the next day—sitting at my kitchen table with a headache, reading my students' ghastly poems. I thought of my students with a sorrowful pang. I imagined them in my living room, watching me as I lay with this too young person. "Look at me," I would say. "This is what I'm really like. I have nothing for you. I'm sorry." The hell of it was, if such a scene could actually take place, my students would only see it as evidence of my thrilling humanity; it would quite possibly raise me higher in their esteem.

We kissed and rolled some more. My excitement was feverish and needy, but that didn't make me feel afraid. I felt as if I could bat my excitement back and forth or turn it up and down, and I was delighted to roll and root in the fun of being pulled in so many directions. I felt as if I could have a small, good experience with this boy, and at that moment a small, good experience was more important than anything.

Then he called the direction. "I'm going to go," he said.

"Please don't," I said.

He kissed me, and I felt a deep, squalid bitterness under the first layer of his kiss. For the first time that night, I felt him in earnest, and he felt very familiar. We were now going in the direction broadly labeled "pain." But of course, pain has many directions too.

I went to the bathroom, and when I came back he was sitting on the couch with his pants on. He said again that he was going to go. I remembered that even pain can be tedious. I wondered if he'd gone through my wallet while I was peeing. I knelt and put my hand on his knee. "Please don't go," I said.

He came back down on the floor with me. He pushed at my wig with a soft, childish gesture. I took it off for him. My short brown hair had been badly mashed by the wig; it probably didn't look very good, but for some reason I didn't mind showing it to him.

"This suits you more," he said. "It's softer."

"Yeah, well, it's actual hair."

He got up on his knees and, putting his hand on top of my head, asked me to go down on him again. Probably he wanted me to get on my hands and knees, but, maybe out of irritation, I merely spread my legs and bent from the waist in a posture that was not very pleasing aesthetically or psychologically. It was also not very comfortable, so I stopped quickly and sat up. He hesitated and then, with a nervous toss of his head, pressed himself against me like a purring cat. I lay down. He lay on top of me. He reached under my skirt, worked his hand down my panty hose and lightly stroked my genitals with the back of his hand. The contempt in the gesture was rich and sensual, and I leaned into it. The numb comfort of humiliation tempted me; I gave him a little mew of encouragement. He answered me with a little mew of his own. He slid his hands under my head and gripped handfuls of my hair and pulled it. Carefully, he placed his prick against my genitals; he rubbed it slowly against me.

"Frederick?"

"What?" His thin voice swelled with greed.

"Would you please fuck me?"

"Oh, all right." He went for his belt buckle with an alacrity that belied his words.

I sat up quickly. "No," I said. "Never mind."

He sat up. We sat there. He blinked several times.

"I guess you want to go," I said.

He sat on the couch and crossed his legs. "It's not that I'm not attracted to you," he said. "I mean, if we had sex, it would probably be really good. But it wouldn't be right."

I was acutely aware of my body, as I might be if I had been knocked on the floor in the middle of a dance movement: first my wind came back, then I made sure nothing was broken, then I was filled with tenderness for my body. I remembered the time my dead lover had beat me up. He had said something unkind to me, and though he often said such things, this time I took offense and slapped him in the face. He slapped me harder; I punched him in the stomach. He knocked me down, fell on me, and banged my head on the floor until I was almost unconscious. When it was over, I had the same feeling of returning to my body, with tenacious animal self-love.

Meanwhile, Frederick was still talking. He said he was seeing a lot of women and that he was obsessed with his old girlfriend. He said that he needed "boundaries." "I'm too guarded to have sex right now," he said.

I thought of how he had pretended to kiss me and then pulled away. His words did not make sense to me, but many things don't make sense to me. "You're probably right," I said slowly. "We don't know each other, and it might be a bad experience. I've had a lot of bad experiences."

A look of indulgent emotionality came over his face, as if he were watching a sensitive movie about the special pain of a lonely older woman who's just been rejected by a younger guy. I felt a little surge of indignation that quickly devolved into pieces of uncertainty and vague goodwill. I was awfully tired. "Can you see what time it is?" I asked.

"It's five o'clock."

"Fuck!" I took his jacket from the floor and wrapped it around my shoulders. "The last time I got involved with a guy we didn't have sex for three weeks, which naturally made me want him desperately. So when we finally did it, it felt like a cataclysm; I went into an emotional frenzy, and he got pulled right into it. Then the sex wore off, and there we were, stuck in all this bogus emotion. It seems like it doesn't work no matter what you do."

Mild surprise overtook his look of indulgent sympathy; his face was shadowed by mournful tenderness. It occurred to me that he might feel pain too. We were both silent. Our silence comforted me. I held my hand out to him, and he took it in his.

"I'd like to see you again," he said.

"I don't think so," I said. "I mean, there's the old girlfriend and the other women and what have you. It sounds like a mess, and I'm pretty busy, actually. But I'm glad I met you. I think you're a nice person."

He almost flinched when I said that. His lips parted and his eyes became bleak and deep. He let go of my hand and stood up. I thought he was going to ask for his jacket, but instead he went to my bookcase and withdrew a book. He looked at the cover and then turned it over. It was my only published book of poetry. I had published it ten years before, won a few awards, and then collapsed. I'd published nothing since.

"Is this you?" he asked.

"Put that back," I said sharply.

He replaced it and stared at me with a look I couldn't read.

"I'm sorry," I said. "I didn't mean to be rude."

"It's okay," he said. "Sometimes when girls come to my place, they pick up stuff, and I don't like it. I say, 'Stop going through my things.' You just told me to stop going through your things." He looked at me as if amazed.

I didn't say anything.

"Maybe I'd like to read your poems."

"I don't write poems anymore. That book is really old."

He got his boots, and as he bent over to put them on he cut a dainty fart. He paused in his bend and made a fussing noise, as if irritated at himself for farting. It was okay with me, though, and I think he realized that. I hoped so. Once, I fell asleep on a train and drooled in front of my fellow passenger; when I woke and glanced at him in embarrassed realization, I saw right away that he had borne with my drool. That subtle acceptance from a total stranger was deeply satisfying to me, and I was pleased to give it to someone else.

He stood up and stumbled over a cat toy. "I'll miss you," he said.

"Oh, please." My words were like quick, shallow water. I handed him his jacket, and he put it on.

"You won't give me your number?" he asked.

I leaned forward and put my head on his shoulder. Sheathed in his jacket, it felt impersonal and kind. He held me for a moment, and I thought I could feel him experimenting with the sensation of kindness.

"No," I said.

After he left, I sat for almost an hour, allowing my body to return to aloneness and safety. Then I took a bath and got in bed. It was almost seven o'clock, and the room was filling with daylight. My moist skin made my pajamas damp and warm. There were sounds from the courtyard outside my window; two of my neighbors were out in the garden, talking in low voices. They were talking about the bonnets and dresses they were making to wear at the Indulgence in the Park Easter celebration.

I wondered why I had told Frederick that I thought he was nice. Probably for the same reason that I had sweet dreams about a petty sadist. I tried to think of my dead sex partner, but my memories of him were truncated, and gray with elapsed time. I could only imagine him with flat, terrified eyes, his hands making a gesture that was too cramped and weak to signify anything. I don't know why I imagined him this way, since I had never seen him make such expressions or gestures. I tried to imagine saying goodbye to him, but it didn't work. I had a sensation of all my memories growing truncated and gray, stretching out over a lengthening span of years, slowly dissolving into broken pieces of imagery weighted with inexplicable feeling.

I turned onto my side and closed my eyes, as if doing so would finally bring the experience to an end. I would've liked to cry, but I couldn't. From the garden, I heard one of my neighbors describe his bonnet as "robin's-egg blue." He must've shown it to the other neighbor, because I heard a second voice say, "Oh, it's *so* special." He was being sarcastic, but he also meant it.

Respect

When I woke it was afternoon. Through my open window, the day felt dull and warm. I turned onto my side and remembered Frederick. I remembered his blithe, half-conscious meanness, the nervous toss of his head, the puzzlement in his voice when he had said, "I like you." Under his silly contempt there had been a little pocket of tenderness, and I had seen it. I imagined that I lay against him, and that he held me. In my imagination, it did not matter that he was thirteen years younger than me. The tenderness was strange and slightly mortifying.

When I went into my living room, I saw the Polaroid that had been taken of Frederick and me lying on the floor, harmlessly reflecting sunlight off its cheap, shiny surface. I picked it up and studied it. The girl who had taken it came into my mind and sparkled for a moment. Frederick posed like a conceited teenager; his face was hard, closed, and very handsome. It looked as if he had struck the pose automatically. Beside him, I was slightly out of focus, and my eyes were woefully large. The picture nonplussed me, but in a curious way it also pleased me. I put it on the kitchen table and looked at it while I drank my coffee.

When I went out to get my mail, I found that he had left a note on my mailbox. I sat on the front steps, smiling foolishly. Sunlight tingled on a tiny, dislocated rhinestone that someone had lost without noticing. The note was badly spelled and almost incoherent, and that, for some reason, endeared him to me. He had given me his phone number.

His voice was warmer and more direct than I remembered it. He said a man who had been at the party had called him that morning to ask how it was to spend the night with me. "And I told him it was none of his business," he said. His words rang with resolute gallantry, but they bewildered me; they sounded completely artificial, yet I sensed that he wanted to believe himself gallant.

We planned to meet for a drink at seven o'clock. He said he had an appointment at ten, which gave us three hours together. Shyly, I said I was looking forward to seeing him. He said he felt the same way. Then he asked me if I felt "compromised." I knew what he meant, but I pretended I didn't; there was vibrant excitement in his voice, which I wanted to resist. "No," I said. "Why would I feel compromised?" I paused. "Do you?"

Half an hour before the meeting, I opened my closet to dress and realized that I was frightened. In part I was afraid simply because I had not been on a date for over a year. But mostly I was afraid that the peculiar absence I had felt in this boy was a harbinger of something worse than absence, something he himself was not fully aware of. But I didn't want to be afraid. I especially didn't want to be afraid of a kid. So I pushed my fear down under my thoughts. In suppressed fear, I chose a high-necked, calf-length dress that once belonged to my mother. It was a quietly beautiful dress, and wearing it usually made me feel both feminine and strong. As I put it on, however, my expectation of feeling good was just barely undermined by a feeling of shame so subtle I didn't identify it for what it was. Before I could, I suppressed it as well.

The bar Frederick had chosen for our meeting was elegant and old, slightly rotted and faintly clandestine. It was furnished with little glass lamps hanging from the ceiling and small tables covered with long, seemly cloths. He was the only person seated there when I arrived. He stood and looked at me with the same stare of ersatz adoration that had made me notice him at the party. "You look like a movie star," he said.

"And you look like a rock star," I snapped. My sarcasm startled me; I hadn't yet noticed how ashamed I felt, so I didn't realize that his absurd compliment had touched my shame.

My tone seemed to startle him too, but he didn't break stride. He helped me out of my jacket with a flourish. He bought me a pale-gold drink in a beveled glass. He took my hand and looked into my eyes and said, "I respect you." He paused with excited relish and then continued. "I don't know why. Maybe it's because you're older. But I respect you."

I tried to understand the feeling beneath his words. It felt as if he were saying two different things with equal force. It felt almost as if he were straddling something. My unease became harder to ignore.

"When I first saw you from across the room I thought you were an extraordinary person," he continued. "And now you look . . . well, you look . . ." He gestured at me in my mother's dress. "Ummm . . ." The hint of a smirk played through his eyes.

I was suddenly shocked and humiliated, too much so to say anything. I couldn't tell if he was being elaborately cruel or very foolish or both. The proportions of the room seemed all at once strange and precious; the little tables looked like cleverly arranged decorations with no relationship to function. "Frederick," I said. My voice was wooden and small. "I'm nervous. I'm scared, actually."

He furrowed his brow slightly. "Why?"

He seemed genuinely puzzled. I tried to think of how to explain it to him, but it was too complicated. "I don't know," I said unhappily.

"Here," he said. He changed chairs so that he was sitting at my side instead of right before me. "That'll make it easier," he said gently. "I'm not, like, staring at you."

"Thank you," I said. His gentleness touched me. Maybe, I thought, my fear was a grotesque projection; I decided I mustn't let the past completely distort my experience of the present. I relaxed, and my tender feeling for him woke and breathed again. The tables looked like tables at which one might simply sit. He raised one hand and, very tentatively, almost as if _he_ were frightened, touched my cheek. He asked if I would like another drink. "No, thank you," I said.

He began talking about a woman he'd had sex with some weeks before. He had never wanted to see her again, so he hadn't called her, even though he'd said he would. She, on the other hand, had been harassing him with phone calls he never deigned to return, demanding to see him. Finally, that afternoon he'd visited her. He'd just come from her, in fact.

"I was arrogant and controlling and cocky with her," he said. "Which just made her want to have sex with me all the more." He sighed as if exasperated. "I was totally different with her than I am with you. I don't respect her, and I'm not interested in her." He paused and lightly gripped the edge of the table with both hands, his long fingers soft and tense, like the paws of a young cat. "I like myself better with you," he declared.

I was not only ashamed for myself, I was also ashamed for him, so much so that I was virtually paralyzed by it—yet I still hadn't noticed it.

"I used to have a lot of relationships like that," I said heavily.

"Like what?"

"With men who didn't respect me. And I can tell you, without even knowing her, that this woman doesn't respect you either. That kind of shit goes both ways."

He looked puzzled, then wary. He retracted one hand slightly along the edge of the table.

"At the time, I would've told you that I loved these men," I said. "But really, I didn't even like them."

"So why were you with them if you didn't like them?"

"Those situations are often erotic. And it's complicated. I mean, why'd you go to this girl's house if you were so uninterested in her?"

"Oh, it's definitely erotic. But I don't like it." He looked vaguely into space. "I don't like it," he repeated. He hesitated. "I want to be a nice person," he said. He looked at me, expectant, almost childish. He looked as though he wanted me to tell him that he was a nice person, and although I would've liked to, I found I couldn't. Silently, I lowered my eyes. The pause was terrible.

The conversation was over and we both knew it, yet neither of us wanted to admit it. With a great effort we changed the subject and lurched into a discussion about books, horror movies, and the construction of Frederick's web sites. When one of us stumbled, the other would clumsily lend a hand, so that we gamely, even chivalrously, pulled each other along. The peculiar thing was, I think we actually liked each other—not that it did us any good.

"I was thinking," he said. "Maybe you could suggest some poets for me to read. I don't know anything about poetry."

"I don't know you," I said. My voice was clipped and hard. "I wouldn't have the slightest idea what you might like."

There was another silence. I felt a shift take place in him. If he had been straddling something before, he had now chosen a position. He looked at his watch; he said he had made plans to go meet another woman. "We have some time," he said, "so I can walk you home." He stood and swung his jacket around his shoulders. "With leisure and pleasure." His voice was voluptuous and charmed by itself.

"I just said that to somebody last week," he added. "Only then I said pleasure and leisure."

I wondered if he'd gotten the phrase from a Japanese merchandising outlet on cable, which went by the same name. I had noticed it on TV, on the channel featuring the electronic program guide; it had a functional bleakness that was almost poetic. Numbly, I admired Frederick's ability not only to appreciate the phrase but to use it as an implement of self-indulgence that doubled as a small, sharp weapon. I remembered his kindness as he held me in his arms just before he left my apartment; it was a feeble, flickering sense memory, and it quickly died.

He insisted on holding my jacket so that I could put it on. Two girls who had just entered the bar admired his gesture. I took his arm and we went out onto the street. He said he'd really enjoyed our evening together and that we would have to do it again. "The time went by so quickly," he said.

"Well, there wasn't much of it," I replied.

We arrived at my apartment building. Frederick kissed me as if there were a television camera trained on us. I responded in a perfunctory daze. It was chilly, but his neck was bare and unprotected, like a little boy's. "So," he said, "what are *you* going to do with the rest of your night?"

"Read, I guess." With the most hopeless gesture of the evening, I stretched up and brushed his exposed neck with my lips and nose.

Faintly, but alertly, he stiffened; I could feel him remember our strange intimacy with a swift, barely perceptible inner twitch. In the dark, I felt his eyes dart uncertainly. "Goodbye," I said. I turned and walked up my front steps.

"Wait," he said. "Do you . . . do you have your keys?"

"Yeah." I half turned to answer him; my voice trembled with anger. "I have my keys." I went in and shut the door.

I went immediately into the bathroom and knelt over the toilet, thinking that I might be sick. But I could not discharge the bad feeling so easily. I sat on the floor and held my face in my hands. I uttered a soft animal moan. My old cat came and sat next to me, looking at me anxiously. "It's all right," I told her. "Don't be afraid. It's not a big deal."

Processing

For the next several days, the memory of my encounter with Frederick lingered like a bruise that is not painful until, walking through
the kitchen in the dark one night to get a drink of water, you bang it
on a piece of furniture. I would be talking animatedly with someone
when I would suddenly realize that I was really talking to and for
Frederick, as if he were standing off to the side, listening to me. This
was a nuisance, but a mildly advantageous one; my efforts to com-
municate with the phantom Frederick gave my conversation a
twisted frisson some people mistook for charm.

The week after I met Frederick, I went to a party celebrating the
publication of a book of lesbian erotica. I was talking to two
women, one of whom was facetiously describing her "gay
boyfriend" as better than a lover or a "regular friend." She said he
was handsome too, so much so that she constantly had to "defend
his honor."

"You mean he's actually got honor?" said someone.

"One should always maintain a few shreds of honor," I remarked.
"In order to give people something to violate."

"I don't know if that qualifies as honor."

"It's faux honor, and it's every bit as good for the purpose I just
described."

"Can I get you a drink?" There was a woman standing off to the side, listening to me. I was startled to see that she was the woman who had taken a Polaroid of Frederick and me. Even in a state of apparent sobriety she emitted an odd, enchanting dazzle.

"Yes," I said. We took our drinks out onto the steps. A lone woman was sitting there already, smoking and dropping cigarette ash into an inverted seashell. When she saw us, she said hello and moved to the lowest step, giving us the top of her head and her back. Because she was there, we whispered, and our whispers made an aural tent only big enough for the two of us.

"I wondered if I'd see you again," she said. "I wondered what happened with you and that guy."

"Nothing," I said. "It was a one-night thing. We didn't even have sex."

"I also wondered if you like girls."

"I definitely like girls." I paused. "Why did you want to get me a drink just now?"

"What do you think? Because I like your faux honor."

"Because it has cheap brio and masochism?"

"Exactly!" I felt her come toward me in an eager burst, then pull away, as if in a fit of bashfulness. "But we shouldn't be so direct," she said. "We should maintain our mystery for at least two minutes."

I felt myself go toward her in a reflexive longing undercut by the exhaustion that often accompanies old reflexes. "I'm Susan," I said.

Her name was Erin. She was thirty-two years old. She was trying, with another woman, to establish a small press and, to this end, was living on a grant that was about to run out. She was reading a self-help book called *Care of the Soul* and *Dead Souls* by Gogol. She had been taking Zoloft for six months. She seemed to like it that I'd written a book of poetry, even if it had been ten years ago. She said that she sometimes described herself as a "butch bottom" but lately she was questioning how accurate that was. I told her I was sick of categories like butch bottom and femme top or vice versa. I said I was looking for something more genuine, although I didn't know yet what it was. She said she thought she probably was too.

"That picture you took of me was sad," I said. "I look sad in it."

I expected her to deny it, but she didn't say anything. She reached between my legs and, with one finger, drew tiny, concentrated circles through my slacks. It seemed a very natural thing. It seemed as if she thought anyone could've come along and done that, and it might as well be her. This wasn't true, but for the moment I liked the idea; it was a simple, easy idea. It made my genitals seem disconnected from me, yet at the same time the most central part of me. I parted my lips. I stared straight ahead. The silence was like a small bubble rising through water. She kissed the side of my lips, and I turned so that we kissed full on. She opened her mouth and I felt her in a rush of tension and need. I was surprised to feel such need in this woman; it was a dense, insensible neediness that rose through her in a gross howl, momentarily shouting out whatever else her body had to say. I opened in the pit of my stomach and let her discharge into me. The tension slacked off, and I could feel her sparkle again, now softer and more diffuse.

We separated, and I glanced at the woman on the steps, who was, I thought, looking a little despondent. "Let's go in," I said.

Inside, we were subdued and a bit shy. We walked around together, she sometimes leading me with the tips of her fingers on my wrist or arm. Being led in such a bare way made me feel mute, large and fleshy next to her lean, nervous form. I think it made us both feel the fragility of our bond, and although we spoke to other people, we said very little to each other, as though to talk might break it. We assumed she would walk me home; when we left, she offered me her arm, and I fleetingly compared her easy gallantry with Frederick's miserable imitation of politeness.

As we walked, she talked about people at the party, particularly their romantic problems. I listened to her, puzzling over the competence of her voice, the delicacy of her leading fingers, the brute need of her kiss. Her competence and delicacy were attractive, but it was the need that pulled me toward her. Not because I imagined satisfying it—I didn't think that was possible—but because I wanted to rub against it, to put my hand on it, to comfort it. Actually, I wasn't sure what I wanted with it.

We sat on my front steps and made out. "I'd like to invite you in," I said, "but it would be too much like that guy—I meet you at a party, bring you home." I shrugged.

She nodded solemnly, looked away, looked back and smiled. "So? I thought you said nothing happened anyway."

"He made out with me and I sucked his dick, and then he acted like he didn't want me."

"That's sort of harsh."

"Yeah. He acted like he was being nice, and I believed him, but then when I saw him again, he acted like a weird prick."

She embraced me sideways. "That sort of turns me on," she said. She nuzzled my neck, and the feminine delicacy of her lips and eyelashes was like a startling burst of gold vein in a broken piece of rock. I slid my hands under her shirt. She had small, muscular breasts and freakishly long nipples, and there was faint, sweet down all along her low back.

I invited her in. She entered the living room with a tense, mercurial swagger that pierced my heart. We sat on the couch. "So," she said. "Do I get to be the bad boy? Are you gonna suck my cock?"

"Don't," I said. "He hurt my feelings."

"Awww." She knelt between my legs, with her hands on my thighs. Her fingers were blunt and spatulate, with little gnawed nails. "If I say something wrong, it's because I'm not sure what to do. I'm not used to this. I want to please you, but you also make me want to . . . I don't even know."

"I'm not sure what I want, either," I said. "I think there might be something wrong with me."

She held my face in her hands. "Let me make it better," she said. She looked at me, and her expression seemed to fracture. Abruptly, she struck me across the face, backhanded me and then struck me with her palm again. She checked my reaction. "Open your mouth," she said. "Stick out your tongue." I did. She started to unzip her pants, then faltered. "Um," she said, "Susan? Is this cool?"

"Yeah."

When we were finished, I walked her out the door onto the porch. Using her ballpoint, we wrote our numbers on scraps of paper torn from a flyer that had been placed on my doormat to remind me to fight AIDS. She held my face and kissed my cheek and left.

When I woke the next day I didn't think of her but I felt her, and I wasn't sure what she felt like to me. I was acutely aware of the artificiality of our experience. It felt like a dollhouse with tiny plastic furniture and false windows looking out on mechanically painted meadows and cloud-dotted skies. It felt both safe and cruelly stifling, and both feelings appealed to me. More simply, I felt as if some habitual pain had shifted position slightly, allowing me to breathe more easily. As the day went on, I thought of her, but gingerly. The thought was like a smell that is both endearing and faintly embarrassing. I remembered how she had knelt and said, "I'm not sure what to do," and I remembered her reckless blow to my face. She seemed split in two, and the memory split me in two. But when she called me, I was happy; I realized that I had not expected to hear from her.

"I would've called earlier," she said. "But last night was intense for me and I had to process. Like I said, I usually bottom."

Her voice was bright and optimistic, but there was something else in it. It was as if she'd made an agreement with somebody to supply all the optimism required on a general basis for the rest of her life, and the strain of it had become almost anguishing. But when she opened the door of her house to greet me, it was with brash, striding movement, and she was elegant and beautiful in a sleek suit.

We went to a Thai restaurant for dinner. It was a cheap place that maintained its dignity with orderly arrangement and dim lighting. Little statuettes and vases invoked foreignness unctuously yet honorably. The other diners seemed grateful to be in such an unassuming place, where all they had to do was talk to each other and eat. Erin pulled out my chair for me.

A waitress, vibrant with purpose, poured us water in a harried rattle of ice. We ordered sweet drinks and dainty, greasy dishes. Erin's smile burst off her face in a wild curlicue. I imagined her unsmiling, wearing lipstick, with her hair upswept, in a hat with a little veil; she would've been formidable and very beautiful. Her jaw was strong but also suggestive of intense female sensitivity and erotic suppleness. Then under that was a rigidity that made me think of something trapped. I reached across the table and took her hand. We were both sweating slightly.

"I haven't been involved with a woman for a long time," I said. "Mostly I'm with men. Although I haven't been involved with men lately, either."

"I don't care," she said. "Basically I'm a dyke, but I like sex with men sometimes so I can understand."

I asked her if she always needed to role-play in sex. I said I was trying not to relate to people in such a structured way. "I mean, I can do that kind of sex, um, obviously, and I can like it. It gets me off and everything. But it's a mechanical response. It's not deep."

"Well," she said, "I hope you didn't feel like what we did was mechanical, because it wasn't for me. I hardly ever top anybody, so it was really new." She drank her sweet iced coffee with ingenuous relish.

"It wasn't really mechanical, because I could feel you under the fantasy. But I've done those fantasies all my life, and I want to try to be more genuine and direct, so whatever we do, it'll really be us. Emotionally, I mean."

"I can respect that," she said. Her voice was like that of a little girl trying to be good for her mother. It gave me a strange, sad pleasure. It made me want to pretend to be her mother, just like another little girl.

Erin was from Kansas. She used to be an Evangelical Christian. She wasn't raised a Christian, but she had converted on her own initiative when she was fourteen. Her parents had separated when she was ten, and her mother had to work brutal night shifts that made her more disappointed with life than she already was. Erin spent most of her time with ardent Christian boys, with whom she went to religious meetings. She was occasionally moved to give bouquets of hand-picked flowers to various bewildered girls, but it wasn't until prom night that it hit her that her repeated daydreams about the elaborate scorn of a certain beautiful brat were actually erotic in nature. She made a successful pass at a drunk, pretty little mouse in the rest room and never wore a dress again—although she valiantly tried to be a queer Evangelical well after she realized it would never work.

I pictured her standing alone in plain, neat clothes in a landscape of dry sunlight and parched yellow earth. Vague shapes were present in the distance, but I couldn't see what they were. She was extending her arm to offer a bunch of flowers to someone who wasn't there. The expression on her face was humble, stoic, and tenaciously expectant, as if she was waiting for something she had never seen yet chose to believe would someday appear. It was the expression she had on her face while she was talking to me. She was telling me that when she told her mother she was gay, her mother said, "I could just shit," and went into the next room to watch TV.

She had other expressions too. When we talked about the ongoing rape trial of a pop star, I made predictable sarcastic comments about people who said that the girl had probably brought it on herself. Erin first agreed with me, then reversed herself to say that maybe the girl *had* asked for it. Her expression when she said that was rambunctious, with a sensual shade of silly meanness—but mostly it was the expression of a kid with her hands in Play-Doh, squishing around and making fun shapes.

After dinner we went to drink. As we walked down the street, we held hands. There was real feeling between us, but it was unstable, as if we had been rewarded with a treat of flavored ice, which we wanted to put off eating for as long as possible so that we could savor it, but which was already melting anyway.

We went to a bar where people in various states of good-natured resignation sat in the dark under crushing disco music. I ordered drinks with lots of amaretto in them. The sweetness gave my mild drunkenness a pleasant miasmic quality.

Erin said she liked what I had said about trying to be more genuine. She said her therapist had recently suggested to her that it might be good for Erin to spend at least a few weeks getting to know women before she had sex with them, and that although she hated the idea on principle, she was considering it.

I reminded her that we'd already had sex.

"But we could start fresh," she said. "And get to know each other before we do it again."

I thought of going with her to restaurants and movies. We would sit and discuss current events, and under all our talk would be the memory of my open mouth and exposed tongue. I moved close to her on the banquette and put my head on her slim, spare shoulder. She held me. Her hair had a tender chemical smell. I pictured her washing it, bent naked over a bathtub, moving her arms with the touching confidence of rote grooming practices.

She walked me to my door and we kissed. Her kiss felt honorable and empty. I asked her in. "We don't have to have sex," I said. She came in and we lay on the living room floor with our arms around one another. We touched each other gently and respectfully, but with each caress I felt as if we became more separated. That made me touch her more insistently and more intimately. I felt her neediness rise through her abdomen in a long pulse; we brushed our lips together in a stifled dry kiss and then opened our mouths to feed.

"I want to do what you said," she whispered. "I want to just be us."

I took her face in my hands. I wanted to say "my darling girl," but I hardly knew her. I pulled up my shirt and pulled my bra down. I pulled up her shirt. I knelt over her and rubbed against her chest and belly, just touching. She closed her eyes, and I could feel her waiting in her deep body, wanting me to show her what "ourselves" might be. And I would've, except that I didn't know. I could remember her at the restaurant talking about her mother and religion, expressing her opinions. Again, I imagined her standing alone, offering her flowers to no one. She was very dear and I wanted her, but I could only see her in pornographic snapshots, stripped of her opinions and her past. I unzipped her pants and pulled them down. I turned her over and positioned her. Her breath subtly deepened; she was taut and vibrant and absolutely present. I lightly rubbed my knuckles against her genitals. I felt an impersonal half-cruelty that was more titillating than real cruelty.

But she wanted to be cruel too, or rather to pretend that she was. She would take her artificial debasement to a certain point, and then she would change direction. She would kiss me and I would feel her tender self in a burst of nakedness that stopped my breath—and then she would veer away, immersing herself in some internal personality that didn't know or care about me. She was a nasty teenaged boy, she was a silly kid, she was a full, deep woman all the way down to her private organs. She slapped me and she pulled my hair—but she demanded that I beat her between her shoulder blades. And when I did she whispered "thank you," her face transfigured with sorrow so abject that I was for one violent second absolutely repelled, and then drawn back with equal violence.

Afterward, we lay against my throw pillows, cuddling and drinking chocolate milk. "Well," I said. "I guess that was us." She giggled and rubbed her nose on my stomach. My feral kitten crept round the bedroom door and peered at us, her wide eyes wistful, curious, and scared.

Later in the week, we took a nighttime walk. We walked uphill to Noe Valley, talking through strained waves of breath. She talked about a book she wanted to publish, even though the author was a nut who called every day to pester Erin with questions about how best to advance her career. Her stride was long and confident, but the inclination of her head was mechanical and deferential. She asked me if I would ever again dress the way I had dressed when she'd first seen me. I said probably, but not to take uphill walks. She told me that a previous girlfriend, who had been molested by her father when she was little, had liked Erin to pretend to be her father while they were having sex; she asked me if I thought that was creepy. I said it definitely didn't seem like they were relating directly as their real selves. She laughed and said it sure felt real to her. She pushed me against a car and tried to make me turn around. I snapped at her to cut it out; there was hurt feeling in her retraction, and I put my arm around her.

We walked downhill and came upon the slovenly burghership of Twenty-fourth Street. People dressed in floppy clothing and carrying lumpy handbags walked up and down in complicated states of distraction. Two men were standing on the corner, each with a telescope, offering people the chance to admire the planets for fifty cents. One telescope was labeled "The Moon" and the other "Venus." A group of children stood around them, looking as if they were willing to be delighted but weren't sure that the moon and Venus were quite delightful enough.

"Do you want to look?" asked Erin.

I said yes because I could tell she wanted to. I did enjoy waiting in line with the kids; their hope for enchantment, glimmering just faintly through their premature disaffection, was poignant in its secret tenacity. Their mothers sat drinking cappuccino on the outdoor bench of an expensive coffee shop, looking pleased to see their children engaged in such a good, simple activity. The moon was cold and beautiful.

We held hands as we walked back up the hill. The city was sparkling and calm in panorama. Erin told me that she'd fantasized about adopting kids one day, but she knew she needed to "work on" herself before that could happen. She asked if I'd ever wanted to have a family.

"No," I said, "not for its own sake." I paused, watching my shoes crease with each steep step. "If, when I was in my twenties, I'd fallen in love with someone and he'd loved me, I would've wanted to have children with him. And I probably would've loved it. But that didn't happen, and I'm not going to be running around trying to get pregnant just to do it."

"It doesn't make you sad?"

"No. Although sometimes, when I hear friends talk about their babies, or other friends talk about how they desperately want to have babies, I wonder if I'm really sad and am just pretending I'm not." My breath chugged earnestly. "I think I'm sadder that I don't write poetry anymore. Although I've been thinking lately that I might start again. Not now, though. Maybe when I'm old."

"Cool." She paused. "I just felt like pushing you up against a car again. But I won't."

Erin shared a large flat with a former girlfriend named Jana and Jana's girlfriend, Paulette. The house had a tiny yard full of saucy flowers. Erin's two large cats sat on the pavement or bounded and promenaded about the area. I loved coming to Erin's house. Every time I rounded the corner and saw it, I felt I was approaching a place where tenderness and good humor prevailed.

One night I came unannounced, surprising Erin in her lavender thermal pajamas. We sat together on her bed and enjoyed the garish comfort of her electric fireplace. To entertain me, she brought a large cardboard box out of the closet and showed me what was in it. There were somber albums of family pictures (tiny, troubled Erin in a ruffled swimsuit, handsome Dad looking absently at something outside the frame, towering, pissed-off Mom), a plaque that had been awarded her in a high school photography contest, a track team trophy, a bracelet her brother had made for her in junior high, love letters, an artificial penis made of rubber, an apparatus with which to strap it on, an odd assortment of small plastic animals, and some Polaroids of Erin naked except for a dog collar and leash around her neck. She explained that the pictures had been taken by a heterosexual couple whom she had met when she'd answered their advertisement for a "slave girl."

"They totally loved me," she said. "It was great, but I got tired of it before they did. They dragged it out too long. They kept making it a big deal that he was eventually going to fuck me with his cock—the way they went on about it, I just lost interest."

I looked at the Polaroids. I was slightly discomfited by her thinness; her ribs showed and her eyes looked starved and abnormally luminous.

"I forgot they even took those pictures until they sent them to me a month later." She put them in a pile and placed them back in the box. She indicated the rubber penis. "I was going to use that on you," she said. "But it reminds me too much of Jana. You deserve your own cock."

Maybe because she had told me a story, I told her one about myself. It was something that had happened when, as a teenager, I had tried having sex for money. I told her the story to excite her, and I could see right away that it did. At first it excited me too; I had never told anyone about it before.

"He didn't want me to take my panty hose off, he just wanted me to bend over and pull them down to about midthigh, which sort of embarrassed me. But I did it, and then I bent over and waited, and he didn't do anything."

"Yeah?" We were lying together, Erin up on her elbow, her eyes dilating slightly as she went into the rigid psychic suspension required by fantasy. She was, I thought, the only person I could tell this story to.

"On one hand, I was embarrassed on account of the panty hose thing, but on the other hand, I was very matter-of-fact—I guess teenagers just naturally are. I said, 'Um, are you, like, doing something or what?' And he didn't say anything, so I said, 'Well, what *are* you doing?' And he said, 'Shut up. I'm doing what I gotta do.'"

"Which was?"

I realized that I was not excited anymore. I was not embarrassed, either. I didn't know what I felt.

"What did he do?"

I put my face against her chest.

She ruffled my hair. "C'mon."

I tilted my head up and whispered in her ear.

Erin yelped with glee. "He jerked off on you?" She fell down on her back and roared with laughter. We rolled around laughing, me tickling her, her little chin pointing at the ceiling. Then she grabbed me and held my head against her chest, and I felt, under her quick breath, her radiant tenderness; it was as if some secret part of her had come out to touch me gently and had then drawn back into its hiding place.

The next day I was shopping in a clothing store and daydreaming about Erin, when a pop song on the sound system took my imagination in a facile grab. It was a flimsy love song, sung in a high, caressing register. There was real feeling in it, but the singer had tortured it into deformed and precious shapes that debased his own emotionality with a methodical viciousness that was quite breathtaking and gave the bland song an odd, obscene jolt. It reminded me of Frederick and the artificial civility just veiling his furious contempt. It also reminded me of Erin, offering her flowers to no one. These images seemed opposite each other but at the same time locked together in an electrical stasis, each holding the other in place.

It was a very popular song. I had seen the singer interviewed on TV. He was a foppish young man who seemed thoroughly disgusted to find himself so liked.

We no longer talked about trying to have sex as "ourselves." Sometimes this was all right with me; we could find a little slot to occupy and frantically wiggle around in it until we were both satisfied. Other times I felt disgruntled and ashamed of myself. On those occasions I was aware that I was offering her only a superficial tidbit of myself, a tidbit tricked out to look substantial. It was dishonest, but our tacit agreement to be dishonest together at least allowed a tiny moment of exchange that I wasn't sure was possible otherwise. And perhaps it was not fair to call her behavior dishonest, since she was so used to it that to her it felt true.

We saw each other two or three times a week, usually for dinner or a movie. Sometimes we went out with her friends. They were loud, lewd, exhibitionistic, and kind. They were a comedienne, an office worker, a photographer, and a waitress who wrote acerbic short stories. They were mostly ten years younger than me, and in their presence I felt enveloped in bracing female warmth that I did not experience with most people my own age, certainly not with my august colleagues. I loved standing around with them in the dark of some bar, talking sex trash. They made fun of me for having sex with men, although most of them occasionally did too.

"When I have guy fantasies, I want it to be a frat boy thing," said Gina, the robust waitress. "I want them to call me bitch and make me suck their cocks and all that."

"I like something more refined myself," I said. "Cruel but refined."

"I'm the reverse about guys," said Lana. She was a curvaceous girl with loud clothes, severe hair, and signifying glasses. "Women can degrade me sometimes, if I really like them. But if I'm with men I want them to get on their knees and worship it. And they have to mean it."

Their talk was like a friendly shoving match between giggling kids, a game about aggression that made aggression harmless. Although I wasn't sure that it was completely harmless. It was fun to say that I liked something refined and cruel, but under the fun was an impatient yank of boredom and under that was indignation and pain.

One night Gina wore a rubber cock strapped onto her body under her pants. She clownishly pressed it against the rumps of men, who laughed and jovially explained that she was doing it wrong. She pressed it against my thigh, and I cooed and groped the rubber thing, arching my back and butt in a satire of narcissism and subservience.

"I'll give Erin ten dollars if she'll get on her knees and suck Gina's cock," said Donna.

Erin smiled and began to move forward. "She doesn't need ten dollars," I said.

"Just for you, baby," said Gina.

"She doesn't need it," I said, and put my arm around Erin's waist. Erin's smile stuck, and she halted uncertainly.

"Aww, Susan loves Erin," said Donna.

We all went to dance, our movements sloppily describing friendship, sex, display, and animal warmth, all in a loop of drunkenness that equalized every sensation. The bar was saturated with dumb, lurid kinesis. Mischievous entities with blearily smiling faces peeped from behind corners. I loved these young women.

But the next day, our posturing seemed stupid. I sat in my office between hours, thinking of the moment when Donna had offered Erin ten dollars, and I felt embarrassed. I imagined my officemate, a hale critic in her fifties, witnessing the exchange in the bar. I imagined her smiling gamely, eager to approve of these young women who were, after all, "gender bending." I imagined her smile faltering as she registered that Erin's eager response had nothing to do with sex, or even with fun. I imagined her frowning and turning away. I closed my eyes and felt this imagined rejection. I wanted to protect Erin from it, to make my officemate see her in all her different aspects—her brave flowers, her swagger, her private tenderness. That way I made my oblivious officemate bear the discomfort I didn't want to feel.

When I got in bed that night I thought of Erin erotically, but my thoughts quickly became inarticulate. I pictured her staring at me like a frightened animal. I imagined a deep, perpetual moan that racked her body but did not come out of her mouth. I pictured the organs in her abdomen dry as old roots, parched for lack of some fundamental nurture that she had never received and was trying futilely to find.

The next night we had dinner together. She pulled my chair out for me, as she always did. Her gestures and expressions were piquant and feisty, but for me they were occluded by the way I had imagined her the previous night. What I saw in front of me and what I had imagined both seemed real, yet one seemed to have nothing to do with the other. I was appalled to realize that I didn't want to see her again.

Still, I invited her into my apartment. We sat on my living room rug, and I brought us dishes of tapioca pudding that I had made. There was subtle discomfort between us; I wondered if she had seen the change in me or if there had also been a change in her. She tried to kiss me, and I said I wasn't sure I wanted to have sex. She said okay. We ate our desserts and talked. I said I didn't think I wanted to stay in San Francisco. I said I thought my apartment was beautiful but that it seemed to me like a way station.

"There are so many doors and hallways in this place," I said. "It makes it seem like a crossroads."

"Is that how you think of me?" asked Erin.

Her question startled me. I said no, and took her hand and kissed her, but I wasn't sure if I was telling the truth. She kissed me back as though she knew this. Kissing, we toppled onto the floor. The moan I had sensed in her was nearly palpable, but I knew she didn't feel it. My kiss became an escalating slur of useless feeling. I kissed her to locate her, but it was no good; she was all in fragments. I took her wrist. "Don't slap me," I said. "I don't want that." She disengaged her wrist and pulled up my skirt. I knew I should not let this happen. She pulled my panty hose and underwear down. Inwardly, I rushed forward, trying to engage her, to find one tiny place we could wiggle around in together. She flew by me in an electrical storm. She had discovered that I didn't want her, but she was ignoring her discovery. Without knowing why, I ignored it too. I rifled my memories of her, all her different faces; none of them stayed with me. She handled me roughly. Tomorrow, I thought, I would tell her I didn't want to be intimate anymore. I closed my eyes. She was doing something strange. I opened my eyes.

She slapped my crotch with a handful of tapioca.

Jerkily, I sat up and stared. "Erin," I said, "what are you doing?"

"Sorry," she said. "It just felt right." She giggled nervously and contracted herself. Her open hand sat in her lap, wet with beads of tapioca.

Absurd tears came to my eyes. I felt almost as if someone had thrown a pie in my face, but that wasn't why the tears had come. "What a gross, inconsiderate thing to do." But that wasn't right, either.

"Oh, Susan, come on."

She reached for me, and I pulled away. My stingy tears went dry. Erin shrugged and self-consciously ate some tapioca off her hand. Then she rubbed her nose with the back of it.

"I'll get some paper towels," she said. "I'll clean the carpet."

"I'll be right back," I said. "I'm going to take a shower."

When I returned, Erin was seated on the couch, her limbs held tight into her body. Even in the dark, I could see she wore the starved face I'd seen in the Polaroids the swinging heterosexuals had taken of her.

"Do you want me to go?" she said.

"I don't know." I knelt and put my hand on her foot. "I think so."

"I'll go if you want. But I don't want you to think I'm a jerk. I didn't do that to be a jerk."

"I know, Erin," I said.

"You know, you seem so vulnerable," she said. "You say you want to be real. But you don't. Not really."

I took my hand off her foot and turned my head away. The silence held varied beats and long, slow pulses.

When she left, she held my face in her hand and kissed me. "I probably won't call you for a while," she said. "But you can call me, if you need to process."

After she was gone, I lay on the floor until I noticed that my old cat was eating leftover tapioca from a dish. I got up to put the dishes away, and then got in bed. I had a puzzling sensation of triumph at finding myself alone, a sensation that took me happily into sleep.

But I woke in two hours, sweating and throwing off the blankets. I wondered if Erin had thrown the tapioca at me because she had been angry. Or perhaps what had felt like anger was just the random overspill of a ceaseless internal spasm. I imagined the terrible moan inside her, like an endless, coughing dry sob. I imagined it so acutely that I was transfigured by it. The pain of it was so ugly it was almost revolting, and yet there was something desperately vital about it. I tried to think what "it" was. My kitten woke and touched me with her small muzzle. She allowed me to stroke her; even in her slumberous state, her small body was quick and fierce with life. She felt her life all the way down to the bottom. Everybody wants it, I thought. Erin has it, but she can't bear it. Again, I saw her low internal organs, parched but tough and fiercely alive, holding on.

Stuff

An acquaintance of mine, a philosophy professor at a neighboring university, had finally succeeded in selling one of the many screenplays he had bitterly toiled over and was giving a big party to celebrate. Friends of his, a married screenwriting couple, gave me a ride to the party. The woman was a thin, excitable person who appeared to be keeping a strict inner watch on an invisible set of perfectly balanced objects, lest any of them fall over or even fractionally shift position. The man seemed to inhabit a benevolent, functional daze. It apparently disturbed the woman that I was single. "You can't just stay at home," she said, gripping the seat back as she torqued herself around to face me. "You've got to go to classes and lectures and meditation groups, places where there might be single men."

"I'm really not interested in that kind of thing," I said. "I'm more of a drinker."

She released the seat back and adjusted herself face-forward. Rather testily, we discussed the current cinema.

The party took place in a spacious studio in Palo Alto. Splendid vases of celebratory flowers stood on short white pillars shaped like building blocks. Almost immediately upon entering, I became engaged in a conversation about antidepressants, which I inadvertently started by casually remarking that I thought a certain administrator at Berkeley was so cranked up on Prozac that he didn't know what he was doing.

"Prozac doesn't crank you up," said a classics professor. "Prozac makes you like you should be."

Her voice was plaintive but resolute. She told me that if it weren't for Prozac, she wouldn't be alive. I told her that sometimes I felt so unhappy that it was hard to live, but that I preferred to sit through it.

"It's like being your own mom sitting beside you on the bed when you're sick," I said.

The woman who had given me a ride poked her head around the corner. "Is one or both of your parents depressed?" she asked.

"I don't know if they're depressed, but they're certainly miserable."

"Then it's genetic and you should take Prozac."

I excused myself and sought out the host. I don't really like him, at least not in the usual sense. In our first conversation, he had asked me why I'd never been married and then told me that he had been married four times, even though he never wanted to get married. He had done it, he said, only because "they wanted it so badly."

"How could you get married for that reason?" I asked.

"Haven't you ever done anything you didn't want to do?" He'd virtually snarled the question.

"Not four times," I'd snarled back.

Whenever I see him socially, I experience a violent psychic hiccup that finally makes me wave my arms and loudly tell him off, even though I'm alone in my apartment and it's days later. Then when I see him again, the bodily memory of the disturbance is roused and starts feebly moving its little feelers, trying to engage the source of the problem and straighten it out. He grabs the tips of those little feelers and locks on. It's an emotional bond, sort of.

I noticed that his two children, each from a different marriage, had come to the party and were standing around, as if presenting evidence of his good and fruitful life. The handsome teenage son lounged affably in a corner. The daughter, a stoic young woman from the particularly ugly first marriage, was serving hors d'oeuvres. A mournful tendril of brown hair played limply against her cheek. I felt a quiet throb of affection for her. I had met her before, at another party. She had gotten drunk and told me that her father had said to her, when she was fifteen, that if he ever found out she'd had an abortion, he'd kill her. "He'll do that," she said. "He'll just spew shit out. It doesn't mean anything, but it's pretty awful anyway."

I said hello to her and selected a canapé with turmeric on it. Her father was standing nearby, railing at some people who were nodding in accord. He was complaining about how nobody wanted to be responsible anymore, particularly those people who went to "therapy" instead of squarely facing the truths of Freud. "'They talk about 'really getting to know themselves,' as if they can come up with a little answer for everything," he said fiercely. "As if any of us can know ourselves, as if any of us can ever explain the brutality of sex. If we ever 'got to know' ourselves, we would be sickened. It is the essence of decency to acknowledge that and keep going." His jaw seemed about to split sideways in a rictus of frustration.

I turned away and fell into gossiping with a fellow who had made his reputation by proving that male and female genitals are really a social construct. He had once been quite a hotshot, but he had since gone to seed in the manner of an old cat who knows where to find the food dish. He entertained me with the details of a spat between two linguistics professors, one of whom had thrown a glass of wine at the other at a recent barbecue.

"We inhabit a nest of vipers," he said, with a happy little movement of his neck and chin.

"Low-grade vipers," I agreed. "But vipers nonetheless."

He vaguely smiled and turned away. I walked through the room, having partial conversations. The public faces of these people were so familiar to me that they were as abstract as a word repeated too many times in rapid succession. Their half-expressions—the gradations of approval or attention or retraction in their eyes as they politely nodded or scratched their noses—were like the surface of quick-moving water, all shiny, slippery pieces. A woman's bright dress flashed with her efficient strides. A department chair from yet another university tucked one arm protectively about her soft, protruding abdomen, while her other arm flailed the air valiantly to exaggerate the argument she made to a man apparently in complete agreement. He laughed with stiff, gaping jaws.

I was seeing them in pieces, and I knew it. I knew that under their words and gestures they must be whole and deep-rooted, with faces and voices I did not know. I stood still, my wineglass a prop in my tense hand, and tried to feel them more fully. I imagined the gesticulating department chair asleep in her bed, her face in the mild furrows of middle age, her body private and innocent as an almond in its special shell. I imagined her, even in sleep, tunneling her way through phantom problems, twisting and turning and valiantly arguing. I knew that she was divorced and that she had a young child; I thought of her at breakfast, touching her child's upturned face with her palm. I pictured the child struggling to make sense of the conflicts surging under her mother's absent, tender gesture.

Meanwhile, light ran and flirted on glass and silverware. Intellectual discussion rose and devolved. A salsa band had arrived and was assembling itself in a slow and professional manner. A pleasant fellow with a hirsute face replaced a part on his horn and frowned as if to frown were delicious. His bandmates moved behind him with sleek, sensory ease.

The classics professor made right by Prozac came up beside me and put an arm about my waist. "I wanted to tell you how good it is to see you," she said. "I like you so much, Susan."

I was surprised to hear this, as we barely knew each other. Still, I put my arm about her. There was a little roll of fat at her waist, which felt sweet as cake.

"You're like me," she continued. "You think for yourself. You see life as it is."

"Life as it is?" My fingers rested gingerly on her sweet fat. "What do you mean?"

She faltered and slightly retracted her embrace. "You know, no bullshit. You aren't fooled by bullshit."

I furrowed my brow.

"Oh, I can't tell you what I mean right now," she said. "I'm a little drunk. But you know."

Her face was uncertain and fractured, but that little fat roll was live and full of feeling. The hell of it was, she was probably on a diet. I withdrew my arm from her, and we changed the subject.

When I got home, my apartment felt pleasing and almost festive in comparison to the party. I lay on my red couch and ate ham and white bean soup from a Styrofoam container. My cats sat happily with their little chests out. I thought of Erin. I wished that I could ask her to visit and that we could lie on the floor together. I remembered her blunt, full-throttle kiss, and a tiny, grateful love flowered in my chest. It had been a month since our stumbling, drunken affair had ended, and Erin was, tentatively, my friend. I could call her, but she probably wouldn't be home. She had just fallen in love with a rambunctious girl whom I had once glimpsed in a crowd, insouciantly bare-legged in a tiny skirt and cowboy boots. She had dumped a glass of ice down Erin's shirt and hopped back laughing, switching her bossy skirt. I smiled and put down the empty soup container. I lay on my back and held a small maroon pillow against my chest. I relished the slight soreness of Erin's memory overlaid with that giddy burst of glimpsed laughter and bare, dancing legs; I felt the laughter almost as if it were mine.

The next day the screenwriting philosophy professor called me to ask if he could give my phone number to a friend of his who had noticed me at the party, a sociologist named Kenneth.

"Normally I wouldn't do this," he said. "But he was quite taken with you."

"How? I mean, we didn't talk."

"He loved your red high heels and your dress. And he . . . well, he noticed this little bruise on your leg, and he thought it was striking against your skin."

"I don't even remember him," I said.

"Well, let me tell you. He's extraordinary. He's a brilliant sociologist, and he's very influential, very respected. And he's a lot of fun. Every weekend he drives around to flea markets and finds the most amazing things. He's got a real gift for it; people beg to go with him on his runs because he can find things nobody else could unearth. He's separated from his wife—"

"I don't date married men."

"He's getting divorced."

I rolled my eyes, but at the end of the conversation I said that the sociologist could have my number. I put the phone down, feeling flattered and at the same time slightly embarrassed by my willingness to talk to someone I didn't remember whose attention had flattered me secondhand. I watched guiltily as the two feelings paired up and slunk off together like snakes. Well, maybe I would like him.

The next day I called Erin. I could hear in her voice that she was glad to hear from me. She invited me to a tiny night haunt where Paulette, Lana, and Gina would be performing as The Better Off Dead Poets Society, which entailed Paulette and Gina's reading poems with titles like "Just Because Your Strap-On Is Big and Brown Doesn't Make You Denzel Washington" while Lana did ironic dances in a leotard.

There were several other acts up before the Poets appeared, so Erin and I refreshed ourselves with beer and Jägermeister. She said her new girlfriend, Dolly, was going to arrive in a few hours. They were going to pretend to be strangers, and Erin was going to try to persuade Dolly to go home with her, which Dolly might not consent to do. Considering the theatricality of their date, it seemed okay for Erin and me to make out, so we did. Her body greeted me with a loyal flicker. Her little hipbone was guileless and friendly against my fatter flank. A woman got on the stage and began to talk about spanking her girlfriend while their friends watched.

"I hope you don't mind," murmured Erin. "It just feels so good to go from you to Dolly."

I said I understood, and I meant it. I imagined Erin rolling voluptuously between two large, fluffy, and unstable masses, blindly nuzzling with her little nose, enjoying the instability as much as anything. I put my hand on her supple low back. She released a burst of tender heat. The woman onstage described how she and her girlfriend had spanked and sexually tormented a third woman while some other people watched. Erin and I smiled nervously; we separated and she took a long drink of beer. She began telling me about her developing relationship with Dolly. The sprightly twenty-one-year-old, the disaffected member of a wealthy family, had already traveled throughout the world and shown in a local art gallery. She had never had intercourse with a man, which to Erin gave her the martial allure of a warrior princess. She had, said Erin, taken to the role of femme top with startling enthusiasm.

"Last night she whipped my upper back, right between my shoulder blades," said Erin. "It hurt so much it was like she was whipping my heart. It connected me with all this deep mom pain and I really cried. My therapist described it as a moment of integration with the primary feminine."

"That's pretty fancy," I said. "Is that what you think?"

She shrugged and drank from her bottle of beer. There was a noise from the front of the room, and she turned sharply. The line of her cheekbone was stark and pure against the darkness. The darkness was like an animal about to lick her with its rough tongue. Her posture was calm, but her mouth was pulled tight and the iris was hard and bulging in her eye. Her rough gold hair was declarative as a flag. Impulsively, I stroked it. She smiled at me, and through all the darkness and declaration I felt something small and intrepid respond to my stroke.

I rose from my bed late the next day, in an unstable mood. I was teaching a summer class that had just begun. I ate my apple and buttered roll without wanting them. When I emerged from the BART station in Berkeley, I purchased a large cardboard cup of tea from a little take-out venue pervaded by an enervated mechanical hum. I loaded it with sugar and cream and drank it as I walked to my classroom, soothed by the sweetness of the tea and mentally tickled by the mechanical hum. I arrived in the classroom several minutes early and sat brooding over my material. While I was sitting there, two boy students came in. They sat and began to talk about another boy, whom they hated.

"And all the girls love him!" said one.

"Oh, no!"

"Yeah! They're, like, all over him!"

"That's disgusting!"

I smiled. "I know just the kind of guy you mean," I said. "They always get, and they never deserve."

"Really!" They looked at me curiously.

"I fall for that kind of jerk myself," I said, "sometimes."

"No! Not you too!" But they looked interested.

"Only sometimes. Mostly, girls get over that when they get older. It doesn't age well."

"Yeah?" One of them looked at me with touching receptivity. He was an overweight kid with responsive eyes. He had an avid, artless delicacy that was striking in contrast to his big, ungraceful body and made him seem vaguely helpless, even though he was probably quite strong. He didn't write very well, but he was a passionate student and so was a favorite of mine. He took me in with a wistful, subtle movement of his eyes. I felt him accept my fondness and shyly give it back. Without knowing it, he comforted me.

Still, I felt disgruntled when I returned to my apartment that evening. The cats walked around with heavy paws, looking as if life with me was taxing their animal tenacity. When the phone rang I picked it up only because I was expecting Erin to call. It was Kenneth, the sociologist.

"Have I caught you at a bad time?" he asked. "You sound a little . . . I don't know . . ."

His voice was tight and complicated, like something faceted and finely wrought that had been compressed into a ball. Making this phone call had probably been difficult for him; I thought I should reassure him, but instead I did the reverse.

"Is it true that you were into the bruise on my leg?" I asked.

"I . . . what?" His voice sprang free from its wad a tad. "That's absolutely ludicrous. I would never . . . I wouldn't—that was Phillip on one of his imagination jags." His voice expanded again, and I sensed a vast array of personality tensed to unfurl itself. "I just said I liked your dress. And your shoes." He paused. "I did notice the bruise, though." The last was said with a meticulous humility that I found endearing.

I told him I probably sounded nervous because I thought the situation was strange. "We haven't really met after all," I said. "Maybe you could tell me something about yourself."

There was an unhappy little pause. "Well, let's see. You know I'm a sociologist. And, uh, I collect stuff. I go out every weekend and find . . ." He coughed. "Look, I'd rather at least meet. It just seems ... I mean, would you want to describe yourself into the phone?"

I wouldn't. I told him that I knew he was married, and that if we did meet, it would have to be for friendship.

"Well, then," he said, "how about a friendly dinner?" The hint of moroseness in his voice was like a slight, perseverant sigh.

I spent the two days between this conversation and our dinner in a satisfying ennui of classes, laundry, pointless walks and telephone calls. At night I would sit on the couch and read my students' poems, with my feet on a chair and the old cat on my lap. In my bland contentment, the presence of the sociologist gave off an obscure little throb, an insignificant signal that nonetheless had to be monitored.

On the evening of our date, I decided to wear the dress I had worn for my two-hour appointment with Frederick. I noticed that when I put it on this time, it made me feel stately and secure. I had complicated thoughts on the relationship between one's outer garments and one's inner state, and the mysterious ways that each can affect the other. The doorbell rang.

Kenneth was tall and had close-cut blond hair like worn wool. He wore an exquisite suit. His shoulders were squared, but his neck and head were habitually in a posture of focus on the ground just before him, and because of that he seemed to be peering up at me when he was actually peering down. I invited him in. He cordially tucked his gaze back down and followed me. I told him I would only be a minute. He asked if he could look around my apartment and walked into my living room. From the back he looked smug and immaculate, but I doubted that he felt that way. He turned sideways; his spine was stiffly curved, and his chest was still and tense. "You live like a kid," he said. But his tone was wondering, not unkind.

He opened the car door for me with a jaunty gesture, and there we were, close together in a small, sealed place. He said he hoped I liked French food. I said I did. He drove down the streets with what seemed abnormal care. There was vacuous delicacy between us.

"Does the situation still seem strange to you?" he asked.

"Yes, but it's okay. It's less strange than meeting somebody through a newspaper ad. It seems all dates get funny after some point in your thirties. It's probably unprecedented and maybe even unseemly, all these middle-aged people with problems out on dates."

"Do you have problems?" he asked.

"Oh, none at all."

In silence, we recovered from my attempt at levity.

"I don't care if it's strange," he said. "It's just a nice thing for me to be on a date at all."

His words gave off a high, sterling tingle. I felt they should've touched me, but they didn't. Still, I noticed them, tingling.

The restaurant was a plain rectangular room muffled in white. The many people seated in it ate with great energy. A woman's sharp nose and tense posture, combined with a glimpse of someone else's long, nimble fingers, gave me an impression of cutting fineness. The waiter who seated us smiled as if he was glad to see Kenneth arrive with a date, and his warmth was startling in the midst of the arranged enjoyment. We studied our menus and selected our food. That out of the way, Kenneth folded his hands and leaned slightly forward with dense shoulders. "You wanted to know about me," he said, "so let me tell you some things."

He had gone to Harvard, where he had studied literature. He had been a founding member of SDS. He had started a rock band and, with the band, had moved to San Francisco, where he helped preside over "acid tests," or public LSD festivals, about which I had read a book and seen a TV special. He had played music and handed tourists paper cups of Kool-Aid with LSD in it, which, to his amazement, they drank.

His voice when he told these stories was oddly perfunctory, as though he were answering a job description. I thought of his phone voice: complexity crushed into a ball. I realized that across from me sat an unknown person, full of thoughts and feelings I had never had. But it seemed that to get to them, I would have to pry them out of their balled shapes. I wondered if I felt the same to him; maybe everybody over the age of thirty balled up without realizing it.

As he talked, I imagined him standing around the Marina with his guitar, handing Kool-Aid to happy, receptive tourists. When I was fifteen, a stranger had given me a tab of acid, but I'd at least known what it was. We were alone in a room together. He sat next to me, watching my pupils dilate. His body seemed both insensible and grossly live, filled with the ignorant majesty of his breath. "If I wasn't such a nice guy," he said, "you could really be getting screwed." I tried to figure out what he meant by that. Eyeless homunculi suddenly spilled out of his nose and sat on his upper lip. The radio sang "I feel free."

The waiter brought wine to our table. Kenneth tasted it and made a small frown of approval. The waiter filled our glasses.

In 1971 Kenneth married the girlfriend of a Yippie celebrity. He went to medical school at her urging. They traveled all over the world together and had children. They were still friendly with the Yippie celebrity, who was now a public relations consultant for environmentally responsible businesses. The food arrived.

We traded information and opinions as we ate. Kenneth ate with fine, tight manners. He ate as if he expected his food to be exquisite, and as if he was almost irritated to find his expectation duly met. He said he'd read my poems and thought they were good. He wondered why I didn't write more. He described a story he had read recently and admired. It was about a man who wanted everything he did, even the smallest gestures, to be perfect. If they weren't, he'd repeat them until they were, which meant that the author had devoted a lot of space to descriptions of such acts as the man repeatedly taking his comb out of his pocket and putting it back.

"I hate that kind of thing," I said. "It's an art school concept."

"I suppose it is," said Kenneth. "But I thought it an elegant description of compulsion."

"Compulsion isn't elegant," I said. "It's ugly as hell."

This seemed to startle him. "Well, yes, it's an, um, illness, I guess." He sat poised over his plate, his utensils suspended in a slight, cute angle of ineptitude, like a pretty girl with one foot turned in. "But the story is also describing a wish for perfection that I share to some extent." He smiled. "In a compulsive kind of way."

"Well," I said, "it is after all possible to be elegant and ugly at the same time."

"I thought you'd understand." He paused. "You know, that dress you wore at the party was a real knockout. I was hoping you'd wear something like that tonight."

When I got home I felt agitated and vacant at the same time. I changed into my thermal pajamas and lay on the floor, eating a candy bar and lulling myself with a television fashion special that was mostly models walking back and forth while music played and high-speed graphics flared and dissolved. I went to sleep at three, and immediately had a nightmare. I was in a room full of strangers with muffled, half-frowning faces that I couldn't quite see. I couldn't hear most of what was said to me, nor could I make myself heard. The room was close and hot, and it was difficult to breathe. I walked around, trying to find an exit, until I realized that there was none. When I woke, I had to turn on the light and sit up, my hand on my rushing chest.

When I woke in the morning, I lay in bed for a long moment, feeling the agitation of the night, now faint and slow, with lots of empty space between pulses. I got up and made myself a mug of tea with a tablespoon of honey in it. I sat in the living room in a pool of live, swarming sunlight, drinking my tea. I thought that maybe I would write a poem about my dream. In the poem, Erin would be my companion in the dark room, a blind companion whom I could not fully see or hear but could feel in bursts of secret radiance.

Kenneth called a week after our date. He called at ten thirty at night. I ensconced myself in bed and we talked about our day. I described a class discussion of a long prose poem about a girl with "peanut-butter-colored hair" who gets gang-banged in a public pool by a band of boobs. The author of the poem, a likable young fellow, wondered guiltily whether it was wrong of him to portray the banged girl as a shallow fool. A subdiscussion had ensued about whether the character was in fact a shallow fool, just because, prior to the pool incident, she'd prattled about doing it with a local musician who later became famous. I told them it was mean-spirited and ill-advised to make a harsh judgment based on so little information, in life or in poetry—mainly because, if I were a teenage girl, I'd prattle about it too, and I wasn't a fool, now, was I?

Kenneth, for his part, had just come from a trying dinner with his two teenage sons and one of their ridiculous friends, a dour young man with unattractive tattoos on his head, who'd gone on about how certain of his tattoos meant something sacred and private to him and then pulled up his shirt to reveal them. Kenneth thought it was stupid, but he had secretly enjoyed the fellow's posturings, as well as those of his eldest son, John.

"John's such a handsome kid," said Kenneth. "He's charming and he plays the guitar and girls just fight over him." He sighed worriedly. "Poor Tom, on the other hand, just doesn't have any of that. He's smart and everything, but he's never even had a real girlfriend, except for one back in high school, and she jumped off a fifteen-story building."

"Well, I was kind of like that in high school," I said.

"You jumped off a building?"

"No. People thought I didn't have anything. Then I wrote a book of poetry that people liked. Gee, do I have something or not?"

We changed the subject. He asked me if I would like to go "on a run" with him that weekend, to scour the flea markets and antique stores for extraordinary stuff. I said no, but when he asked if I would like to have dinner with him again, I accepted.

The restaurant he chose for our second dinner was elegant and quiet. A couple in early middle age sat next to us, handling their cutlery with the careful, vaguely grateful manner of people unused to eating in restaurants. The man was like a happy animal in his suit. The woman's hair flared up and her loud, finicky skirt flared out.

Kenneth fussed over the wine menu. His forehead sweated faintly in the light. "So," he said, "there has been one other person I've been on a date with besides you—it was a year ago, when I first started the divorce. It's a story I think would interest you."

The woman next to us kept stiffly brushing imaginary crumbs from her skirt. She had a brittle, wounded sweetness that the man seemed very solicitous of.

"I was really anxious because I knew I didn't want to be in the marriage anymore, but I was afraid that I couldn't find anyone else. I looked around; there was nothing."

"But there's a ton of single women who want—"

"You always hear that, but really, there aren't." He ordered our wine. He spread his napkin in his lap and made an expansive reach for the bread. "My friends asked me, well, who did I want to meet? And I said, 'Uma Thurman.' "

"Really."

"And you know, like magic, that's who I met! Well, not really Uma, but a twenty-four-year-old model who looks just like her!"

He had met this extraordinary young woman at a gallery opening. Her pale-blond hair was piled upon her head. Her loose, cream-colored pant legs wafted with her stroll. She wore white open-toed sandals, and her toenails were painted pink. She frowned at a piece of sculpture and toyed with the raised mole on the back of her perfect neck. "Oh," said someone. "That's Zoe. She's either an actress who's trying to model or the other way around."

Kenneth secured an introduction; with a graceful grimace, she told him that, although she supported herself as a model, she wanted to be an actress, and that she was studying to be a lawyer too. He thought he felt her gently score his palm with her fingernail as she slowly withdrew her hand from his grasp.

She joined Kenneth at a small dinner party, and at the end of the evening, she allowed him to drive her home. He invited her to go out on a run with him, and she said yes.

"It wasn't just that she was beautiful," said Kenneth. "She's an aristocrat—quite literally, from Poland. She speaks six languages. She can converse intelligently on virtually any subject. And she's got flawless manners. If she needed some salt at dinner she wouldn't just ask you to pass it. She'd say, 'Excuse me, do you mind if I ask for the salt?' Or if she had to go to the bathroom she'd say, 'Please, do you mind if I use the bathroom?' Everything was special with her. I took her to the same restaurant we went to. The waiters went crazy over her."

The man at the next table glanced at Kenneth and then at me. He saw me notice his glance.

Zoe had told him on their first date that she liked to have friendships with "old men" because she knew that they wouldn't "come on" to her. He had found this remark irksome, but it didn't matter; just to be in her presence made him feel reverent and sensitive. They went on run after rapturous run, and he bought her carloads of stuff.

"Being with her was like nothing else," he said. "It was like having a beautiful Cartier watch on your wrist."

I wondered if he was trying to disgust me. I wondered if I had any right to be disgusted. The bald spot on his head appeared oblivious and vulnerable in the overhead light. The woman seated next to me sighed restlessly.

But then, he went on, he began to notice subtle character flaws. Once, when they were out on a stuff run, she asked him if he thought she should get breast implants. "It shocked me," he said, "because I thought she didn't take that modeling stuff seriously. I thought she wanted something more genuine. I told her that, and she didn't really have an answer."

It only got worse. They went to a dinner party and, on being introduced to "a European has-been director," Zoe virtually dropped Kenneth and spent the evening fawning on the director. On another occasion, he was sure he saw her trade lewd winks with some absurd boy. Then, when they went to an art opening, she abruptly canceled their dinner afterward because someone she had just met had invited her to a screening. When he complained, she got snippy. "I decided I wasn't going to see her again until she called me and apologized," he said. "And she never did, so . . . like Phil put it, Cartier watches don't hurt your feelings."

"Cartier watches don't *have* feelings, either," I said. "Please, would you mind if I—excuse me—go to the bathroom?"

I sulked in the rest room, loathing Kenneth. My loathing was grating and frustrating. It made me feel like a small animal trapped in a maze as part of a science experiment. I thought about how everybody tried so hard and how it never worked. I thought of the woman at the next table brushing at imaginary crumbs. I remembered my mother standing in front of a mirror, trying to pull her short jacket down over her protruding abdomen, her face anxious and sad. I remembered the way Frederick had first looked at me, as if beholding an object that ideally filled a perpetually empty place. I remembered how I had touched him in quite the same spirit, except that my touch had been even more peremptory than his look. I pictured Kenneth pulling a comb out of his pocket and putting it back, over and over again. My loathing depressed me. It seemed arrogant and stupid.

I returned to the table. The people sitting next to us had gone, leaving a dainty wreckage of cutlery and waste. Kenneth looked diminished and sad, picking at his fancy dinner. He looked up mournfully. "You think I'm an asshole, don't you?" he said.

"No," I said. "No." I sat down. "I just—"

"I told you that story because I thought you would like it. Believe me, I know I made a fool of myself over that girl. I learned my lesson. I thought you'd appreciate it."

"I do. I mean, I understand." My tone was obnoxiously kind and judicial. "I can fall for superficial things. Sometimes I wish everything could be like a pop song, like *fine*, like white sugar. But it just doesn't work that way. And besides, that Cartier watch thing was a bit much."

"But what I meant was that she was like magic. I mean, since I met her, I open the passenger door for every woman who gets into my car. It's a tiny thing, but things like that create a sense of dignity and—"

"It's just that pop song thing. Also, how come you like her exaggerated manners and you don't like it that she wants fake boobs?"

We ate our food and discussed the complex allure of the artificial. He said he didn't think his attraction to Zoe was entirely false, because he'd respected her law studies and her desire to excel mentally. I said I thought that was just another objectification, and he seemed to consider this. We were beginning to be excited by each other. The waiters enjoyed our excitement. When we finished eating, they brought us small, festive balls of cotton candy on cardboard sticks for free.

We walked back to his car, a subtle membrane of feeling spanning the air between us. With a sudden movement, he took my hand and held it. His palm was fleshy, but it felt brittle anyway. I held it and tried to ease its brittleness. But later, when we stood on my front steps and said good night to each other, he tried to kiss me on the lips and I turned my head. I glimpsed his limpid, bewildered eyes as his mouth lighted on my cheek and then drew back in an open, stifled purse. He coughed and looked away. "I'll call you again," he said.

A blurry impress of his eyes and his lips, open and moving away, was still on me when I lay down to sleep, and that may've been why I dreamed of kissing a boy I had known when I was thirteen. In life, he had looked down on me because I had been shy and plain, and I, in turn, thought him an empty-headed snot. But in the dream we were in love. We sat together and kissed. Our hands were at our sides, our shoulders just touched. He came near and drew away and nervously played with his honey-colored hair. His T-shirt had a rip under one faintly pungent armpit. He extended his mouth again, stretching his long, supple throat. He brushed his lips against my cheek, and the dream slowly fell into nothing.

I rode to Berkeley in a state of melancholy. The passenger seated sideways in front of me on the BART was a slouching, unhandsome young man with pale-brown hair and a weak, somehow derisive chin. Still, there was something pleasing in the dull brown stubble on his thin white skin and the sardonic loll of his head against the rattling plastic window of the car. He turned, met my eyes, then looked away, and I remembered my dream with a funny rolling sensation, almost as if, half asleep, I had turned over and rubbed my face against an unexpected softness. I remembered Frederick then, and to my embarrassment and mild sadness, it occurred to me that the dream had been at least partly about him. How maudlin, I thought, to have conflated two drunk, unhappy adults who had casually mistreated each other with tender, kissing children. I remembered how Frederick had touched my cheek, his hand sensitive and bare as the paw of a friendly animal. The memory was plain and blameless as a glass of water. It made me remember my fear and shame, also as something plain and blameless. Then it occurred to me that the dream had been, in some less clear way, about Kenneth as well.

Erin decided to stop seeing Dolly, because she had revealed herself as a shallow brat who "jerked people around." We discussed it over drinks at a crowded boy bar.

"She decides she wants to see other people and we have to have this interminable discussion of it and I'm crying and tearing my hair and finally I agree. Then next week she wants to be monogamous. Then two days later she's fucking some bitch down the street. Who needs it?"

Her voice was defiant, but her eyes were stunned and fixated, her chest hard and shrunken. She wore black cigarette-leg pants that were too short at the ankles and a black leather shirt that was too short at the waist, and the clothes made her look desiccated, almost ridiculous.

I remembered my glimpse of Dolly, dumping ice down Erin's shirt; with a slight shock, I intuited her vagina, a rude girl that would've stuck out its tongue if it could.

"It's really painful," continued Erin, "but I'm trying to work with it in a creative way. I've done all these healing rituals with candles and shrines and stuff. I tore up the whole backyard and planted a garden with petunias and snapdragons and, um . . ." She looked into the room, trying to remember what she had planted.

"Is it helping?" I asked.

"I don't know. I know it's going to hurt for a while, and I don't want to wallow in it. But I don't want to run away from it, either." She brightened. "Last week I ran a personal ad in the *Guardian*. I answered a few too. I'm not looking for sex; I feel too vulnerable for that. I just want somebody to hurt me and humiliate me." She took an enthusiastic drink. "It's harder to find than you would think," she said. "I've met a few women for coffee dates and they were nice, but I didn't really want them to do anything to me. I'm supposed to meet a dominatrix from Germany tomorrow. Mainly, she's into cutting."

We went to a peep show known for its humane and feminist work environment, where we poured quarters into slots so that a dismal panel of lead would rise, revealing naked girls dancing and showing their genitals behind a thick pane of plastic.

I came home very drunk. I turned off all the lights and lay on the floor, listening to music. I thought of Erin and Frederick and Kenneth. I sang along to the music. I thought of the boyfriend whose death I had learned of the night I met Frederick. He had once shown me a photograph of himself as a baby, held against his father's shoulder. He rose eagerly out of his father's arms, grinning like a wolf cub. Everything in him went up and outward in a bright, excited rush. In its raw form, what he'd had was beautiful and good. But it hadn't helped him. Probably he'd never even known it was there.

Frederick had that fierce upward movement in him, but more muscular, less bright. I had sensed it when I put my hand on his midsection; it had felt angry, and bitterly wounded, but also vigilant, dignified, and determined to preserve its form. He was a lot like me, actually. I thought of a medieval painting I had once seen of a young man holding a torch high over his head, his eyes focused upward into darkness. Frederick had dishonest, petty meanness, but he also had an idea of honor, and if he had put these qualities together in an odd, tacky combination, then that combination must have held some deep, secret sense for him. He was certainly no more odd or tacky than I, a woman who would debase herself trivially, for sport, and yet who sought, in the sheltering darkness of her debasement, passion, depth, and, most ludicrous, even tenderness.

Erin's image suddenly shimmered through my thoughts, dispersing them. I saw her smiling, radiating her sweet, skewed gold light. Then, more faintly, I saw Kenneth, his face focused and busy, as if bent on the pursuit of his stuff, a pursuit that held some deep, secret sense only he could see.

My young cat approached, sniffed me cautiously, then walked away. I fell asleep on the floor and woke an hour later, disturbed and anxious, with a buzzing head and a dry mouth.

The next day I wrote Frederick a letter. I didn't try to describe the things I had thought about the night before. I just said I felt bad about our last meeting. I said I knew I had behaved strangely and that I had done so because I had been afraid. I said that even though what happened between us had been uncomfortable, I had felt touched by him and hoped that if we met again, we could be nice to each other.

I didn't think Frederick would answer my letter, but writing it nonetheless made me feel pleased and relieved. I pictured him reading it. I pictured him reacting to it with uncertainty and maybe even slight agitation, but I also pictured him being secretly pleased and relieved by it as well. I looked in the phone book and found the address of the computer consulting firm that employed him. After I sent the letter, I bought two expensive cookies from the deli next door and sat on my porch steps and ate them.

Erin called, very excited, to tell me about her cutting experience with the dominatrix.

"We took it slow," she said. "We had a few coffee dates and got to know each other, I explained about being too vulnerable for sex, and she understood. I told her I'd never been cut before, so the first time she took it really easy. Just a little bit on my stomach."

Her voice was jubilant, even triumphant.

"But last night she made me beg to be cut and stuff. And then she carved this whole elaborate pattern on my butt in the shape of a snake curled into an S—for 'slave,' I think. Want to come see it?"

I went to her house and she dropped her pants. The snake had fancy diamonds all up and down its back. Its mouth was open, and a happy little tongue popped out.

"Is it permanent?" I asked.

"No. She did it shallow, so it'll fade in a few months." She pulled up her pants. "I took some pictures," she said. "So I could look back on it." She pointed to the bulletin board, to which Polaroids of her cut buttock had been affixed. Her expression as she pointed had the minor, easy pride of a workman indicating a newly repaired phone or dishwasher.

Kenneth called two or three times a week, often late at night. Usually I let him talk into my answering machine while I stood in the hallway, listening. Sometimes I answered, and we would talk for an hour or more. He offered to find furniture and other stuff for me, for my household. "I could help you upgrade your apartment," he said.

"There's nothing wrong with my apartment."

"Well, no, I'm not saying there is. I'd just like to make it better." He paused, and I could feel him tensing, as if before a jump. "I'd like to make your life better."

I rolled my eyes.

Our conversations were much like the one we'd had about the model who wanted to be a lawyer or an actress. They were amiable and opinionated, and sometimes he said things that irritated me, but the irritation didn't stick: first I wanted to tell him what was wrong with him, then I felt foolish, then I accepted him, and then I lost interest. Under the awkwardness and the arrogance, I knew there was generosity and kindness and that he was trying to give it to me. Not because he wanted anything in return, but just to give it. Still, I couldn't feel it. I tried. But I couldn't.

I was walking on the street one afternoon when I saw Frederick again. I was with a colleague, a likable, loudmouthed creative writing teacher named Ginger. We were gossiping so avidly that I didn't see Frederick until he was right before me. He was with a big man who had a hard, void face. Frederick's face was also hard, but when he saw me, his eyes became startled and alert, almost fearful. I looked at him, and the expression in his eyes became shapelessly emotional while his face and body retracted and became harder. For a moment, his nonfeeling and his emotionality ran quickly parallel, and again he matched me. Then his eyes hardened too, and as he walked by me, he quite unmistakably sneered. "Hi, Susan." His voice was soft and caressing, but he said my name like an insult. I was hurt and shocked beyond any sense.

"What was _that?_" said Ginger.

"This guy I had a one-night thing with."

"Jesus, Susan, how old is he? He's not a student, I hope."

"God, no. I wouldn't do that."

Ginger looked over her shoulder. "He's looking back this way," she reported. "Guy looks like a fourteen-year-old skeezer."

"Don't," I said. "I liked him."

She was quiet, and I thought I could feel puzzled embarrassment in her silence. She put her hand on my back and rubbed me. "Sorry," she said.

I didn't answer, because I felt terrible. I experienced my tenderness for Frederick as a gross, gushing thing that had oppressed and offended him. It occurred to me that he had sneered precisely to make me feel that way. I hoped that wasn't true. But even if it wasn't, it seemed that I had been very stupid to see such complexity in what had happened between us. It seemed equally possible, though, that he was even more stupid not to see it.

Kenneth invited me to have dinner at his house with Phillip and his girlfriend Laura, a young blond woman with a small face full of timid hope. Kenneth's wife, with whom he still shared the house, was away for a month, and he wanted to celebrate. We sat in the kitchen and drank wine while Kenneth prepared steaks and salads. The kitchen was gleaming and precise. Every bright knife, every cork and dish and bag, was meticulously and aesthetically arranged. Kenneth washed and dried the lettuce; his hands were white with cold from the water.

Phillip harangued us about President Clinton. He said he knew his presidency was a disaster when he tried to make the army accept homosexuals. Had he succeeded, Phillip went on, it would've been an unprecedented cultural cataclysm, a fact that no one but religious nuts would acknowledge.

"It's not that I have anything against them," he said. "I don't care what they do. You see them in the johns all the time—who cares?"

I hated his words, but his voice and face had a desperate, emotionally distended quality that made me involuntarily sympathetic. I did not think he believed what he was saying, yet he continued to expel words as if from a violently churning pot.

"But if homosexuals ever become truly accepted, just normal like everybody else, do you know what will happen? Heterosexual men and homosexual men will band together, and male power will be felt in this society like never before. Women will be knocked off their pedestal and ground underfoot. Then we'll see sex for the horror it really is. There'll be no romance, no—"

Laura frowned and picked up the cork from the wine bottle. Her pale hair fell forward and covered her face; she tucked it behind her small, very red ear. Kenneth concentrated on the lettuce.

"Phil," I said carefully, "you aren't making any sense."

"Have you read Thomas Aquinas or Aristotle? Because you should have. Even though they're dead white males." His dignity rasped horribly. "Do you know the story of the warrior who had a cute little slave girl that he kept around for fun, and then there was the man he truly loved? And—"

"Spell it out," I said. "What are you trying to say?"

"That all these stupid liberal women who think they have some kind of alliance with gay men don't understand. Gay men aren't interested in women. They care about men." He looked at me as if he hated me, except that his eyes were focused inwardly.

"Yeah," I said, "and lesbians are a lot more interested in women than in men. In fact, sometimes even straight women, frankly—"

"I'm interested in women," said Kenneth brightly, "whether or not they let gay guys in the army."

"Phil," said Laura. She looked at him with all the focus and force she could put in her little face. She looked as if she was trying to remind him of something he had accidentally forgotten.

Abashedly, he dropped his eyes, coughed, and turned his chair so that he faced her, not me.

We moved into the dining room, to eat around a big table. We all helped to set the table and bring out the food, and those gestures of goodwill made us seem like friends. The thick, rare steaks were served on large, expensive plates. Laura said that her mother, who lived in Kansas, would be glad to hear that Laura had eaten a steak dinner, because she thought Laura and Phil ate too much pasta. Her voice included us all in its bright, gentle touch. The men looked at her almost gratefully, as if glad to be reminded of the special place where mother and food were. Phillip began talking about the scourge of political correctness and how it had made honest talk impossible in the academy.

I examined the decorations on the buffet next to the table. They included vases, little books upheld by bookends, several different kinds of matchboxes, and statuettes of animals and girls. They had the potential for the kind of luxuriant aesthetic spewage I enjoy, but they were positioned with a stifling judiciousness that ruined the effect. Amid the fuss, I noticed a small framed photograph of a very handsome young man. He had long hair and wild eyes and an open, imperiously yelling mouth. He looked as if he were riding a roiling, swift-moving current of joy and triumph and satiety, yelling out his pleasure as he rode.

"Kenneth," I said, "is that your son?"

"No," he said. "That's me. Almost thirty years ago."

Sherbet was served, with slices of mango. Kenneth put on a CD. As each song played, he told us about each musician who played it, his history, his technical strengths and weaknesses. Then he told us about each of the instruments. Then he discussed the sound quality of each cut on the CD as opposed to vinyl.

When we finished eating, he said, "So. Are you ready to look at some stuff?"

We followed him upstairs, past darkened rooms full of furniture and boxes heaped together. He took us to the spare bedroom, where he had been sleeping since the separation. There, he kept the small things: drawers filled with sunglasses, cupboards of slumbering hats, boxes of jewelry in grand knotted lumps—gold, silver, glass, and plastic—ashtrays, matchboxes, paperweights, and figurines that fussed and promenaded. There were bags of shoes, chests jammed with women's underwear, a deep closet full of suits and dresses. In the corner, a small, hard bed stood assailed by the teeming stuff; I wondered how he could sleep in such an uproar.

We walked through the room with cordial exclamations of delight. Kenneth rummaged magisterially, concentrating on finding things that each of us might especially like: an Armani suit for Phillip, a velvet gown for Laura, gray suede shoes, cuff links, scarves, an amber necklace. He kept saying, "Here, this is perfect for you." He handed me a pair of sunglasses with elegant, winged eyes, a fey spray of rhinestones on each wing, the occasional bare indentation where a stone had dropped poignant as the bad teeth of an aristocrat. "Take them," he said.

Phillip went into the bathroom with the Armani suit and came out wearing it, pleased and resplendent as a child at his own birthday party. Laura took a purple silk blouse and a zebra-striped handbag. Somewhat guiltily, I pocketed the sunglasses and an enormous pale-blue glass ring.

"Here, Susan," said Kenneth. He went into the closet and emerged with a big gold coat in his arms. He unfurled it and held it out to me; it was a ridiculous, beautiful coat. "When I met you, I pictured you wearing this," he said.

I looked at the coat and felt the same shy, greedy pleasure I had seen in Phillip's face, as if I were a kid receiving a treat simply for being myself. "Thank you," I mumbled. I turned around and offered him my arms. He put the coat on me, and his hands briefly closed on my shoulders. I turned to thank him; his face was private and mundane, but his eyes were full of emotion that was shallow and deep at once. The mixed quality of it reminded me of the expression I had seen on Frederick's face when he passed me on the street, even though it was not the same mix.

During the drive home I asked Phillip and Laura why they thought Kenneth was so dedicated to collecting stuff. "It seems kind of compulsive," I said.

Laura snorted mildly. "Oh," she said, "you think?"

Phillip spoke, his voice insistent, almost bullying, and at the same time absolutely defeated. "When Kenneth was at Harvard, he was a leader," he said. "He was at the center of a charmed circle. He had parties that were legendary—to be invited, you had to be extraordinarily intelligent or beautiful. He went through girls like they were nothing. They used to come crying to me afterward, and I'd say to him, But she's a lovely girl, don't you want to give her a chance? And he'd laugh. He'd just laugh." As he spoke, the insistence gradually drained from his voice, leaving only the defeat. His hands on the steering wheel looked helpless and somehow hurt.

The summer term ended. My students brought a bottle of tequila to class, with lemon and salt, and we shared it while we talked about poems. They were full of themselves and affectionate, and tensed to fly away forever.

That night I celebrated with Erin, Jana, and Paulette in a bar crowded with women and girls. Erin and I stood on the edge of the dance floor, arms about each other's waists, drinking and basking in the vibrancy of the dancing girls. She felt so light in my half-embrace, as if she were made of bright, fluxing atoms, forming and disintegrating in secret patterns, determined in their private purpose and delighted if it made no earthly sense. I imagined lying on top of her, supporting myself with both elbows, so that I could look into her eyes. I imagined cradling her head in my hands. "My sweet girl," I said. "You don't deserve to be hurt. You don't deserve to be cut. You don't have to beg for anything, ever." I imagined her looking at me with the scared, disbelieving eyes of a small, starved wild thing looking at a dish of proffered food, one paw extended forward, the rest of the body poised to fly. I pulled her into a corner, and she pressed herself against me. Full on, she felt too quick and light, as if she were racing inside, gathering speed to blow apart and scatter in a burst of sparkling motes. We kissed.

"I was thinking about you," I said.

"Yeah?"

"It upsets me that you do all this stuff. Like cutting and whipping and having to beg for whatever."

"It *upsets* you?" She pulled back and looked at me almost with distaste.

"It's not that I think there's anything wrong with it," I said. "I've

251

done it, and it's . . . it's human and everything. But it's like you want that stuff because you think you deserve it. And you don't. You just don't."

She embraced me, and she felt solid and human, with a corporeal, beating heart. "Susan," she said, "you're so sweet I just want to tie you up and torture you. But that stuff is what gets me off. It's not about self-hate or anything icky. It just gets me off."

"I know," I said. "I know." But we were separating.

"Come back to the house with us," she said. "We're going to release the ladybugs."

I wondered what she meant, and my wondering went in an aimless spiral. The music turned raucous and absurd. Two tiny, feverish girls in torn shirts slammed against each other, leapt apart, and slammed together again, giggling drunkenly. More girls moved through my line of vision, their private selves breathing through the lax shape of their drunken public presentations. A beautiful dark girl at the bar drank from a shot glass and urgently ran her mouth, shifting her big butt on the barstool and stabbing her finger at the floor as if ordering someone to kneel. As she spoke, her full mouth took harsh, abrupt shapes, as if everything had to be said with a lot of force and then chopped into pieces.

Erin came and took my hand. "Come on," she said. "Let's go."

Jana and Paulette were kissing on the hood of the car when we emerged from the bar. Jana wore chipped purple nail polish on her splayed, grabbing fingers; a beggar walking by said he liked her purple paws and then asked us for money. We lavished him with change. Erin and I got in the back seat, and she embraced me from behind. I took her hand and kissed it. I felt her subtly respond, as if a clear bell had sounded in her chest and passed its reverberation into mine. Paulette turned on the radio; they were playing the love song that had so grabbed my imagination at the clothing store, months before. This time it sounded harmless and childishly sweet. I pictured the pop star singing it into a microphone, his eyes closed and his nose thrust slightly up and forward as he reveled in his tiny loop of bliss. Vaguely, I wished him well. Jana sang the song out the window as we rolled through the noise and activity of night.

When I emerged from the bathroom in Erin's flat, I found her busily handing Jana and Paulette clear plastic bags filled with crawling bugs. She laughed at my perplexed face. "Didn't you hear me? We're going to release the ladybugs."

I stared stupidly.

"For the healing garden!" yelled Erin. "These are special store-bought ladybugs, and we're going to release them out into the garden to protect it from mites. Because it's night, they'll settle in to sleep and then wake up in paradise."

We went down the rotted gray back stairs, each holding a bag of bugs. Erin's cats came with us. My dalmatian-spotted fur shoes looked fey and ridiculous on the steps. When we stepped into the yard, my heels sank into the dirt and I almost fell over. Verdant and sibilant, the garden lurked in the dark. In patches of gray light, we could see leaves trembling.

"Wait," said Erin. "I want to say a poem first."

Jana belched, and Paulette shoved her.

"Shut up," said Erin. "It's Eliot."

"Oh, well, then," said Paulette.

Erin coughed and began to recite.

"I said to my soul, be still, and wait without hope
For hope would be hope for the wrong thing; wait without love
For love would be love of the wrong thing; there is yet faith
But the faith and the love and the hope are all in the waiting.
Wait without thought, for you are not ready for thought."

There was a soft, jumbled silence. Jana contemplatively sniffed.

"Shit," said Erin. "There's something more about a garden, but I can't remember."

"Isn't Eliot that turd who made his wife think she was crazy?" asked Paulette.

"Yeah, I think so," said Erin. "But it's still a great poem. Anyway, come on."

We went among the sleeping plants. The ladybugs tumbled from our bags and tooled about on petal and leaf with all their diligent legs. My friends giggled and joked. I dropped two ladybugs on the soft flesh of a petunia; it bobbed gently as the tiny creatures alighted. I thought how vast and deeply textured the surface of the flower must be to them, how huge and abstract the garden. My imagination opened in one small deep spot. For a moment I felt I was in a limbo of shadows and half-formed shapes which would dissolve into nothingness if I touched them. I felt loneliness so strong it scared me. Then Jana laughed and Erin brushed by me, thoughtlessly caressing my spine with one hand. I was in a garden with my friends. I could not fully see what lay about me, but still, I knew it was there, abundant, breathing, and calm.